RIVER OF LOVE

The days passed quickly. Sometimes the river stretched out lazily like a woman without her corset stays; in other places, the Colorado narrowed to a gushing faucet pouring over rocks. Sometimes it was frightening . . . a matter of survival.

"What's the matter?" Morgan asked her as they sat beside a campfire one dark night. Her eyes had grown round with terror. "You're shivering. You're not afraid of ghosts, are you?"

She shook her head.

He chided her gently. "Some of the things that should scare you don't, and other times you act like a child afraid of the bogey man."

His tightened grip on her waist and his nearness fired every nerve ending. She had never been with a man like this before.

"What's the matter?" He tipped her chin up so he could see her face. As he looked into those sea-green eyes, he was lost to a need he could not define. Abruptly, he pulled her into the warmth of his arms. "Trish?" he whispered. Then he lowered his mouth to hers.

For a moment, Trish did not know what to do. Then, slowly, her hands slipped around his neck and threaded the thick strands of hair that fell upon his neck. She kissed him back . . . then locked her arms behind his neck.

Like the roar of the river's wildest rapids, all thought, all reason was drowned out in a cataract of passion.

TODAY'S HOTTEST READS
ARE TOMORROW'S SUPERSTARS

VICTORY'S WOMAN (4484, $4.50)
by Gretchen Genet
Andrew—the carefree soldier who sought glory on the battlefield, and returned a shattered man . . . Niall—the legandary frontiersman and a former Shawnee captive, tormented by his past . . . Roger—the troubled youth, who would rise up to claim a shocking legacy . . . and Clarice—the passionate beauty bound by one man, and hopelessly in love with another. Set against the backdrop of the American revolution, three men fight for their heritage—and one woman is destined to change all their lives forever!

FORBIDDEN (4488, $4.99)
by Jo Beverley
While fleeing from her brothers, who are attempting to sell her into a loveless marriage, Serena Riverton accepts a carriage ride from a stranger—who is the handsomest man she has ever seen. Lord Middlethorpe, himself, is actually contemplating marriage to a dull daughter of the aristocracy, when he encounters the breathtaking Serena. She arouses him as no woman ever has. And after a night of thrilling intimacy—a forbidden liaison—Serena must choose between a lady's place and a woman's passion!

WINDS OF DESTINY (4489, $4.99)
by Victoria Thompson
Becky Tate is a half-breed outcast—branded by her Comanche heritage. Then she meets a rugged stranger who awakens her heart to the magic and mystery of passion. Hiding a desperate past, Texas Ranger Clint Masterson has ridden into cattle country to bring peace to a divided land. But a greater battle rages inside him when he dares to desire the beautiful Becky!

WILDEST HEART (4456, $4.99)
by Virginia Brown
Maggie Malone had come to cattle country to forge her future as a healer. Now she was faced by Devon Conrad, an outlaw wounded body and soul by his shadowy past . . . whose eyes blazed with fury even as his burning caress sent her spiraling with desire. They came together in a Texas town about to explode in sin and scandal. Danger was their destiny—and there was nothing they wouldn't dare for love!

Available wherever paperbacks are sold, or order direct from the Publisher. Send cover price plus 50¢ per copy for mailing and handling to Penguin USA, P.O. Box 999, c/o Dept. 17109, Bergenfield, NJ 07621. Residents of New York and Tennessee must include sales tax. DO NOT SEND CASH.

LEONA KARR

STOWAWAY HEART

ZEBRA BOOKS
KENSINGTON PUBLISHING CORP.

To Karen Graffenberger
With love and affection.

ZEBRA BOOKS are published by

Kensington Publishing Corp.
850 Third Avenue
New York, NY 10022

Zebra and the Z logo Reg. U.S. Pat. & TM Off. The
Lovegram logo is a trademark of Kensington Publishing
Corp.

First Printing: October, 1994

Printed in the United States of America

One

The two riverboats were only black dots upstream when Trish Winters first spied them rising and falling in the turbulent waters of the Colorado River. She leapt up, abandoning the spot where she had been dangling her feet in a cool eddy. Her curiosity almost overcame her caution, but she grabbed her high-top shoes and long black stockings, lifted the folds of her skirt and hastily took cover in a thick stand of cottonwood trees. Trish had been warned about the danger of her solitary walks along the sandy banks of the river that bordered Colorado and the Utah Territory. In 1867, only the roughest of frontiersmen dared to challenge the belligerent Colorado River filled with devilish cataracts as it roared southward on its way to the Gulf of California.

She couldn't keep excitement from overwhelming her as she peered through the leafy cover and watched the boats come nearer and nearer. Trish had never seen anything like the trim crafts slicing through the water. Over twenty feet long, she reasoned as they swept past her hiding place and she glimpsed a huge, blond-bearded man working the oars in one boat and a dark-haired man in the other, both moving with frantic rhythm to keep the boats in the center of the river. She darted out into the open and gazed after them as the boats disappeared around the next curve in the river.

Bend River was only a couple of miles downstream and Trish knew that there would be plenty of excitement in the ugly, dusty settlement when the river men put to shore. Except when an army patrol from Fort Laramie stopped in Bend River, or a wagon train went through, there was nothing to relieve the dreary monotony of the frontier town.

She grabbed up her sunbonnet from the rock where she had been sitting and quickly tied it over her fiery brown hair. Holding up her skirts with one hand, she ran along the sandy bank after the disappearing boats. She was breathless when she bounded over the last rise of a small hill cupping the sprawling settlement along a wide curve in the river. She stopped and let her gaze travel the river's edge where a few canoes and rowboats were tied. No sign of the riverboats. Disappointment swept over her. And puzzlement, too.

She frowned as she descended a dusty path skirting patches of sagebrush and yucca plants. Surely, the river men hadn't gone past Bend River without stopping since the course of the Colorado below Bend River still hadn't been fully charted. Trish knew a great deal about the Colorado River because her father had made several attempts to explore its banks and her older brother, Teddy, had been drowned on one of her father's excursions on the river. Her mother had never been able to accept the loss of her only son. She wasted away and two years ago, when Trish was fifteen, her mother had died. Shortly after her death, her father had decided to start someplace else anew. Despite Trish's pleas not to leave her in Bend River, her father had refused to take her with him.

"I lost my son to the Colorado," he told her. "I'll not chance it with my daughter. You stay here, honey—with the parson and Gertie. I've talked with them. They're willing to look after you."

Trish had flung herself into his arms, begging, "Take me with you, Poppa. Don't leave me here. I'm not afraid of the river.

I'm fifteen. Old enough to be of help. Let me go with you."

He shook his head. "I've got important business to take care of. The government's interested in exploring the Colorado from the Gulf of California up to the Big Canyon." A robust man in his forties, smile lines creased the corners of Benjamin's eyes and weathered cheeks. His broad mouth parted under a graying mustache, and he gave his pilot's hat a rakish tilt. "Guess your old man knows Big Mud as good as anybody." A passionate glow touched his eyes. There was a lustful, possessive passion in it, the kind usually associated with a woman.

"I wouldn't be a burden to you," she pleaded.

He set his jaw. "I told you, Trish. A river trail is no place for a woman." He kissed his daughter goodbye. "I'll come back for you when I'm settled. I hear things are really booming around Fort Yuma at the mouth of the river. I'll buy a nice little place and you can come keep house for me."

Two years had passed since that day he kissed her goodbye. A couple of hastily scribbled letters reached Trish from Fort Yuma the first year. He sent money from time to time for her keep. She continued to live with Parson Gunthar and his wife, Gertie. Now, at seventeen, Trish's future stretched out in front of her like the never-ending lifeless desert. She would have run away, but there was no place nor anyone that she could run to.

Her excitement over seeing the river men was gone and a sense of emptiness had taken its place. Her steps slowed as she came down the hill toward a row of crude wooden buildings lining a dusty, rutted road. Her heavy shoes made a hollow sound on the wooden sidewalk that ran in front of several saloons and a few stores. She paused in front of Jeb Stubbens's Mercantile and Feed Store for a moment and glanced at a clutter of merchandise offered in a window display. Her eyes lingered on a bolt of lovely floral gingham and her fingers unconsciously fingered the worn fabric of her brown calico dress.

Even though her father had sent money for her keep, the parson and Gertie had treated her as an object of charity. All her clothes came from the rummage boxes sent to the Reverend Gunthar from a church back East. And for the Christian hospitality of their home, Trish was expected to cook, clean, sew, and present a humble and supplicant demeanor at all times. Unfortunately her willful, stubborn nature refused to bend to the restrictions of such a pious, dedicated life. She readily slipped away from her unfinished duties to walk barefoot along the river and visit a saloon gal, Winnie May, who had become her dearest friend. She would have hurried to Winnie's small cabin at the edge of town to tell her about the riverboats, but she knew that her friend slept in the afternoon and left for the Rawhide Saloon about eight o'clock every evening. Winnie May was not a woman who met with the parson's approval.

Trish had been about seven years old when she first heard the word "whore" and with her usual curiosity at work, she had hunted up Winnie May to see what one looked like. When the bosomy, middle-aged woman ambled out of her one-room cabin at the edge of town, Trish had stepped forward and asked, "Are you the town whore?"

Winnie stiffened and swung around, her hand ready to cuff the impertinent brat. When she saw only wide-eyed frankness on the little girl's face, she stayed her hand.

"Who wants to know?" she demanded in her deep, throaty voice.

"Me . . . Trish Winters. I never saw a whore . . . but *they* say you're one."

"Who says?" Winnie's full mouth tight-ened.

With the open honesty of childhood, Trish readily named the three women. "My mother, Mrs. Stubbens, and Gertie, the parson's wife." Trish gave her a mischie-vous grin. "I was hiding behind the flour barrel. I heard everything they said."

"Well, my friends call me Winnie May," answered the prostitute with a slight lifting of her double chin.

"Then I'll call you Winnie May, too. And you can call me Trish."

A smile eased the deep lines in Winnie's face. And a strange friendship was forged.

In time, Trish learned that Winnie had been left stranded in Bend River by a wan-dering frontiersman who decided to hit the fur trail and never returned for her. She warned Trish not to give her heart away to any man with dust on his shoes.

Trish drew her eyes away from the pretty cloth and sent a quick glance through the dusty glass into the store. She blinked. Two strangers were standing at the counter talking to Jeb Stubbens. One had wild blond curly hair and a beard. The other was clean shaven and dark-haired. The river men! She was positive of it. They must have pulled in their boats above or below the settlement. Maybe they were go-

ing all the way to Fort Yuma through the
Big Canyon just as her father had done.

She spun on her heels, intending to go
inside and corner them with questions, but
a small boy about seven came barreling
out of the store and grabbed her hand.
"We gotta get Miz Gertie."

"What's the matter, Timmy?"

He pulled on her. "Ma . . . she's
abirthin'."

Trish flung a look inside the store.

"We gotta hurry," the little boy cried.
His face was scrunched up with fear.

"It's all right, Timmy. We'll find Gertie."

This was Mrs. Stubbens fifth child and
her labors were always long and dire.
Gertie Gunthar was the nearest thing to
a midwife that Bend River possessed. The
meager medical training given to missionaries scarcely qualified her to deliver babies, but she was better than the
alternative—delivering a baby without any
assistance whatever.

Gertie was a gaunt woman who carried
her religion in plain view like a heavy
knapsack. Her shoulders were rounded
and her chest was as flat as her stomach.
An habitual pained expression put deep
furrows in her forehead and narrowed her
mouth to a straight line. Trish had felt the
sting of her sharp tongue so often that she

had grown impervious to the woman's dis-
pleasure. She didn't blame the parson for
becoming a circuit preacher and spending
a lot of time away from Bend River. In
truth, Trish didn't like Reverend Gunthar
any better than she liked Gertie. In some
ways, he made her life more miserable
than his sour-faced wife. He had become
bolder and bolder in invading her privacy,
pretending an avuncular affection that had
an edge of lust in it. Trish had learned to
keep his wife's presence between them.

Gertie's mouth was drawn in an angry
tight line when she saw Trish coming up
the path toward the house. She had
thought Trish was in the wash shed,
scrubbing the week's laundry until a moment before when she had discovered everything soaking in chilled water and no
Trish in sight.

"Run off again, did you? The good
Lord who had shed his bounty upon you
and—"

"Mrs. Stubbens needs you," Trish said
quickly, hoping to deflect Gertie's rage and
cut short her hell-and-brimstone sermon
about Trish's ingratitude. "Timmy says it's
time."

"Yes, um." The little boy nodded his
head. "She's screaming like all get out!"

"You'd better go, Gertie. I'll finish up

here," Trish gave the hostile woman a soothing smile.

"A devil's child, that's what you are." Her eyes were points of flinty black. "He'll claim his own one day."

"You'd better hurry," Trish said without giving Gertie the satisfaction of seeing how much her cold rejection hurt her. There had never been any love or warmth given her in the two years she'd lived in the Gunthar home.

"You finish up the washing, scrub the kitchen floor, and get that chunk of venison cut up for jerky. Hear? Most likely I won't be back till morning."

Even as Gertie collected her things, she listed a half-dozen more tasks to be finished before Trish turned in for the night. "The parson won't be back until Saturday and I want everything the way he likes it before he puts a foot in this house."

After she'd gone, Trish gave a happy twirl in the middle of the floor. She had the house to herself for the whole evening. Humming a tune, she went out the back door and across a small clearing to a shed that served as a washhouse. She had to pump another bucket of water, return to the kitchen and heat it on an old blackened stove. She promised herself that after she finished her chores she'd have herself a nice leisurely bath in front of the fire.

She tackled the washing, scrubbing the clothes on a washboard until her arms were weary and then hung them out to dry. She sharpened a kitchen knife and cut up the venison someone in the congregation had given the parson. She decided the kitchen floor could wait.

Being alone was a luxury she intended to enjoy to the fullest. She lit a candle, set the wooden tub in front of the kitchen stove and heated up two kettles of water to a delightful, soothing warmth. Then she stripped off her faded brown dress, worn petticoat, and mended cotton drawers. Candlelight burnished the ivory softness of her young body as she stepped into the tub. With a contented sigh she eased down into the water.

She cupped the water in her hand and let it run down her neck and pink-tinged breasts. Like a nymph under a waterfall, she closed her eyes and poured water over her head and face, laughing softly from the pleasure of washing herself all over.

A half-caught breath was the first hint of a presence behind her. Her breath caught. She jerked her head around.

Parson Gunthar stood in the kitchen doorway. There was a mesmerized expression on his round, sweaty face. He was a short man, solid except for a paunchy middle. And light on his feet. In a second he was across the kitchen to the side of the tub and his shadow fell over her like the wings of a predator. A hungry glint in his eyes devoured her young, supple body.

Trish tried to sink lower in the water. "What . . . what are you doing home?"

His moist mouth curved. "A change of plans. I met a wagon train that will be pulling into Bend River tomorrow. Need to hold a revival. Where's Gertie?"

"With Mrs. Stubbens . . . helping with a birthin'. We weren't expecting you. She said you'd be gone . . . a couple more days."

His eyes held a glassy stare as they traveled over her glistening bare shoulders and breasts barely covered by her crossed arms. Her supple legs could not be hidden under the water in the small tub.

"Bathsheba." He quoted in a husky voice. " 'And as David walked upon the roof of the king's house, he saw a woman washing herself and the woman was very beautiful to look upon,' " he quoted in sonorous tones.

"Please . . . leave me alone."

His eyes were glazed with lust. "And he

inquired after the woman and she came unto him."

"No . . . please, go . . ."

"Come, my own lovely Bathsheba."

His thick hands pulled her out of the water. She fought but her slender body was no match for his bull-like strength. His moist mouth was all over her as she struggled against his torturous embrace.

"Let me go!" Trish writhed in the iron circle of his arms. Her hands beat against his chest. "You can't do this."

"God understands the temptations of the flesh."

"No . . . no!"

His full mouth descended on hers. His broad hands splayed across her back. The abhorrent kiss sucked at her breath. In desperation, she caught soft flesh of a lip between her teeth and bit down as viciously as she could.

He jerked his mouth away and she shoved him as hard as she could. The wooden tub turned over, spilling water all over the floor.

She almost twisted out of his grasp but his hands clutched her waist and held her tight. His eyes were glazed with lust and blood trickled over his mouth where she had bit him.

She struck out at him, clawing and hitting. They crashed against the table, tipping it over and scattering the remnants of her supper across the floor.

Desperately she caught him behind the knee with one of her legs and succeeded in throwing him off balance for a second. His grip tightened around her waist as he struggled to catch himself. Then his boots slipped on the wet, soapy floor and they went down together.

For a moment the breath was knocked out of her. With a muttered oath, he rolled his thick body on top of her nakedness. His heavy breathing bathed her face. " 'And she came unto David and he lay with her.' "

He secured her arms above her head, holding her down with one hand and reaching with the other to unfasten the buttons on his black, dusty trousers.

"You can't do this!" she cried but she knew her protests were in vain.

His expression was one holy dedication. "And she came unto him and was purified from her uncleanness."

Trish screamed, twisted her body to one side as he tried to sweep her legs apart. Then she raised a leg and kicked him. The grip on her wrists loosened. She jerked free and her hands scraped on the kitchen floor. In the midst of spilled clutter, her fingers touched a bread knife that had fallen from the overturned table.

She grabbed it. His eyes widened with disbelief as she plunged the knife into the soft flesh of his belly. With a choked cry, he rolled off her. Blood spilled out all over the floor.

She scrambled to her feet, swept up the pile of clothes and her shoes lying on a chair, and fled from the house.

The evening stars were already splashed across the night sky, and a cool breeze touched her trembling body as she darted across a small clearing. Wet hair clung to her head and sent trickles of water running down her naked body. When she was a safe distance away, she huddled in the darkness of a drift of cedar trees and dressed. Her arms and legs were seized with an uncontrollable trembling. Even her teeth chattered as deep sobs clutched at her throat. She didn't know what to do.

Who would believe her story? Reverend Gunthar was a respected man of God. No one would believe he had attacked the young woman he had befriended as his own daughter for the last two years. Trish knew frontier justice. Sure and arbitrary. She would be condemned as murderess no matter if she pleaded just cause. There

was only one person she could go to for
help . . . and understanding.

Winnie May.

Two

Moonlight gave faint illumination to the dark forms of rocks and trees hugging the river. Trish darted over the rough terrain like a threatened doe in flight. Even though she knew every rocky rise, mud pit, and thicket, terror brought every shadow alive and every sound became a warning in her ears. Winnie's crude cabin stood isolated in a drift of piñon pine trees only a short walk from the Rawhide Saloon where she served drinks. The site was private enough for her nightly visitors and far enough away not to taint the respectable ladies with her presence.

When Trish burst into the cabin, Winnie was in the process of struggling to lace herself up in a skimpy velvet gown that was becoming too snug for her ample figure.

"Winnie . . . Winnie," sobbed Trish.

"Land's sake, girl. What on earth?"

Trish's mouth wouldn't work. Wet hair

clung to her cheeks and tears spilled out the corner of her eyes.

"What is it?" Winnie took Trish's wet hair. "Did you fall in the river?"

"No . . . he . . . I . . ." she stammered.

"Someone's after ya?"

Trish's body shook like a sapling battered in a vicious wind. Winnie May enveloped her in the circle of her soft cushion arms. "It's all right. Winnie's right here. Ain't nothing going to harm you," she soothed, stroking her head. "Hush, now. Hush. Nothing's that bad. Tell me what happened."

"The parson," Trish sent Winnie a panicked look.

The older woman's expression tightened. "What about the parson?"

Her eyes hardened as she listened to Trish's sobbing account of what had happened. It didn't take many of Trish's fractured sentences for Winnie to get the picture. The holier-than-thou Parson Gunthar had come upon Trish naked in her bath and tried to rape her on the kitchen floor.

"The two-faced bastard!" swore Winnie. The hypocritical preacher had slithered over to her place late one night. She'd cussed him out good and proper and told him to go home to his wife. She'd never trusted him and had been worried about Trish living in the same house with him. "You ain't going back to that house," Winnie told Trish firmly. "I'll tell the parson myself."

Trish's frightened eyes rounded. "I killed him, Winnie."

For a moment Winnie looked too stunned to speak. Then she croaked, "You what?"

"I stabbed him . . . with the kitchen knife. I was so frightened, Winnie," she sobbed.

" 'Course you were, honey, but how could you . . . kill him?" The man's lust didn't surprise Winnie but Trish's murderous response did. "You shouldn't of done it, girl. He's a bastard for coming at you like that but to stick a knife in him. Land's sake, you shouldn't of killed him . . . set yourself up for a hanging." Even as she scolded, she stroked the russet head buried against her ample bosom.

"I . . . I couldn't get away . . . and the knife . . . it was there in my hand." She lifted her head and her anguished eyes pleaded with Winnie. "I had to stop him."

Winnie remembered how an uncle had introduced her to the ways of men in the same way. She sighed. "Sure you did, honey. Now let old Winnie May think a minute.

Got to act quick, honey. We can't let some-one find the bastard and start a posse . . . you say Gertie's helping Mrs. Stubbens with a birthin'? Good, that will give us a little time . . . can you get yourself lost till mornin'? Give Winnie time to handle this?" She put her full cheek against Trish's tear-ful face. "It's going to be all right, hear?"

Trish nodded, straightened her shoul-ders. "What are you going to do? I don't want you to get in trouble."

Winnie snorted. "Don't be a worrying about me. I've been taking care of myself for a long time. It's you that we have to worry about now. But we ain't got no time to dally."

"Gertie will probably be gone all night. I'll figure out something that'll keep that pretty neck of yours out of a noose. You hightail it out of sight, keep yourself scarce, don't be blabbing to anyone about what happened. When it's safe to come back tomorrow, I'll put one side of my cur-tain up . . . like this. Understand?"

Trish nodded.

"Here, take my shawl. You'll need it against the night's chill." She wrapped a knitted shawl around Trish's shoulders and gave her a quick bear hug. "Don't you worry none. Now git!" She gave Trish a gentle shove out the door.

Trish was still trembling when she left Winnie's shack. She headed for the only other place of solace she knew—the river. As she stumbled along its bank, uncertain moonlight filtered through a gauze of fast-moving clouds and sent her shadow playing upon the bleached sand. Her thin dress, cotton shift, and drawers were not much protection against water-chilled breezes. In her haste she had failed to put on her long stockings and her feet were bare in her buttoned black shoes. She hugged Winnie's shawl around her.

She walked for a while, then sat down and hugged her knees. She closed her eyes, put her head down, and tried to shut out the picture of the parson lying in a pool of his own blood. Her stomach churned with nausea. Everything had happened so fast, like a horrible nightmare.

As she cowered in the shadows of rocks and scrubs, raw terror curled her insides. "Set yourself up for a hanging" Winnie had said. *A hanging.* Was there anything that Winnie could do? A sickening bile swept up into her throat just remembering how a posse had brought a horse thief back to Bend River and strung him up. She'd seen his body dangling from a noose, turning slightly in the breeze, his head dropped forward and his bloated face turned black.

Once Gunthar's body was found, the outraged inhabitants of Bend River would be searching for her. The parson was a man of God, dedicated to bringing the Holy Word in this uncivilized land. No one would listen to her. No one would believe her story. Men who used women freely and then tossed them aside would have little patience with her pleas that she had the right to defend herself.

Her nerves were like frayed hemp ready to snap. Her head came up with a jerk when a quiet snapping in a stand of cedars behind her sounded like the quiet footsteps of someone creeping toward her. She jumped to her feet, darted forward through a thicket of scrub oak. Winnie's shawl caught on the nettles and she left it dangling there.

She ran and ran, finally slumping to the ground, her chest burning and sobs choked in her chest. She buried her head in her arms. A hushed silence was broken only by her frantic breathing and the soft lapping of water at her feet.

Night was beginning to give way to the first pearly white of dawn when she got to her feet again and began walking downstream—and that's when she came upon the boats.

She froze for a moment as her eyes identified the two crafts she had seen earlier that afternoon. They were pulled up in a sheltered bend of the river. Darting quickly behind a cottonwood tree, she held her breath and then cautiously peered around its thick trunk. The riverboats rocked slightly in the water, and she spied a brown army tent pitched a short distance away under a canopy of straggly willow trees.

For a long moment, her eyes scanned the boats and out of her desperation came a decision. As quickly as a shadow playing upon the ground, she sped across a narrow clearing to the nearest boat. Hunching down beside the hull, she waited, stiffening against any sound that would warn her she'd been seen. The wings of a nighthawk and the call of an owl were the only intrusion in the waiting silence.

She stood, slipped over the side of the boat and felt it dip under her weight. Her hopes for concealment rose when she pulled back a canvas hung over a small hatch at the stern of the boat. Thank heavens, she was small and agile enough to fit in the storage space—if she emptied out some of its contents. Her heart wedged in her throat like a hard lump of bread dough as she removed one box, and then a small canvas bag, and finally a rolled-up tarp. Making three trips over the side of the boat, she hid the objects in a nearby thicket. Returning to the boat, she curled herself up in the tiny space and pulled the canvas back down in its former position.

"Please God, let me get away," she prayed, waiting like a hunted creature as the light of dawn crept under the edge of the canvas.

When she heard men's voices, she held her breath until her lungs burned. Her heart seemed to stop. She closed her eyes, her ears straining for every sound. She couldn't hear what they were saying. Their conversation seemed to be short, precise sentences. Every terrifying second she expected the canvas cover to be pulled back and a rough pair of hands to drag her from the hiding place.

She heard footsteps and a moment later, her head jerked forward as a sudden shove of the boat sent it sailing out into the water. Then she felt the boat dip as one of the river men jumped in.

She could hear the man's labored breath above the squeaking of oars in their oarlocks as the river current caught the boat and sent it plunging through the water.

The cramped-up position and the constant movement of the boat brought a fiery ache to every part of her body but she told herself that she could endure any torment. Every mile down the river widened her chances of escaping a posse's noose.

As she began to think ahead, her joy of escape was tempered with growing apprehension. What would happen when the two men discovered her presence? She would be totally at their mercy . . . and helpless. Civilized behavior was rare in a lawless territory where women were little more than chattel of the rugged men who dared to settle it.

My God, she thought with a silent cry. What have I done?

Three

Trish felt the boat rise and fall in the water but couldn't tell how fast they were moving. As the hours passed, she had no idea how far they had left Bend River behind. Her whirling thoughts were halted by a sudden yell from the man in her boat. The next instant the craft reared up almost perpendicular.

Trish's panicked cry was lost in the tumult of crashing water spilling into the boat. Her head was flung back so viciously that her neck nearly jerked out of her collarbone. Oak timbers in the hull crackled and groaned as if threatening to pull apart. The boat seemed to be falling through space.

She was going to drown! The same river that had taken her brother's life was going to claim hers, but unlike Teddy, she was going to meet her Maker with the blood of murder on her hands. A terrifying dizziness enveloped her as the craft shot forward, bucking and spinning.

Water poured under the edge of the canvas cover. Then, as suddenly as the upheaval had begun, the boat righted itself.

Trish gasped for breath.

The boat moved smoothly over the water and then bumped to a stop with a scraping of its hull upon land. Immediately the craft dipped as someone jumped out. Not even fear of what awaited her could make Trish stay where she was another minute. She lashed out frantically against water, cloth, and suffocating air.

"What in the hell—?" A man's deep voice accosted her as she scrambled into the sunlight and wavered to her feet at the stern of the boat.

Momentarily blinded by the sudden shift from darkness to bright sunlight, she squinted through dangling strands of wet cinnamon hair. Before she could say anything a dark-haired man whose face had been bronzed by the sun grabbed her by the arms and pulled her out of the boat. His deep voice vibrated like thunder. "I don't believe it! A goddamn stowaway!"

She looked up into angry eyes, smoldering darkly with a fiery glint. The man was soaked from his recent battle in the rapids, wet doeskin trousers clinging to long, muscular legs. His shirt had been torn open where several buttons were missing and dark hair curled on his tanned chest. Even in her shattered state, his anger did not reach her. The feeling of relief that she had escaped the wrath of the river blotted out everything else. She tried to smooth back the tousled hair tumbling loosely around her face.

Morgan Wallace choked on his next oath as he stared at her. He could not believe it! A stowaway who had the audacity to look up at him with beguiling green eyes and a soft smile. Her hair glinted in the sun, a flamboyant color of reds and browns; dark eyebrows were slightly winged, giving a saucy look to her sea-green eyes. At the moment water droplets tipped her long eyelashes and bathed her face in luminous softness.

"Where in the hell did you come from?" he demanded with controlled fury.

Somehow Trish found her voice. "I . . . I . . . got in . . . upstream." She was ready with her story. "My parents—my parents were killed," she lied. "By Indians. I fled to the river . . . and found your boats." Memory of her frantic flight made her voice shake. "I—I had to get away," she finished honestly.

"If that's the truth—why hide yourself? Why not tell us what happened . . . and that you needed help?"

"Would you have let me come with you—if I'd told you?"

"No! Of course not, but—"

Her slender chin jutted upward. There was courage, defiance, and sharp intelligence in her bold look. "That's why I hid in your boat . . . without saying anything."

"I guess she's got you there, Morgan," his companion said in a midwestern drawl.

Trish's gaze swung to the man who was chuckling. He was a huge man. Arms, legs, chest, and shoulders were of mammoth proportions. Curly, sun-streaked hair sprang out from his round head like a lion's mane and a thick beard of the same bleached tawny color curled over his jowls and chin. He stood with his weight settled on two gunboat feet. His side alone made him intimidating but there was something diffident, subordinate in his manner, which identified the man he called Morgan as the one in charge.

Trish looked back at the dark-haired, handsome man. Yes, he was the leader. It stuck out all over him, she thought. His stance and the way he held his head hinted of an aristocrat used to controlling men . . . and women. Tanned skin stretched tightly over bold cheekbones; a wide mouth held deep crescents at its corners as he glared at her and she knew that it could spread in deep laughter, but he wasn't smiling now. He stood there handsome, dangerous, invincible—and angry! A hard lump of fear built in her chest as his puzzled gaze passed over the simple calico dress hanging in wet folds against her breasts and outlining her slender waist and thighs.

"Indians?" Morgan questioned, raising one eyebrow. The way she had stumbled over the word "Indians," he suspected that she was lying about the reason she had hid herself away in the boat. Right now, it didn't seem to matter. After all his careful planning, this unforeseen complication could ruin everything. What was he going to do with her? They were miles from any civilization and they sure as hell couldn't dump her like an unwanted kitten.

Trish pushed past him. Her arms and legs were cramped from long hours in her hiding place. She stretched them as best she could and then sat down on the warm sand to empty her shoes of water.

Morgan turned his back to her with muttered swearing. "We'll have to check that hatch and see what's missing. She must have dumped some stuff or there wouldn't have been room for her."

Jens massaged his full curly beard and nodded his head in agreement. His round hazel eyes slid over Trish and he shook his massive head. "Imagine that? A pretty river wench sitting at my feet all that time and me not knowing it!"

Trish realized then that she had been in his boat and not the dark-haired man's. As the two men unloaded the rest of the things from the compartment where she had been hiding, she sat down on the warm earth a few feet away and watched them with anxious eyes. Trish was almost certain that the man called Morgan had not believed her story about Indians. Whatever happened, she mustn't let him know she was a fugitive from the law. He'd turn her over in a minute if he knew she'd knifed a man. Her only hope was to appeal to his sympathy. Not an easy order judging by the cold, speculative glare he had given her when she was babbling about Indians.

"My God, she dumped a box of ammunition—and some of the tools!" Morgan stared at the pile of supplies they had gathered on the bank. "How can we bring down any fresh game? And with vital tools gone, no way to keep the boats in repair!" Morgan ran a hand through his thick wavy hair in an exasperated gesture as if he couldn't believe his own words.

"I'm sorry," Trish gulped. She realized now how terribly important the items were that she had taken from the boat. But she'd had no choice, she told herself. None at all. She'd taken the only escape offered to her.

"Sorry!" Morgan repeated the word like a demand that she give him some reasonable explanation for putting his well-laid plans in jeopardy. He stood over her, his hands clenched as if struggling to keep from strangling her.

"Please try to understand," she said quickly, trying to stay his mounting wrath. "I never meant to cause trouble. I had to get away." If only she could explain the real reason for her flight. She swallowed hard. How much understanding would she get from this commanding river man if he knew she was guilty of murder? Even as she searched for words to soften his expression, she knew it was hopeless. She had to keep her secret. Her life probably depended upon it. She lowered her eyes and clamped her mouth shut.

"Where did this Indian attack take place? What wagon train was it? What tribe?"

"Paiutes," she said quickly for she knew they had been on the warpath recently. "They attacked our wagon . . . outside of

Bend River . . . and I ran away . . . to the river. That's where I found your boats."

Morgan snorted. His gut feeling told him she was lying. More likely some rough frontiersman was trying to put his brand on her and she took flight. He had to admit that her supple body was something to stir a man's blood. Her wet dress clung to rounded curves of her thrusting full breasts and he felt his own virile body responding to the sight of her long, supple legs and rounded hips. Even in his anger, he was not immune to her tempting body and the pleasure it could offer a man.

Jens sauntered up. "Maybe we should have split everything evenly between the two boats, Morgan," he offered, looking at the small pile of provisions from his boat. "Then we wouldn't have lost so much of one thing."

"I tried to do that," countered Morgan, "but we didn't have duplicates of all the tools. We've been using my box of ammunition. It's nearly empty. We'll have to save what I have left for hostile Indians. Forget about fresh game, now."

"At least we didn't lose anything going over those rapids—"

"Except one of my oars, damnit," swore Morgan. "I'd never have made it to the bank if you hadn't caught me with your boat and guided me in. How in God's name are we going to make another one—without any tools?"

"Who told you this river was navigable anyway?" demanded Jens. "Hell, these waves ain't anything like an ocean's. A boat can't stay in one place . . . can't get loose from that crazy forward motion. No way the Colorado's going to take to river travel."

"How do you know? No one's charted the course of this river nor any of the land spreading away from it. I aim to do just that! I won't be satisfied until we make it to the Gulf of California," Morgan countered aggressively. His diction was crisp, with the clipped vowels of the eastern seaboard. "Settlers in this territory are looking for an outlet to the sea and anyone who can find it will make himself a fortune and be master of all he surveys."

"Good Lord, Morgan, if the old river is this cantankerous all the way to the the Gulf of California, she ain't going to take a liking to any boats trying to go up and down her. And we sure as hell ain't going very far until we scare up another oar for you."

Morgan squinted up at the midday sun overhead. "Better fix some grub first." He glanced at Trish as if he couldn't bring himself to handle all the complications of an unwanted stowaway on an empty stomach.

Trish had listened to their conversation about the river with great interest. They were going to explore the Colorado River all the way to the Gulf of California. Excitement leaped into her breast. She was her father's true child, for she had been always fascinated by his adventures and had longed to go with him on one of his river trips. Now she was here, with two men who were really going to ride the river as far as its mouth. Was there a chance that they would take her on as a member of the exploration? She knew the answer to that. She was just a vulnerable female, not of as much value as a mule in these uncivilized parts. She had watched Morgan's eyes traveling over her body. Her thin, faded calico dress had torn away at one shoulder and her cotton shift and drawers clung damply to her skin. She began wringing out the soaked edges of her dress and shift spreading the layers of cloth out around her. Thank heavens, she wore no stays, she thought, as she felt the warmth of the May sun evaporating moisture from her clothing. Her spirits revived and her agile mind began to work on the problem at hand.

With fingers lacing her hair, she spread

out damp strands over her shoulders like a dark chestnut fan, trying to get it smoothed out enough to braid. Then her fingers worked nimbly as she wove the heavy, russet strands. She wasn't dead! That knowledge lent a foolish buoyancy to her thoughts. She was alive and far enough downstream to be safe from anyone searching for her. Her father had told her that not many men had the courage to run the Colorado for any distance so she knew it was unlikely that anyone would be coming after her. She savored the safety of the moment, leaned back her head and sighed.

"Pretty little thing," mused Jens, watching Morgan's puzzled gaze settling on her. "What are we going to do with her?"

"God knows! Leave her here, I guess."

"We can't do that, Morgan."

"I know it." He sighed. "But that's the only choice beside taking her back upstream. God knows how far it is to anything like a settlement downriver." Morgan was not superstitious but he couldn't rid himself of the notion that disaster had crawled into the boats with them. The success of his expedition was perilous at best. Fury raged within him. All his careful planning jeopardized by a green-eyed beauty was something that challenged his ability to control his emotions.

He began to make a new inventory of all the supplies they had brought and made new calculations. Without ample ammunition to bring down fresh food, they would have to rely on what meager provisions were left. They would have to dry out the cornmeal or it would be too rancid to use. One slab of bacon remained, some jerky, coffee, dried apples, and about two messes of beans. That was about it. There was scarcely enough for two. No extra provisions for a conniving river urchin.

As the men worked, Trish raised her eyes to colorful lichens coating nearly vertical sandstone cliffs that hedged in the river. Festoons of yellows, greens, and red-oranges blended with the ruddy walls. Some of the tension eased from her shoulders as the warmth of the sun dried her clothes. Bright, midday sunlight poured straight down into the canyon and she squinted against the bold colors of cliffs and water. Brassy orange rays of the sun spilled over her, easing away her chills. The bleached blue sky was heavy with a windless heat. Rocks, dirt, and water radiated heat and a glaring brightness. She gave a self-mocking laugh. How ironic that she was now fleeing down the Colorado River that her father loved so much. Her thoughts lurched to a stop. An idea burst in her head like a fiery explosion. A decision was formed full blown as she sat on the warm sand beside the river.

She would find her father!

The decision was made without any consideration of her total lack of resources. She hadn't heard from him for months but he would be somewhere near the banks of his beloved river—she was certain of that. He had mentioned Fort Yuma in his letters. Somehow she would get there. She had to! She couldn't go back to Bend River.

Trish's thoughts swirled frantically as she watched the men. The one called Morgan had caught her interest. Even in his anger, she had glimpsed the kind of strength that captured her imagination. He was a river man . . . like her father. And not someone who changed his mind easily, she thought with a leaden feeling in the pit of her stomach. He was angry about the loss of the vital tools and ammunition and she feared he had dismissed her tale about fleeing from Indians for the lie that it was. When he looked at her, it was as if those intense dark eyes could see right through her. He was not a man to be manipulated and yet she knew she must match wits with him if she were to get her way.

The smell of boiled coffee and fried bacon tantalized her nostrils and her stomach growled in empty protest. Part of her dizziness was lack of nourishment. "I'm hungry," she said.

"She's cost us our ammunition and tools—now she wants to eat what she hasn't thrown overboard," said Morgan as he filled up a tin plate. He still couldn't believe it. He was angry, dazed, and thrown off balance by her sudden intrusion into his life.

Jens squatted on his thick haunches Indian style and brushed a hand across a mouth moist with bacon grease. "I reckon river rats can fend for themselves . . ."

"I'm sorry, I really am—" Trish cajoled in a pleading tone.

"Sorry don't change nothing," countered Jens and for the first time Trish saw an ugly expression on his placid, broad face. "Gals lie really pretty . . . when it suits 'em. Takes a while to see behind them soft eyes to a barbed trap." His round hazel eyes centered somewhere beyond her and she knew his thoughts had sped to a memory that had nothing to do with her. Trish shrank back against the rocks. She didn't want to antagonize either of them even though the smell of the food was pure torture and twisted her stomach in empty knots.

She was surprised when Morgan carried a plate over to her. If only he would give her a chance to talk with him, thought Trish. "I didn't mean any harm. Please try to understand."

"I hope *you* understand how dire our situation is," he countered as he watched her eagerly eat the food. He was already feeling added responsibility for her safety.

"I'm not afraid," she said with a lift of her chin. "I'm ready to ride the river."

"Don't be an idiot. I'm not going to jeopardize this expedition with an unwanted stowaway. I've decided that we'll take you back upstream as far as we can. You'll have to hike back to Bend River and find help there."

"No!"

"You're not going with us! And that's final."

He walked back to Jens, his jaw set in a hard line. "We'll have to find some wood that will make into another oar to replace the one that wildcat of a river jerked right out of my hands."

"Ain't going to be easy."

While Jens washed the tin dishes in the river, Morgan looked up and down the canyon. Upstream the narrow bank disappeared completely without even footing along the stark, sun-baked walls hemming in the river. He tipped his head back, looking high above where some pieces of dry wood were caught in high crevices, probably left there the last time rampaging floodwater raised the river's level. Even if one of the logs were suitable, there wasn't any way to scale the cliffs and bring it down. The other side of the river didn't look any more promising. He turned to Jens. "We'll have to go downstream and see what we can find."

"We've only got a hunting knife left for whittling." The big man rose from his haunches.

"It'll have to do," said Morgan. "Maybe we'll find a tree of sorts."

"What'll we do with her?" He tipped his tawny lion's head toward Trish.

"Can't leave her here," answered Morgan. "She might be fool enough to shove off by herself in one of our boats . . . or eat up a month's rations while we're gone. She'll have to come with us." He strode over to Trish. "Come on, we're going to take a walk."

Hours cramped up in the small hatch of the boat had left Trish unsteady and she wavered as she got to her feet. Morgan's firm arms automatically shot out to support her.

She pulled away. "I can walk."

"Good." He glared at her. He hadn't liked the way her soft flesh felt in his hands. Warm and soft, and damn it, just touching her reminded him he hadn't had a woman for a long time. Good God, what on earth was going to come of all of this? They had to get rid of her and fast. A desirable woman would put restraints on the easy camaraderie between him and Jens. That's all this expedition needed! He cursed silently as he motioned her to follow Jens while he took up the rear.

"Don't see a blasted piece of driftwood that'll do," said Jens as his gaze scoured the riverbank.

"Keep going," ordered Morgan.

The cliffs were stark and empty of any vegetation. How far downstream would they have to go to find anything suitable for an oar, Morgan wondered as they rounded several curves in the river.

Once Trish's muscles stretched out again, she easily kept up with the men. There wasn't a hill around Bend River that she hadn't climbed. She had scrambled up and down the rough terrain with a delight that had been a constant challenge to her mother's idea of proper upbringing. Even Teddy, her older brother, had not been able to scale a rocky gorge or hop across a creek as fast as she could. She walked in front of Morgan with an easy, graceful gait. Her long plait of her newly braided hair swung on her back and Morgan tried to ignore the pleasing rhythm of her arms and legs as he followed her.

Swift currents had undercut the sandy bank and weakened it so that in places great sections of the soft ground had fallen into the muddy Colorado, earning its nickname, Big Mud. Jens led the way around several bends and still no large pieces of driftwood clung the river's edge and the only sign of vegetation was high up on the precipice of vaulting cliffs. It seemed to Trish that they had walked at least a mile along the narrow bank before Jens's voice jerked her head up.

"Look at that." He pointed downstream. The scraggly branches of a weathered willow tree hung out over the river. Half of its gnarled roots were exposed and it seemed ready to topple into the river at the next high water.

"Whatcha think?" asked Morgan walking around it when they reached the spot where it tottered on the bank's edge. His gaze assessed the tree from every angle. "See a branch that might do?"

Jens pointed to one limb that looked firm and straight enough for whittling into an oar—the one that dangled the farthest out over the rushing water.

"No way to crawl out and cut the limb

off. The damn tree won't take any weight,"
declared Morgan.

"Maybe I can lasso the end of it—a quick
jerk might break it off," said Jens, stroking
his beard in a thoughtful fashion. "See how
rotten the wood is next to the trunk. Looks
like the whole tree might split in half with
just a little pressure."

Morgan's dark eyebrows knitted together. "It might work. You'd have to give
it a good hard snap." His frown deepened.
"But if it fell, you could lose the branch
and rope." He studied it carefully and
then said, "Hell, might as well give it a
try. Don't see another piece of wood that'll
do."

Jens took some rope coiled at his belt and
stood as close to the desired branch as he
could without slipping off the bank into the
swirling current. Very carefully he threw a
loop into the air toward the branch hanging
high above the water. He missed, pulled the
rope back and tried it again . . . and again.
Muscles in his thick arm rippled with each
throw but he was always short of the target.
Finally he shook his head in exasperation.
"Can't make it reach without the danger of
losing the rope."

Morgan swore and squinted downstream.
"Maybe we can find another one that—"

"I could do it."

Both men turned to look at Trish as if they had forgotten she existed. Their faces hardened. They stared at her as if this unwanted female was somehow responsible for their bad luck.

"I could do it," she repeated in an even voice, keeping her gaze on Morgan's scowling features. "It wouldn't be hard. I could do it . . . climb out on that limb . . . tie a rope on the end. Then Jens could pull it in. I've shimmied up trees worse than that." Her mother had claimed that she was half monkey and had repeatedly admonished her daughter that ladies did not climb trees—to no avail. Trish had never outgrown her love of hiding away in some leafy tree with only the birds to keep her company.

Jens rubbed his beard thoughtfully. "She might be light enough for it, Morgan."

The men surveyed the tree again, looking longingly at the desired branch hanging like a delicious plum out over the water. "Maybe you're right . . . she's small . . . that rotten section might hold," Morgan contemplated, his handsome brow furrowed.

Or snap off as I climb out on it, thought Trish. Her offer had been pure bravado born out of desperation. The whole tree could pitch into the river! She looked up to find Morgan's gaze fixed on her and his forehead furrowed.

"I don't know." He hesitated. He knew what the danger was and as much as he wanted to be rid of her unwanted presence, he sure as hell didn't want to be responsible for drowning her.

"I can do it," she insisted again. The chance to bring any kind of begrudging thawing in those deep, dark eyes was worth the risk. A translucent glow in her sea-green eyes challenged him as she elevated her firm chin.

Morgan's expression wavered. "The tree's rotten . . ."

"I know that . . . but I'm light . . . and willing to try . . . a kind of payment for the things I dumped. Are you afraid to give me a chance?"

Her mocking tone challenged him and brought a wry smile to his lips. "All right. Let's shore it up, Jens."

The men stacked some large boulders against the tree in an effort to strengthen it up and slow down its movement if her weight pulled it over. Then Morgan nodded to Trish. "Ready?"

Trish bent over, reached through her legs and grabbed the back hem of her skirt. Deftly she drew the material through her legs and then tucked the skirt's hem in at her waist, making a kind of pants. She was conscious of her dirty bare legs showing below the ruffled edge of drawers and she knew a young lady should not be showing her limbs in this fashion. Still, there was no help for it—she couldn't climb the tree with folds of material flapping all around her. She had always been practical about social mores—which usually meant ignoring them whenever it was convenient.

She kicked off her shoes and then caught Morgan's eyes traveling over her supple legs exposed by the draping of her skirt and petticoat. Warmth crept up into her sun-burnished cheeks. She had never exposed her legs like this before a man but it was too late to back out now. "I'm ready," she said in a firm voice, daring him to say anything lewd about her appearance.

Morgan cupped his hands to give her a boost up. Gingerly she put her hand on his shoulder to steady herself. His muscles were firm under her touch and she could feel his warm breath upon her heated cheeks.

For a moment he just held the small foot she had placed in his hand, her body brushing against his. With her arms raised, he was aware of the full ripeness of her breasts curving softly and sweetly above a waist he could span with his hands. For an absurd moment Morgan found himself wanting to explore her young, vibrant body. Her hand on his shoulder invited an intimacy that sped warm desire coursing through his veins. It had been a long time since he felt such an urge to bed a woman. As if she were deliberately arousing him, he tightened the hard sweep of his cheek and jaw and growled, "If you hear the tree begin to crack . . . get down fast . . . and don't do anything stupid!"

She let her breath out, shaken by feelings she didn't understand. In response to his own clipped tones, she snapped, "I'll get your precious branch for you!"

Morgan lifted her up and kept his arms protectively upward until she had scrambled into the crotch of the tree. Then she grinned down at him, like some fey creature poised in the leaves of the old tree. Her dark russet hair, her pixielike features, and the mocking smile she tossed at him captured his senses. "What's your name?" he asked as if she might not be real but some momentary fancy, an enchanting hallucination.

Trish hesitated—should she tell him her real name? A first name shouldn't do any harm. "Trish," she called down. "What's yours?"

"Morgan Wallace."

"Nice to make your acquaintance, Mor-

gan Wallace," she said in an impudent
tone that used to get her in trouble with
her mother and the Gunthars. A heady
feeling made her laugh down at him.

His mouth curved in return. An intriguing cleft in his chin deepened, then disappeared. Because his emotions were suddenly
confused, he said quite crisply, "This could
be dangerous . . . do what I tell you! Jens,
throw her up the end of the rope."

The big man moved as close to her under the tree as he could and gave the rope
a toss. She caught it. The rope was already
looped at one end, so Trish put her head
and one arm through it and then gave
both men a cocky wave of her hand as she
began climbing upward, staying near the
trunk. When she reached a rotten section
of the tree where the desired limb jutted
out toward the branch they wanted, she
paused.

"How does it look?" he called up.

"Rotten . . ."

"Will it hold you?"

"I think so," she answered but she could
see where parasites had riddled the trunk
until it was nearly hollow. She was not at
all sure that the branch would hold her
weight when she eased out on it. She swallowed hard to get a dry cotton feeling out
of her mouth. Very gingerly she began to

scoot out on the limb. Immediately it bent downward under her weight. With every inch, the branch dangled her closer and closer to the rushing water below.

"That's far enough!" yelled Morgan. "Throw out the loop."

"No, I can't reach the end of the branch you want from here. I'll have to go out farther . . ."

At that moment the tree gave a threatening creak.

"It's not going to hold . . . come back!" ordered Morgan.

Stubbornly she moved out farther on the branch, shutting out the commanding tone of his voice.

"I said to come back!"

Carefully she righted herself. "I think I'm close enough to—" Before the last word was out another warning shift in the tree lowered her closer to the water.

"Damn it . . . do as I tell you! Get back before—"

The old cottonwood gave a lurch forward. If it hadn't been for the boulders weighing down its roots and the additional weight of Jens's body pressed against the trunk, the tree would have pulled free from the weakened ground. The sudden jerk almost unseated Trish as she pitched forward into a prone position on the branch she was straddling.

Frantically she hugged it!

Below her, water swirled and frothed and the roar of the river filled her ears. The limb bounded up and down as if trying to shake her off! She shut her eyes as a sickening dizziness threatened to send her plunging downward. She knew from Morgan's yells that he couldn't tell whether she had fainted or was immobilized by fear.

"Move! Damn you, move . . . the whole tree's going to go in a minute." He swore. He shouldn't have let her do it. The river would suck her away out of sight once she hit the water. At the moment, nothing in the world was more important than getting her down from that damn tree before it broke in two. "Come back."

Trish ignored his bellowing orders. She righted herself on the slanting branch and tried not to look at the river below as she took the rope off her shoulder with one hand and kept the other clutching the tree branch. Every time she looked at the foaming current below, the whole earth rushed dizzily under her. The rope . . . throw it out. You're close enough. Throw . . . throw. A brisk inner voice gave her the crisp orders.

She took the loop in her hand, and gingerly threw it forward, hoping to snag the end of the limb that the men wanted. The toss was too short and too flaccid. Her throw would have to be longer and more energetic to catch it. She tried again, throwing it with such force this time that she nearly unseated herself—but it caught!

"Yahoo!" Jens's booming voice congratulated her.

She heard Morgan's surprised laugh. It was a wonderful, resonant sound coming deep within his throat. "Good . . . now climb back down." He backed up, making the rope taut so that he had the branch securely tethered. "I told you I could do it," Trish taunted him, enjoying this moment of victory. Her laughter was cut off by a sharp crack, like a gunshot coming. She screamed as the limb on which she sat broke off between her and the trunk. The branch dropped out from under her. Frothy spumes rose in the air with the force of a sudden, upward waterfall as the limb crashed down into the river—and she with it.

She hit the water and went under.

Then up! Gasping. Choking.

Down—under again!

An undercurrent of the river jerked at her, spinning her in a churning maelstrom.

Blinded by the foamy water, she once more bobbed to the surface.

Something grazed her face. The rope! Fire laced her hands as she grabbed it and clung to it as she went under again. Her lungs filled with water but she felt herself being dragged toward the bank along with the limb she had lassoed. Then she was out of the river coughing and gagging.

Her chest burned with the raw pain of red coals searing her flesh. Rough hands turned her over. Water spurted from her mouth. Then a blessed unconsciousness claimed her and she slipped away beyond the torment.

Four

Possessive purple shadows hung low, enveloping the canyon as Trish floated in and out of consciousness. Red-orange rocks had lost their daytime colors and only a narrow expanse of night sky was visible between burnt umber cliffs. The sandy bank was damp under her as she lay on her back. A numb, floating sensation gave her body no boundaries. Her arms and legs seemed detached. She ordered them to move, but they remained listless, connected to a body too exhausted to move.

Except for the monotonous flow of the river, an ominous silence filled her ears. No movement in the night. She was alone. Abandoned. A wavery grayness drew her down in a restless sleep. She stirred fitfully and when she finally opened her eyes, vaulting cliffs were silhouetted against the misty light of early dawn.

Night was over.

"She's coming to." Morgan knelt down beside her.

Trish frowned as his face wavered into focus, trying to gather her thoughts into some kind of pattern. "I—I thought you'd gone . . ." she stammered.

He pushed back tangled wisps of damp hair from her forehead. Her face was drained of color; her lips blue. He remembered how cocky she had been sitting up there in the tree, grinning down at him, triumph flashing in her eyes. Only her dogged determination had kept her clinging to the rope as the river tried to sweep her away. She had guts. More than he'd been prepared to acknowledge. He didn't like the feeling of being beholden to her and nothing was going to change his mind about getting her out of his sight as soon as possible.

"I thought you'd left me," she said with relief shining in her eyes.

"Seemed best to let you sleep while we brought the boats down from above," he said in a gruff tone which he hoped masked his concern. "How are you feeling . . . after nearly drowning yourself?"

"Did you save the limb?" she asked anxiously.

"Yes. The rope held."

"Now you'll have your oar."

He ignored the edge of bragging in her voice. "Do you feel like sitting up?"

She nodded. As he helped her, she wanted to lean back against him and hold onto this moment of joy and relief. They hadn't left her! The realization that she had not been abandoned flooded her with renewed strength. "Thank you," she said weakly and then strengthened her voice with a deep breath. "I feel fine now."

He took his arm away. "Good. I'm glad we fished you out in time."

"So am I." She smiled at him.

He steeled himself against the temptation to trace the sweet curve of her cheek with his fingertips. He reminded himself of the months he had spent getting ready for this expedition and how his own future depended upon its success. "Trish," he said, sitting down on the ground beside her. "We've got to take you back upriver."

"I can't . . . go . . . back."

"Why not?" His intense gaze and commanding expression demanded the truth. "You lived in Bend River, didn't you? Who are you running from?"

She worked her mouth. She swallowed. How could she tell him that she had killed a man of God? And what was worse she knew that this commanding, self-disciplined captain would never take a murderess with him.

"I—don't have anybody to go back to," she managed. That at least was the truth. "I can't go back—ever! Please take me with you—I'm not afraid of the river."

"Crissake, you ought to be. It's been hell all the way down from Green River and you can bet that the worst is still ahead. No way of knowing if we'll even make it another five miles."

"I'll take my chances. I know about the danger. If I end up at the bottom of the river, so be it. Please . . . please. You have to take me with you." She almost told him she hoped to find her father somewhere on the river but that wouldn't fit in with the lie that he was dead.

Morgan searched her face. He'd known plenty of women, some in silken gowns, some in harlot scarlet, all of them willing to tease and please him. Some of the loveliest and most respected ladies had gambled on matrimony—and lost. Even the most sophisticated of his conquests had never gotten beyond the defenses that he raised against deep involvement or commitment. Morgan Wallace prided himself on never having been manipulated by any woman. He couldn't understand why this stubborn, beguiling stowaway was getting to him. Nothing more than carnal appetite, he thought, angry at himself for not being immune to the physical hunger she aroused in him and the vulnerability he saw in her face. He realized she was truly afraid . . . of something. "Tell me the truth."

"I . . . I can't."

A shuttered hardness came down over his eyes. As he turned away, Trish knew the moment had been lost when there could be honesty between them. He walked over to where Jens was whittling the cottonwood limb into a crude oar. "That should do it," the big man said with satisfaction. "It won't be as heavy as your other one . . . may take a little time getting used to it. I'll trade with you, if you want."

"No, I'm the one who lost the other one in the river. Fix Trish some gruel—that ought to set easy on her stomach after her dunking. I'll start packing the boats again."

"Are we going back upstream?"

"Yes," Morgan answered as he strode to the river.

Jens smiled as he handed her a tin plate filled with corn gruel. "The captain says stowaways get to eat this morning, Trish." She was uneasy as his eyes lingered on the damp cloth stretched across her breasts. His expression seemed good-natured enough but a spurt of fear caught Trish in the stomach. She kept her eyes on her plate until he moved away.

She ate with her usual enthusiasm even though she would have preferred a breakfast of something else besides a thick mush that nearly gagged her. Still, it was food—and the boiled coffee was strong enough to overpower the mush's bland taste.

When she had finished eating, she watched the two men load the boats. Her heart thumped loudly and her mind scurried in every direction trying to formulate some scheme that would keep them from returning upstream. If they returned her to Bend River, they would put her right into the hands of the posse she was certain would be waiting for her. She had little faith that Winnie May had been able to come up with a story that would save her neck. Nervousness brought Trish to her feet and she ambled over where the remaining provisions waited to be stored in Morgan's boat. She sat down in the middle of them and watched until the last item was stored away and the hatch covers tied securely down.

Morgan studied Trish sitting quietly on the sand and drew a heavy breath. "What do we do about her, Jens. Shall we take her back?"

Trish caught her lower lip with her teeth. Her heart was beating loudly against her rib cage in a frantic, wild rhythm. He was wavering. She choked back pleas mounting in her throat.

"Seems as how, we have three choices," Jens said. "Take her back, leave her here, or take her on with us to the first settlement."

"Who knows if there's anything between here and Jacob's Ferry," Morgan answered. "I'm told that's only a river crossing for settlers going up the Little Colorado. Only one family lives there . . . A fellow named Sutton."

"Well, maybe Sutton wouldn't mind having one more under his roof."

Trish went white. Her cheekbones were stark and angular in her taut face. Would she find herself another helpless victim of charity? And God forbid, would Sutton be anything like Parson Gunthar?

Morgan saw fear chase the color from Trish eyes and set her lower lip to trembling. "I think it's best if we take her back upstream. Somebody in Bend River will take care of her."

"No, please don't," she begged.

The fear in her eyes was real. Whatever it was that had sent her fleeing down the river was enough to send her slender body trembling. She was hiding the truth but there wasn't any question about her genuine terror. As much as he wanted to, he couldn't bring himself to ignore her pleas.

"All right. Then we'll take you on to Jacob's Ferry. That's the best we can do, Trish." His jaw was set.

She nodded. Whatever lay in wait for her at Jacob's Ferry would have to be handled when she got there. At least, she'd be safe from a posse and given a little time, she should be able to find a way to go on down the river and hunt for her father. Relief brought a relaxation of her tensed muscles. "Thank you," she said. "Thank you for taking me with you."

Her eyes deepened with a luminosity that put Morgan off balance as she smiled up at him. She had conquered her fear, whatever it was, he thought. In fact, he was certain a flicker of triumph hovered on her lips. As if somehow she had bested him in some way he didn't know about. It was not a pleasant feeling. He was used to being in complete command of himself and others. "All right. Get ready to shove off."

"Just a minute—" She started digging in the sand beside her. Quickly she uncovered something buried there.

"What the—?"

"Your compass. I took it from the stuff

piled here. I thought I . . . I might have to bargain with you . . . to take me on down the river," she finished lamely.

Morgan looked as if she had slapped him. Red-hot fury blazed in his black eyes.

Trish's mouth was suddenly dry. She knew she had made a terrible mistake. "I didn't want to do it," she said quickly, afraid of the fury that twisted Morgan's face. "Don't you see, I was afraid you wouldn't take me with you. You can't blame me trying to bargain." She began backing up toward Jens's boat. "You would have done the same thing in my place."

There was a weighted silence and then Jens chuckled and massaged his jaw. "I guess she's got you there, Morgan. Well, are we going to take her or not?"

Morgan couldn't bring himself to answer for a moment. No woman had ever bested him with such brash, audacious conniving. In spite of himself, a begrudging admiration tempered his anger. "I guess we have no choice. She rides with you, Jens. I'm afraid I'd be tempted to throttle her before we went five miles."

Trish would have preferred to ride in Morgan's boat but she knew that he was too angry with her at the moment to grant any favors. With an anxious look at him, she climbed in Jens's boat. The big man pushed it away from the bank and then leaped into it as the current thrust the craft forward. Jens's huge shoulders and arms began working the oars, sending the craft down the middle of the canyon, gliding on polished ripples that caught the sun.

Morgan kept his boat in the lead position, watching for any signs of approaching rapids, relieved that for the moment the river was running smoothly in its southern direction. Being on the river helped him put matters in perspective. It was a good thing that the incident with the compass had reminded him not to be fooled by Trish's feminine wiles. Her blackmailing efforts had put some sense back into his head. She'd not get by his guard again. He'd get her safely to Jacob's Ferry and then his responsibility toward her would be over.

In the boat behind his, Trish let out her breath. She had weathered the crisis. At the moment nothing else mattered but that she was on the river again. Her father had ridden these very waters and now she was going to share that river lust which had taken him away from her and her mother. She began to fantasize about what a glorious reunion they were going to have once she found him. How proud he would be of her! She couldn't hide her excitement as her gaze followed the river.

Every curve in the Colorado brought new breathtaking vistas as the small boats shot through deep-cut gorges in the earth. The magic splendor of the river seeped into her very soul like nourishment. All around her the colors of the landscape were raw and stark. Ruddy rock battlements, rounded towers of monolithic sandstones and gigantic natural sculptures rose so high above them that she often had to crane her head backward even to glimpse a small ribbon of blue sky visible between the dramatic cliffs.

For several hours the river flowed complacently, accepting tiny tributaries and crystal-clear waters from hidden springs. These rivulets flowed through glenlike ravines thick with green rampant vegetation before they tumbled into the muddy Colorado and swelled its banks.

Walls on both sides of the river were nearly vertical, thousands of feet high. Trish was like a child "gawking and sighing" as they passed deep depressions extending back into the rock walls. From the top of those awesome cliffs, their boats must look like two black specks gliding down a narrow greenish-red slate, thought

Trish. She gave the bearded Jens a broad smile. "It's unbelievable!"

Jens grunted. He didn't know what to make of her. She was as tricky as a polecat when you thought about the way she'd planned on bargaining with Morgan about the compass. He had to laugh silently. Most females would have been weepin' and wailin'. And the way she skidaddled up after that branch was something to see. She'd be a hard one to handle, he thought as he watched her tip her head back so she could see to the top of the cliffs. He wondered if the story she told about Indians was true. Something had her on the run, but he wasn't sure what.

Trish saw Jens's calculating look. If only she hadn't lost Winnie's shawl, she lamented, she could have kept her bare neck and arms covered. As it was the rents in her clothes and her disheveled hair kept her in a state of dishabille. She kept her back straight and her head elevated as if she could put some decorum into her carriage if nothing else.

She turned so she could watch the movement of Morgan's broad shoulders and arms as they gracefully worked the oars in rhythm with the flowing water. Under a straight brimmed hat, sunlight turned his thick dark hair to a shiny blue-black. She glimpsed his bold and vigorous profile, deeply tanned, and she wondered what he was thinking. Was he sharing this deep mystic communion with river, sky, and cliff? Did he feel the spirits reaching out to them from some primeval antiquity? She regretted that she wasn't riding in the bow of his boat so she could watch his expressions. If she hadn't tried to trick him, she would be there now and maybe that intriguing mouth would smile at her instead of hardening with threatening fury. She knew she had made a mistake but how could she have known that Morgan was going to take her on down the river with them without any bargaining? Given the same circumstances she would do the same thing over again.

They didn't stop for their midday meal— there was no bank along sheer canyon walls cupping the river. Jens handed her a piece of jerky and a drink of water from his canteen. The dried meat was salty and so tough she had to tear it with her teeth. About an hour later, they reached a new stretch of the river where narrow banks edged the water. Morgan motioned Jens to the side and they pulled their boats up on the sandy ground.

With some embarrassment, Trish headed into the bushes to relieve herself but both men ignored her departure and return. Morgan busied himself with a sextant and compass and some charts that he protected in a leather portfolio. She'd seen her father working on charts like that. Morgan was determining latitude and longitude and making maps of the river's course.

"Can I help?"

"I hardly think so," he retorted crisply.

"I bet I can add those figures faster than you can. My mother was a teacher. Taught school right in our little cabin. My father said she was the smartest woman this side of the Alleghenies."

"And, of course, you take after her," he said with a wry grin.

"Yep." Trish smiled. "Want to give me a try?"

"All right. Add up those readings for me and tell me what you get."

She did the mental calculations and came up with a correct answer.

Morgan raised one eyebrow.

"I told you so," she said smugly.

"So you did. Anything else you'd like to tell me about yourself?" He watched her guard go up. Those sea-green eyes of hers lost their shine.

"No." She knew that Morgan was smart enough to figure out a posse was after her if she didn't keep her mouth shut. Let well enough alone. After all, she was on the river, moving farther and farther away from Parson Gunthar's bloody body and every mile brought her closer to finding her father.

"All right. No more questions. A truce."

"A truce," she agreed with a light lift to her heart.

Jens had watched the little exchange between her and Morgan and when they were on the river again, he saw how she kept her eyes on Morgan's boat. "Won't do you no good to go mooning after him," he told her. "He ain't for the likes of you . . . comes from New York, he does. Family's right up there with the Goulds, Astors, and Vanderbilts. The Wallace Transportation Company used to own half the ports on Long Island Sound and up the coast to Boston."

"What's he doing here?" She had already guessed that Morgan Wallace came from money and good breeding. His speech, his carriage, and air of command had the touch of the upper class.

"He and his pa had a falling out. Old man Wallace sold out the company Morgan had built from nothing. Sold it to competitors. Right out from under Morgan's nose. Never gave Morgan a chance to say "aye" or "nay" about it. Dirty deal.

Guess blood doesn't matter when it comes to business—not by the rich, anyways."

"But how could he do that to his own son?"

"Easy enough, I reckon. Anyways, the old man is buying into railroads now . . . but Morgan lit out. Refused to go along with the new company his pa's got all set up for him. Turned his back on a fortune, he did. Got some idea he's going to show his pa a thing or two by building a waterway on the Colorado." Jens shook his mammoth head.

"But you don't agree?"

"Not from what I've seen so far. The river's been cantankerous all the way. It's a fool's dream—"

"Then why did you come along?"

"Needed the job. Hired on because the pay was good and . . ." He shrugged. "I guess Morgan's fancy speeches got to me. I wouldn't mind getting in on something good for a change. Morgan's got money. Have you seen that money belt he's got around his waist?" Then Jens sobered. "Guess I shouldn't be talking this way to a . . ."

"Stowaway?" she finished for him. "I'm not interested in his money."

"Unless you needed it."

For a moment Trish didn't answer. She was without any resources except her own determination for survival. All of her life she had felt alone; her mother had never really understood her, her father had never been around for any length of time during her upbringing, and her brother had thought her a pest and nuisance. Gertie, the parson's wife, had made a scullery maid out of her and the parson had pretended avuluncar affection—and then tried to rape her! How could she deny that she wouldn't steal if she had to in order to stay on the river and find her father?

Her expression must have given Jens the answer to his question because he nodded. "That's what I thought."

That evening they camped in one of the fern-bedecked recesses she had viewed from the river. A tiny clear stream ran along the bottom of the ravine flanked by mossy banks. As soon as the men had unloaded some supplies, Morgan thrust a fishing pole into Trish's hand. "Don't come back until you've caught your supper."

His tone brooked no argument. She didn't want to fuel his fury by returning empty-handed. As she trampled through patches of feathery ferns and green cane, a flurry of birds took flight. Jays, swallows, and bobwhites rose in flocks around her.

Canyon wrens piped frail songs from hidden perches in the rocks. As always Trish's spirits lifted when she was surrounded by unspoiled nature. She'd catch his damn fish if she had to jump in the stream after them.

She'd been fishing lots of times but usually she was too impatient to wait for any to swallow her hook. Her brother, Teddy, had managed her pole while Trish hopped barefooted on rocks and fallen logs, squealing and laughing as cold water splattered her feet. Now, as she turned her back on Morgan and walked over to the edge of a small clear stream, she tried to remember how Teddy had cast upstream and let the current carry the hook along, hoping it would sweep by some deep hole where fish might be waiting.

Clumsily she threw the line out . . . and watched the water sweep it right back to the bank. She cast again . . . getting it farther out this time . . . and again . . . and again . . . until it seemed her arm was going to break off. An hour lengthened into a frustrating eternity. She wasn't going to catch anything!

From time to time, she glanced back at the men. They were busily collecting wood and making camp. Unexpectedly her pole dipped with a sudden jerk. Squealing she fought with a silver-scaled trout, about eighteen inches long, and brought it to the bank with great wonder and delight. Not the least squeamish, she took the hook from its gasping mouth, baited the hook, and threw it out again. In less than twenty minutes, she had two more fish. They weren't trout but they looked eatable. She took them victoriously back to the campsite like a warrior returning with booty.

The expression in Morgan's eyes might have been surprise and pleasure, but before she could identify it, he said curtly, "Why didn't you gut them in the stream?"

"Gut them?" She had forgotten all about cleaning the fish. Her brother had always taken care of that distasteful chore. Now, Morgan handed them back to her.

"Clean them," he ordered. He handed her a sharp, curved knife.

Trish just stared at it. She couldn't take it from his hand. The last time she'd grasp a knife she had thrust it into a man's gut and in her memory blood like warm red syrup had gushed out over her hand. Her face blanched, her hands trembled. She took a step backward. She couldn't do it. "No. Gut 'em yourself," she said in a choked voice.

The look of pure anguish in her face stunned Morgan. Maybe she hadn't been lying. Maybe she had seen her parents die under an Indian's knife.

Jens was thinking the same thing. "I'll do it." He took the fish from Trish's trembling hand.

Morgan touched her shoulder. She jumped at first but his strong grip sent a flood of warmth through her. "Are you all right? Do you want to talk about it?" he asked with unusual softness.

She didn't dare meet his eyes. It took all the resolve she could muster not to pour out the sordid story. Only the fear that he might turn her over to the law kept her body rigid. "No, it's all right. I'll catch the fish . . . and cook them . . . but I won't gut them."

"Fair enough," he said. What was she hiding? She was like a frightened child in need of reassurance. Impulsively, he let his hand slide along one arm. She jerked away as if fearful of his touch. He knew she had misinterpreted the gesture and he cursed himself for offering it. He turned away abruptly and gave his attention to the fire.

"If the river stays the same, we should be no more than a few days away from Jacob's Ferry," he said after they had eaten and the evening clean-up was finished. "The map I got in Salt Lake City shows where the Paria River flows into the Colorado. Frontier settlements are springing up all over that area."

"I thought that was all Indian country," said Jens, his beard shining with grease from the fish fry.

"It is . . . several different tribes, all warring with one another. Settlers from the East seem to be willing to gamble their scalps just to get land."

Suddenly Trish felt the skin on the back of her neck begin to crawl. In the dark shadows beyond the circle of the campfire, she could almost see moving figures, naked savages with painted bodies and feathered tomahawks. Once she had seen a dead Indian brought in by a couple of trappers. He had been caught stealing grub from them. A bloody blond scalp had been hanging from his belt, small enough to be a child's. Trish's mother had lectured her long and hard about staying in the settlement and Trish had obeyed—for a short while. Then she forgot all about the Indian and resumed her climbing, hiking, and long treks along the river's bank.

As she listened to Jens and Morgan talk about the miles of hostile country ahead of them, she realized how she had jeopardized their safety by dumping part of their ammunition. No wonder Morgan was ready to scalp her himself.

Then all thoughts of Indians was pushed out of her mind as the men prepared to bed down for the night. She felt moisture leaving her mouth. Earlier fears about her vulnerability in the hands of river men came back. Winnie had educated her as to the appetites of men. Visions of them taking turns with her sickened her. The fish dinner sat queasily on her stomach. With her eyes darting like those of a trapped animal, she watched them take blankets from the boats and spread them on the ground.

Morgan was well aware of her growing uneasiness. It was obvious in the way she was avoiding their eyes and watching their preparations for bedding down. All evening he had been conscious of her as she sat by the fire, her supple body relaxed and graceful. Soft flickering light burnished her face and neck and highlighted the beautiful structure of her face. She had a lovely straight nose, smooth cheek planes, and a bold little chin that enhanced full, sensuous lips. He had felt a warm stirring of desire just looking at her. The thought of cupping those full, ripening breasts and burying his face in their delicious softness mocked the indifference he sought to maintain against her. She would be a woman worth taking. She would love as fervently as she did everything else, but he was determined to control his thoughts and to put her desirable body completely out of his mind. Nothing she could do would change the fact that she was bad luck . . . an albatross around his neck. Trish slipped out of the flickering circle of light and went down to the riverbank. Her heart lurched into an erratic rhythm as she waited for one of them to shout at her and order her back. She knew that Morgan did not trust her anywhere near the boats, as if she were idiot enough to try and navigate this river alone. He ought to give her more credit than that. Apparently he did, for he made no objection to her lying down in Jens's boat.

She stretched out on a tarpaulin she had placed on the hard oak planks. Lying there, she stared overhead. Thousands of stars blinked against a purple velvet backdrop. As she stared up at the lovely heavenly canopy, her tired muscles began to responded to the hypnotic movement of the boat. No sounds came from the campfire circle where the men had bedded down. She relaxed and closed her eyes.

She didn't know whether she had just dropped off to sleep when her eyes flew open! A cry of terror caught her throat.

A man's form was silhouetted against

the night sky as he bent over the boat. Morgan! Her hands flew up to push him away and her nails clawed at his arms.

"You little wildcat! Calm down, Trish. I was just bringing you a blanket. You'll sleep cold without something over you."

His face was close enough to feel his warm breath upon her face. "I . . . I thought . . ."

"I know what you thought." He spread the blanket over her. "Get some sleep. We have a hard day ahead." He turned away.

"Thank you," she called after him.

He didn't answer but threw himself down on the ground. The thought of her lying on the cold bare boards of a boat had made him jerk off his own blanket and take it to her. And look at what had happened! The back of his hands smarted where she had raked her nails.

As Trish clutched the blanket to her and stared up at the twinkling heavens, she felt exhilarating excitement race through her young limbs. He had brought her a blanket! He had not wanted her to sleep cold. A smile curved her lips as her fingers played along the edges of the blanket like a contented child who feels warm and protected in the night. Tears and laughter got all mixed up inside her chest. "Good night, Morgan," she said softly.

The gentle swaying of the boat and lapping water echoed a sudden singing in her heart.

Lynn Kerr

Five

The next five days passed quickly, some smooth, some crazed. The cliffs disappeared and the land stretched out like a dry desert on both sides of the meandering river. The bright sun was blinding and even evaporation from the water failed to cool the river travelers. Sometimes the river stretched out lazily like a woman without her corset stays and in other places, the Colorado narrowed to a gushing faucet pouring over rocks.

At each campsite Trish was given chores to do. Unabashedly she listened to Morgan's and Jens's conversation as they talked about the next day's run or reminisced about something that had happened earlier in the trip. The Indians they had met on the upper Colorado, called the Green River, had been friendly and had warned them in pantomime about the river that "bucked."

"I guess they were right about that," Jens drawled.

Trish eagerly asked all kinds of questions. Sometimes the men answered her and sometimes they didn't. Just about the time she thought Morgan was ready to throw her overboard to save rations, he would do something unexpected—like giving her a comb or sharing his piece of unleavened bread. She didn't understand him at all.

One night around the campfire, he asked her about her parents.

"They were born and raised in Iowa," Trish told him. "My father was working on a small farm and my mother was a school-teacher." Her expression softened. "They met at a barn dance. My father said his Nancy was the prettiest gal there, light as a butterfly, turning and spinning . . . the belle of the ball. He couldn't believe she had eyes for him."

"And you were born there . . . in Iowa?" Morgan asked, throwing anther piece of dry wood on the fire.

"Oh, no. After they were married, they lived on the farm . . . until Teddy was born and then they came West."

"Good farm land in Iowa," Jens said with a longing in his voice.

"I guess so but my father wasn't a farmer.

He didn't have his heart in it. Never was the kind to be tied to a plot of ground," Trish told them. "He didn't want Mama to come West with him but she wouldn't be left behind. I guess she knew she'd never see him again, always said her husband had wanderlust in his veins. Anyway, he ended up trapping in Wyoming near the White Wind Mountains. That's where the headwaters of the Green River are, you know." Then she added proudly. "That's where I was born."

"No wonder you turned out to be a river rat." Jens laughed.

"Do you look like your mother?" Morgan asked, watching the way her reddish-brown hair caught a million copper highlights.

"Heavens no." Trish laughed. "She was tall, dark-haired, with pale blue eyes. My brother, Teddy, took after her. I don't look like anyone in my family." A touch of sadness crept into her voice. "My father said I was a changeling . . . you know . . . a baby left by somebody out of a fairy tale. Nobody likes the color of my hair."

"I do," said Morgan with one of his rare smiles.

Most of the time he seemed to have more interest in an unusual rock formation than he did in her. Morgan was aware of his vacillating behavior. He was chafing under the added worry of seeing to her safety. Every time they ran a series of bad rapids, he had to assure himself that she was unharmed before his heart would quit pounding. It surprised him that Trish didn't seem worried in the least. At the bottom of each run, she would wave to him victoriously and the sight of her glowing face, water-drenched hair, and clinging damp dress made him laugh back in relief.

Day after day they shared the excitement and challenge of the river and this added to a bewildering fascination she held for him. Women who attracted him on a sexual level had rarely touched him in any other way. He had always kept his romantic interludes separate from the rest of his life and forgot them rather easily but somehow the stirrings he had for this russet-haired stowaway threatened to go much deeper. When her laughter floated over the water to him, he foolishly wished that she were sitting in his boat instead of Jens's and only his pride kept him from ordering her to change boats.

Trish's relationship with Jens thawed as the hours passed on the river. She learned his last name was Larsen. He began to talk about the Ohio farm where he had been born and raised. His full name was Jens Owen Larsen. He spoke affectionately of the grandmother who had raised him but there was a tightening about his full lips when he described his Swedish father. "A hard man . . . owning land . . . more land . . . that's all that mattered. Pa worked his kids as hard as his mules. Put me to pulling stumps out of the ground with a team. My mom was sickly and my grandma taught me my letters and read the Bible to me. When she died, I left the farm. Hiked up to Lake Erie and got me a job as a mule hand, guiding those ornery critters as they pulled canal boats through locks. Sometimes, I'd get tangled up in harnesses and get pulled into the river. Some bastard would shout, 'Watch out, mules, there's a dumb ox in the water . . .' They all started calling me 'Ox' and then run away before I could bash their heads in."

Jens's hands tightened on the oars, big knuckles rising white. Trish shivered. She knew those hands could become lethal weapons if anger put his huge frame into a murderous rage. Although most of the time he seemed good-natured, a hint of violence surfaced in those round hazel eyes when some memory was dredged up. It was probably a woman, she thought, for he swore a couple of times about cheating, no-good sluts. Shivering to think what

those hands could do to a soft neck, she'd
quickly let the conversation drop.

Jens gave her a long scarf that his
grandma had knitted for him of yellow,
twisted yarn. It had shrunk up, probably
in one of his dunks in the river, but it
made a nice cover for Trish's shoulders
and her torn bodice. She appreciated its
warmth when the threat of rain brought
bands of cold air down into the canyons
and dropped night temperatures to a shivering degree.

Every time they beached the boats, Morgan told her curtly, "You stay here—and
don't go wandering off by yourself, hear?"
He'd take his sextant, compass, and maps
and sometimes be gone for hours.

She didn't dare beg to go with him. She
knew her best chance to make it to Jacob's
Ferry was to remain in the background,
keeping his attention away from the stowaway who had thrust herself upon him.
But he made her so mad! Why did he always keep his guard up, watching her? She
had tried to apologize for taking his compass but he refused to listen to her. Sometimes she caught his gaze lingering on her
and she felt a peculiar wash of sensation
as their eyes met. Then he would tighten
his jaw, and glare at her as if he'd gladly
dump her overboard. Late one afternoon

she couldn't believe it when he came back for her.

"There's something up on one of the ridges you might like to see," he said without preamble, as if their relationship called for this kind of companionable exchange.

Her mouth dropped open. For a moment she thought her ears had deceived her. Then she jumped up and scrambled after him before he could change his mind. They climbed over a steep talus and worked their way up a ravine. Deep in the recesses of the canyon they found a cliff that mounted to a precipice about fifty feet above their heads.

She couldn't see what the excitement was about at first. A depression hundreds of feet deep ran back from the edge of a sandstone cliff—and then she saw it! An Indian pueblo.

"Deserted . . . hundreds of years ago. It's been protected back in that canyon." Morgan pulled her forward to the base of a rising cliff. "Look at this!" He pointed to some scratched indentations in the rock. "Early pictures . . . pictographs, they're called. Indian writing."

Trish bent forward to see faint figures scratched in straight lines . . . one looked like a stickman with a spear, another like a basket, and some other markings that were surely characters of some kind. "What do you think it says?" she asked in hushed wonderment.

"Don't wait dinner for me," he quipped, his eyes crinkling with levity.

"Or, don't come home without the bacon," she responded dryly.

They laughed together.

"Come on. Let's give it a closer look."

He grabbed her hand and she walked eagerly beside him, smiling up at his handsome face. Too late she realized that he might have brought her here to see what her reaction was to this area that had been inhabited by Indians. If her parents had really been killed by Indians, she would not be making facetious remarks about pictographs, she thought. Well, she didn't think he had believed her story anyway. Her natural curiosity made her eyes bright with anticipation as they reached the ruins.

"Can I trust you not to break your neck or fall down a pit?"

"I'm as surefooted as a goat," she assured him.

A full smile creased his face and a boyish glint in his eyes surprised her. "Yes, you are. Let's take a look around."

A hushed silence greeted them as they entered the deserted, ancient ruins. Protected under the shelf of the cliff, the adobe structure stood firm and solid after hundreds of years. Built on several levels, with numerous doorways opening on the front, they peered inside.

Once they descended into an underground kiva by means of steps chiseled into the stone wall. Only a round patch of light illuminated the empty, echoing chamber. "Probably a place for religious ceremonies," he said. Part of his preparation for this trip had been reading and studying what little was known about the red man who inhabited these regions. He knew that prejudice colored much of the information but what he had learned he shared with Trish.

She had never thought about uncivilized Indians having a history or culture of their own. Parson Gunthar had been sent out as a missionary to convert the savages and make them into decent people. His sermons had been filled with the wicked ways of the heathen Indians. Listening to Morgan brought a new perspective of a people she had been taught to consider inferior. Ghostly voices echoed through ruins that had been silent for the passing of many years. As they explored in almost a hushed, reverent silence, Trish could almost hear the sound of children playing, old men talking, and women busy at their pots and looms.

"Easy . . . careful . . . that staircase is narrow!" He warned as she scrambled up hewed rock steps that had been worn away by years of weathering. When they reached the top of a high ledge, he put his arm around her waist.

"I guess I've never thought about Indians as people before . . . living together like this," she said thoughtfully. "Why did they leave here, do you think?"

"Something drove them away, obviously. A hostile tribe . . . or drought . . . or some fear. Undoubtedly, it was a matter of survival."

Survival. She knew all about that. "Yes, survival," she echoed and her voice caught.

"What's the matter? You're shivering. You're not afraid of ghosts, are you?"

She shook her head.

He chided her gently. "Some of the things that should scare you don't and other times you act like a child afraid of the bogey man."

His tightened grip on her waist and his nearness fired every nerve ending. She had never been with a man like this before, talking and sharing an exciting experience. The only fellow who had come calling on her had been a young cavalryman whose detail had been posted in Bend River a short time. Billy McIntyre had been a year younger than she, a Kansas farm boy who had joined the U.S. Cavalry when he was sixteen. Trish would have married him just to make her escape from the Gunthars but he had been sent on to Laramie before they had exchanged more than a little hand-holding and a couple of adolescent kisses. She had never felt excitement surge through her veins the way it did when she was close to Morgan. Oh, she had dreamed that someone like Morgan Wallace would come riding into Bend River and carry her away. And in a way, that's exactly what had happened. How ironic it was. She started to chuckle.

"What's the matter?" He tipped her chin up so he could see her face.

"I was just visualizing you as my knight in shining armor, carrying me away like Lockinvar. Silly, isn't it?" For some reason, there was a sudden fullness in her eyes and she blinked rapidly against it.

As he looked into those sea-green eyes, moist with tears, he was lost to a need he could not define. Abruptly, he pulled her into the warmth of his arms. He raised a hand and smoothed her hair's vibrant thickness. "Trish?" His voice was soft and wondering, as if it contained all the questions for which he had no answers. Then he lowered his mouth to hers.

Trish was not prepared for the devastating sensation that enveloped her when their lips met. For a moment she did not know what to do. His mouth was working hers with a hunger that was both bewildering and wonderful. Cautiously, her hands slipped around his neck and threaded the thick strands of hair that fell upon his neck. She couldn't breathe. Her heart beat wildly and she was conscious of his quickened breath. She kissed him back. Passion that had lain dormant within her vibrant body now fired her senses. There was too much hunger, too much desire flowing between them for her to be passive in his arms. She locked her arms behind his neck and her fingers pressed into his flesh. Like the roar of wild rapids, all thought was drowned out by a cataract of feeling.

Her scarf slipped from her shoulders. His hand touched the warm skin exposed through the rents in her bodice and then cupped the fullness of a breast that swelled and tingled under his pulsating fingers. She gasped from the sheer delight of it. At the same time his tongue explored the sweetness of her mouth, questing, deepening his kiss.

"Yahoo!" Jens booming voice floated up

the draw. "Morgan . . . Trish. Where are you?"

Like falling glass, the moment shattered, bringing them back to harsh reality. Morgan set Trish away from him and picked up her scarf from the ground where it had fallen. His hands lingered for a split second as he placed it on her shoulders. Then he turned away just as Jens's thick frame came into view.

"Here we are." Morgan walked toward him. "See what we found."

Jens showed only a passing interest in the Indian ruins. "No wonder they moved out. Not an acre of ground around worth farming."

When they returned to camp, Morgan acted toward Trish as if nothing had happened between them. She was confused, bewildered, and half angry. Maybe kissing a girl senseless was something he did all the time, she thought. With her own emotions in such disarray she couldn't keep from feeling resentful. The rejection she'd experienced all her life from people she cared about fueled her anger. Damn him! Why had she let him kiss her like that?

On the surface everything was the same as it had been every other night. After they had eaten their evening meal of dried apples and cornmeal mush, Morgan told her to get some sleep for a hard day ahead. She bade him good night, hoping for an intimate smile but he just nodded and said, "Sleep well," without looking directly at her.

Morgan stared at the fire, remembering how she had felt in his arms. Thank God, Jens had come along when he did. He knew he had been lost to his own desire and she had responded with an explosive fiery passion. He would have taken her in the shadows of the ruins if nothing had stopped them. Even now, he desired her with an all-exploding need. Her luscious body promised a man's delight. Angry with himself for having given in to the temptation to hold and kiss her, he threw himself down on his bedroll and tried to put her out of his mind.

Night descended in the canyon. Trish waited, every nerve ending firing with anticipation. Would he come to her? She lay in the darkness and stared up at the silver-spangled heavens. A deep indigo sky held fast-moving clouds to its bosom. Her newly awakened passions brought sensations to her with a bewildering intensity, as if every pore in her body was open, waiting to be filled. Watching the filmy cloud sculptures shape and reshape against the moon, she wondered if Morgan lay awake, looking up at the same sky, with a hot flush invading his body. She was frightened of this new awakening in her body and yet for the first time in her life, she felt totally alive. She couldn't stop thinking about what had happened between them and sleep was a long time in coming.

The next morning when she climbed out of the boat Trish saw that Morgan and Jens had already eaten the horrible mush that was their morning fare. She looked around. Neither Jens nor the handsome and intriguing Morgan were in sight. Morgan always shaved daily and she loved to watch him whip his straight razor in and out of the water with the flourish of a baton. He must have already left on one of his solitary reconnaissance explorations, she decided, disappointed. Then her spirits brightened. It was another wonderful, glorious day and there was no place on earth she'd rather be than on the banks of the Colorado River.

As she came back from her morning walk, she heard Jens whistling. The sound came from a narrow ravine where a fresh stream flowed into the river. Jens stripped to the waist, kneeling over the flowing water as he washed his face. He looked like a thick-shouldered animal as he scooped up water and poured it over his head, splattering drops in every direction. He wasn't aware of her presence as she tiptoed quietly up behind him. When he lowered his head again, Trish gave it a hard shove down into the water.

He came up blubbering. She darted back laughing. He swung around and grabbed her with his giant-size hands.

"Want to play, huh?" He swung her up in his arms.

"Jens . . . no—!"

"How about a little bath?" He held her out over the water.

She shrieked, laughing and giggling and protesting.

His round face spread in a broad grin, he plopped her down in the shallow stream.

"You—You—!" she gasped as she scrambled to her feet, trying to get her legs under her as her dress spread out around her like a water-logged blanket. She finally scrambled out on all fours.

"No, you don't!" He gave her another shove that landed her on her back in the water again. Laughing, he put his hands on his hips. "That'll teach you to start something." Then he held out his hand and pulled her out. "You spend more time getting wet than anybody I ever saw, river rat," he teased, laughing as she stood there sopping wet.

She lifted up the hem of her skirt and tried to wring out some of the water. Jens watched her, his lazy gaze taking in her bare legs, rounded thighs, and the feminine curves of her slender waist and firm breasts. Trish was so engrossed in what she was doing that she didn't see his expression change. It was the husky timbre of his voice that sent a warning.

"I'll help you do that."

There was no teasing gaiety in the offer. Her playful companion was gone. A narrowing of his round eyes frightened her and she knew she was looking at a man who had been aroused—a man who wanted her! She stepped back as Jens made a move to grab her skirt.

"What's going on here?" Morgan's commanding voice sliced the tense moment. He had heard Trish's shrieks when he was coming back to camp. He had bolted back to camp, only to find a scene that stabbed him with its intimacy. The sight of Jens with his hands on Trish sent a red poker stabbing through his head.

Jens dropped Trish's skirt and stepped back as Morgan strode toward them. His thundering black eyes took in Jens's flushed expression and then raked Trish's bewildered face. Jealousy was an emotion completely foreign to him and he didn't recognize it for what it was.

Trish was so stunned she just stood there, a hunk of her wet skirt still clutched in her hand. Morgan's gaze fell from her stunned expression, traveling down her rounded, sensuous torso to supple legs showing below clinging wet drawers tied under her knees.

"You don't understand . . ." she stammered, aghast, dropping her skirt. How could she explain that a little harmless horseplay had gotten out of hand . . . that she hadn't deliberately enticed Jens. Dark fury burned like hot coals in his eyes. She knew he was thinking about the passionate intimacy that they had shared yesterday. He thought the same thing had happened again . . . only this time with Jens.

"It's . . . it's not what you think," she stammered. "We . . . we were just having fun. I ducked Jens's head in the water . . . then he threw me in and . . ."

"And—?" His voice was coated in Arctic ice.

"And then you came."

"I'm sorry to interrupt but I heard you shrieking and I didn't know you were just having 'fun.'" He was so angry that he couldn't control the spiteful words that came spewing out. "You'll not make a fool out of me—or this expedition."

"I wasn't trying to make a fool out of anybody," she flared. He was as much to blame for what had happened between them yesterday as she was. The accusation was in the look she gave him.

He reddened. "No conniving stowaway is going to put a wedge between me and Jens. Do you understand? Another scene like this and I'll dump you in some thicket the way you did all our supplies."

Jens had been silent during their fiery exchange. Now the two men faced each other. "From now on she rides in my boat so I can keep on eye on her deceitful little hide," Morgan said, a challenge in his tone. "You have some objection, Jens?"

For a weighted moment the command wavered between them. Morgan's posture was pure martinet, stiff, commanding, with a poise of inbred authority. Even though Jens's huge stature was a physical advantage, it was Morgan's attitude of firm control that dominated the confrontation. His intense ebony eyes never wavered and a flicker of a jaw muscle was the only perceptual sign of emotion.

Jens shifted his weight and then shrugged his thick shoulders. He wasn't about to get in a hassle with Morgan over a gal. Sure, he'd been thinking that she felt mighty nice and soft in his hands. It had been a long time since he'd had a woman. He wasn't immune to a pretty little thing laughing and playing around but that's all there was to it.

"Fine with me." Without even looking at Trish, he lumbered away and began breaking up camp as if it were an ordinary morning and everything was just as it had been before.

For a moment Trish and Morgan stared at each other. He couldn't believe how shaken he was. The thought of Jens taking her had made him want to plunge his fist into Jens's round face. He had been ready and willing to fight like a stag protecting his female. He felt like shaking her. Didn't she know what those mermaid eyes did to a man? Or how her wet clothes molded her figure seductively? Was she aware of her power to drive a man crazy? Or was she as innocent as her pleading expression indicated?

Six

The next week passed and as if the weather were endeavoring to match the sour mood of the river travelers, days turned cold and wet. Low gray clouds swept down the canyon and the sky, cliffs, and river lost their colors to chilly gray mist that penetrated bone-deep.

Trish huddled shivering in the bow of Morgan's boat. As misty rain descended upon them, Morgan dug out an army blanket and tossed it to her but his face remained impassive as if he were steeling himself against any display of emotion. Her longing to share the river with him was a mockery to his stiff, silent attitude. She didn't know how to put things right between them.

If a strong wind had accompanied the rain and buffeted the boats about, they would have been forced to a bank to wait out the storm but only intermittent gusts of wind swept across the water. The river remained its complacent self of the last few days. For hours the boats ran silently through the soft drizzle of rain.

Morgan was worried as he watched the canyon walls. When soft rocks, like limestone, lined the water's edges, the current ran smoothly but when hard formations like granite held the river, they could expect huge boulders jutting up out of the water to form swiftly running cataracts. Late that afternoon, they heard the crescendo of water ahead. Morgan gave the signal to pull the boats to a shelflike strip of sand that hugged the darkening rock walls.

"We'll have to make a portage," said Morgan.

"It's the only way to get past those rocks," agreed Jens.

Trish had heard her father used that term. "A portage?" she echoed, trying to remember exactly what was involved.

"Right. We carry the boats along the bank past the rough section," Morgan answered briskly. "We'll empty everything out of the hatches, carry all the stuff downstream and then come back for the boats."

Jens scratched his woolly head as he eyed the darkening sky. Then he nodded. "Better get at it. Looks like we might get caught in a real goose-drowner."

The men began unloading the boats, endeavoring to make them as light as possible for carrying.

"Here, put these on." Morgan handed Trish a wide-brimmed, army-style hat and a man's rawhide jacket that hung to her knees.

"Thank you," she said, searching his face for some sign that his anger was a thing of the past. "What shall I do?"

"Pick up some stuff . . . but not too much," he warned. "You don't want to get off balance; some of that rocky bank looks treacherous . . . one slip and—"

There wasn't any need for him to finish. One false step and there would be nothing to save her from being battered to death in the raging waters. For the first time, she felt icy fear creep up her spine. She would have rather taken a chance going over in the boat but she dared not question Morgan's authority.

Jens shifted a box onto his back and started walking along the narrow bank that descended abruptly beside the plunging river. Trish followed Jens with Morgan bringing up the rear, all three loaded down with contents of the boats. There was no sandy bank to walk upon and they were forced to climb over a rocky talus made by debris that had tumbled away from the cliffs. The boulders were wet, slippery, jagged, and coated with slimy mud that made footing extremely precarious.

"Watch your footing," Morgan yelled at her when she misjudged the slant of rock and her feet nearly slipped out from under her. "Don't look at the water." The roar of the river was deafening. Sprays of white cataracts leaped upward in the channel around granite boulders. Trish could see why the men had decided a portage was the only way to get beyond the tumbling rapids—anything else would have been suicide! She begrudgingly admitted that Morgan had made the right decision.

She lost track of how many trips they made from the boat, over the treacherous talus to a section of widening river below the rocks and back again. She hated the slow, demanding task of transporting every item over the slippery rocks. Finally, the boats were unloaded and all their provisions piled in stacks below the rapids.

Morgan peered up anxiously at the lowering sky. Dark clouds had grown more ominous and now broken streaks of lightning pierced the black shrouded sky. Thunder rumbled in echoing crescendos through the canyon's black abyss.

"We've got to get the boats down," Morgan shouted over the roar of the falls.

"Yep, it's going to break any minute!"

"You stay here, Trish," Morgan said as he and Jens hurried back upstream.

Thunder and lightning moved closer. Like cannon volleys, the heavens sent deafening roars vibrating between the canyon walls. As the moments passed, Trish strained her eyes for signs of the returning men. Maybe something had gone wrong. Had they lost their footing? Dropped the boat? They could have been swept past her in the churning water and she would have never seen them. Mist was getting heavier every minute. She fought rising panic.

It was a torturous eternity before she saw them coming with one of the twenty-one-foot boats upside down, each of them carrying one end on their shoulders. Her heart was a wild bird beating in her chest as she watched them descend the wet, rocky talus. She began to breathe again when they reached the bottom of the falls safely and tethered the boat in a smooth eddy. Then another excruciating wait began again as they went back for the second boat. The wait didn't seem as long this time and when the task was finished, they reloaded the boats. The mist had changed to a steady light rain.

"Better make camp here," said Morgan,

eyeing some sandstone formations close to the river. He pointed to a huge cavelike indentation that could have been made by wind and weather. "Let's see if we can bed down there for the night."

They took the things they needed from the boat to make camp and climbed to the shelter of the rock cave. Jens built a fire just inside the opening and smoke trailed upward, finding its way out a small fissure in the rocks above. Trish huddled close to the fire, grateful not to be sleeping in the boat as the wind rose and fell, sending a wailing cry above the rain. The presence of the two men was reassuring even though Morgan had little to say and Trish knew his thoughts were centered on getting them down the river alive.

She curled up in her army blanket even before the men had settled in for the night. Every muscle in her body ached from the strenuous hauling and climbing and an emotional exhaustion made her even more ready for the solace of sleep.

She heard the men talking in quiet tones and she stiffened when Jens brought up the morning's incident. "We were just playing around. I admit I let it go too far. Sorry."

"I guess I got out of hand," Morgan

admitted. "I don't know what came over me."

"I do," answered Jens, turning away from the fire.

The next morning the sky remained leaden with gray clouds but the rain had stopped and a valiant sun was trying to dry out the canyon. Trish's spirits rebounded with her usual resiliency. Morgan and Jens had regained their easy, companionable relationship and Trish felt that the ugly incident had been put behind them. Morgan continued to treat her with an indifference that belied his concern for her well-being.

They had been on the river less than an hour when a roar of impending falls brought them to the bank again. This time they couldn't make a portage past the rock-choked river. Fast-moving water poured over a fifty-foot drop. There was less than a foot of bank hugging stark granite walls . . . not enough room for two men to carry a boat on their shoulders.

"We'll have to let the boats down by lines."

Trish didn't know what that meant but Morgan wasn't in any mood for questions.

She knew he was worried about diminishing rations, which included hard flour that had been wet and dried to a musty paste. High waters had ruined the streams for fishing. They had eaten the last of the dried apples and mush that morning for breakfast and the portions of gruel had been so small her stomach was still growling in protest.

He ordered her out of his boat and Trish stood on the narrow bank with her back pressed up against the rock walls and watched as the men attached bowlines to one of the boats. Somehow they were going to lower each craft over the falls to the bottom of the rapids where a tranquil pool waited. She couldn't see how they could maintain control of the boats lowered over the foaming white cataracts. Only Morgan's commanding figure gave her any confidence in the situation. The safety of the boats was in his hands.

Morgan instructed Jens to take one of the lines and climb down a shelf of rocks that descended along the plunging waterfall. When he had made it safely to the bottom, he told Trish to follow.

"Don't hurry. Test each step and don't go looking at the falling water."

She nodded.

He gave her shoulder a reassuring

squeeze. "Should be easy for a mountain goat."

It was. Trish made the descent quickly and easily and in a few minutes she was standing beside Jens at the bottom of the rapids. She gave Morgan a triumphant wave of her hand. He returned her wave and then disappeared.

Jens set his feet solid on the edge of the bank, took the rope off his shoulders and gave a tug on the line to signal Morgan that he was ready for the first boat. The huge man braced himself against the weight and pull of the boat.

Trish's mouth went dry when one of the boats appeared at the top of the falls, then slid over the edge, swung in the air, and came down as Jens let it drop into the water below the rapids. Pulling on the rope, Jens guided the craft toward the bank near the quiet, shallow eddy where Trish waited. She splashed out, waist deep, grabbed a bowline and eased the craft to shore. When she had it securely moored on the bank she gave a triumphant laugh and then took her place to catch the second boat. Her reddish-brown hair whipped wetly around her face. Her face glowed with the wonderment and excitement of the moment. She much preferred a "lining down" to a "portage."

Jens gave a booming "Yahoo" when the second boat made it safely down. And a moment later Morgan joined them and they were on the river again.

Trish didn't know that as she sat in the bow of his boat, Morgan was well aware of every breath she drew. His admiration for her had grown with every crisis and he was angry at himself and at her for the struggle he was having to keep his priorities straight. This expedition had to be carried out with a clear head. There was no place in his emotions for the kind of upheaval he had been experiencing since she had first looked up into his face with those wide, compelling mermaid eyes. Day by day she had worked her way under his skin and he had begun to look at danger in terms of her safety. He couldn't allow himself to be weakened by such sentiment. If he could get her safely to Jacob's Ferry, he would have carried out his responsibility. She'd be safe there and if she behaved herself, the settler's family would surely look after her. What happened to her after that was none of his concern.

The next three days they battled the weather, granite cliffs, and rapids. They were constantly faced with portages and

Trish had never been so weary in her whole life.

"How . . . how much farther to the Ferry?"

"God knows," he swore, worried about the dwindling food supply. "If the river widens . . . only one or two . . ."

She didn't know if she was glad or sorry they were almost there. She wondered what waited for her at Jacob's Ferry—and how she would be able to continue her search for her father. Suddenly the hopelessness of the task she had set for herself swept over her. Her shoulders began to shake and she buried her face in her hands.

"Here." Morgan handed her a linen handkerchief with an embroidered *W* on it. He was exhausted and discouraged and felt like letting his own emotions go. This river was not the navigable waterway of his dreams but a devil's nightmare.

Trish fingered Morgan's soft handkerchief, dabbed at her eyes and drew on the warm memory of his kisses. She'd never been in a man's arms before. Oh, she had let Billy McIntyre, the freckled-faced cavalryman, kiss her a few times when she was deciding whether or not to marry him so he could take her out of Bend River. She really hadn't liked it. Billy had pimples on his face, grease in his hair, and his mouth had felt kind of like soft fish. The experience was nothing like the wild sensation that had engulfed her in Morgan's arms. She had wanted to stay there. He had brought her whole body alive, vibrant, and surging with desires she had never imagined existed. He was so handsome, so splendid, so confident and brave that just thinking about his kisses, she felt a pang of longing so strong that she put a fist up against her mouth to keep from crying out. She closed her eyes tightly as a swelling of tears dribbled down her cheeks. He was going to dump her at Jacob's Ferry and she'd never see him again.

The foul weather lasted several more days and then gave way to clear skies. A metallic orange sun warmed the depths of the canyon and dispelled a bone-deep chill the rains had brought. Spectacular walls rising nearly three thousand feet in the air were wetly polished by rain. Little rills of fresh water ran down their surfaces bringing out their saffron tones and hues of white, pink, and purples. Everywhere was an iridescent beauty that was lost on Trish. She had withdrawn into herself, trying to pretend that Morgan's rejection of her didn't matter.

They had been on the river about an

hour when the river widened and hard marble rocks lining the canyon changed to layers of soft sandstone. Desert vegetation began to appear. Rounded red buttes replaced canyon walls, rising in natural sculptures of every shape, plane, and line. At last the tongue of the river carried the boats down the middle of the broad river—and out into nearly open country!

Trish saw the same glow on Morgan's face that she had seen many times on her father's. The old river had cast its spell once more and when river lust ran through a man's veins, she had learned that no mere female could hope to compete with it.

"Are we . . . almost there?" she asked, a tight constriction in her throat. She pushed back Jens's scarf from her shoulders. Her breasts rose full and firm against the thin fabric as she warmed herself in the welcome sun.

He nodded. "A small river named the Paria makes a junction with this river according to my sketchy map. That's where the Jacob's Ferry is. We made it! By God, I think we've made it."

She gave him a luminous smile that shook him. His gaze traveled over her russet hair and beautifully tanned skin, softened by the recent high humidity. She was

as dangerous as a coil of dynamite waiting
for a charge. And yet, there was something
vulnerable about her that challenged any
defenses he raised against her.

"Jacob Sutton will look after you,
Trish . . . if you keep a civil tongue in
your head. He might even believe that
tale about your parents being killed by
Indians. You gave yourself away that day
at the ruins. You made up that story,
didn't you?"

For a moment she was ready to tell him
the truth. Then she pictured the revulsion
that would flare in his eyes when she told
him she'd thrust a knife in a man's stomach and left him dead on the kitchen
floor. Her face paled as she thought of
the hanging noose that was waiting for her
back in Bend River.

"What is it, Trish? Why won't you tell
me? You're not married, are you?"

She managed a short laugh. "No, I'm
not married. My parents were killed by Indians . . . and I ran away," she said in a
leaden voice as if repeating the lie often
enough would make it sound like the
truth.

"I don't believe you."

She shrugged. "What does it matter?
You're going to leave me in Jacob's Ferry

and finish your expedition. You don't care what happens to me."

"You'll be safe with the Sutton family," he said gruffly. "They'll put a roof over your head and Jacob Sutton will look after you."

"I don't need Jacob Sutton . . . or anybody else to look after me," she said with her chin jutted out pugnaciously.

Before Morgan could reply, Jens shouted in the boat behind them. "Yahoo." He pointed ahead.

A small river flowed from a northerly direction into the Colorado. Variegated clusters of trees grew where the two rivers met. Trish saw a drift of cottonwoods and a scattering of sturdy Judas and small hackberry. The landscape stretched in every direction as far as she could see and land was barren, dry, and sparsely covered with desert flora. A log house and several outbuildings stood near the confluence and cultivated fields stretched up a delta. No other signs of civilization that Trish could see softened the harsh, arid terrain.

"Jacob's Ferry," breathed Morgan in a reverent whisper as if he couldn't quite believe that a few strokes of his oars would bring him to this indistinct spot on a smudged map.

There was nothing reverent about Trish's horrified expression. It couldn't be! This desolate spot on the river couldn't be Jacob's Ferry. She had expected a growing settlement—where sympathetic ears could be bent to her story. This spot on the river was the most godforsaken place she had ever seen.

As they neared a crude wharf, an assortment of people came running down to the river. A tall man in work clothes, graying dark hair, and a thick beard stood beside the large woman wearing a severe black dress and holding a baby on her hip. A girl about Trish's age stood in the midst of several young children who danced about, waving and shouting. A young man galloped up on a buckskin horse and swung down from the saddle. Sandy hair jutted out over his ears under the brim of his dirty cowboy hat. He quickly took a rifle off his saddle and held it readily in his hands as he joined the welcoming throng.

Morgan jumped out and secured the boat but Trish did not move.

Jacob Sutton extended a handshake as Morgan quickly introduced himself. "Morgan Wallace. We've run the river from Green River, Wyoming. We plan to make an expedition down the Colorado to the

Gulf of California. This is my companion, Jens Larsen."

"Glad to see you made it safely to Jacob's Ferry." The settler shook hands with Jens. Then his eyes slid to Trish still sitting motionless in the bow of Morgan's boat and his weathered face wore a questioning look as his gaze came back to Morgan.

It was Jens who answered. "She was escaping from Indians, sir. Upstream. They killed her family."

"And we hoped that you would take her in," added Morgan.

Sutton's wife stepped forward. "She is welcome. We've had a number of people find sanctuary in our home," she said in a soft voice that belied her thick arms and torso.

"But none as pretty as she is," said the young man. He had lowered his rifle, and his stance was one of deliberate arrogance. His eyes held an avaricious glint as he boldly surveyed Trish. "She's some looker."

Morgan suddenly tensed.

"You must excuse my son, Dirk . . . and his bad manners," said his father quickly, sending the smirking young man a warning glare. Then Jacob stretched out his hand to Trish. His eyes were kindly. "The

Lord has delivered you safely into our hands. His will be done."

Trish heard one of his children giggle, "Dirk loves red hair."

Seven

Jacob Sutton led Trish over to a young girl standing in the midst of the gawking children. "This is my oldest daughter, Rebecca. She'll see to your needs." Then he turned to Morgan and Jens. "Come with me, gentlemen. Three of my oldest sons are gone so there are empty beds in the bunkhouse."

They walked across a clearing to a long narrow structure behind the house. Jacob left them there, telling them to make themselves at home. Jens took one look at a feather mattress placed on a narrow cot and stretched across it with a sigh. "I do believe I've died and gone to heaven. This bed's softer than an angel cloud. Wake me up when the trumpets start blowing."

Morgan laughed. The bunkhouse was about as crude as they came, unfinished lumber, walls put together with chink and groove. Narrow windows that kept the room shadowy and cool. And yet, after weeks of hard ground and dank caves, it was a palace.

Two young boys about ten and eleven years old brought in kettles of hot water and filled a couple of large washbasins. "Pa thought you'd want to wash up for supper," said the older one. Then they scooted out as if they had been warned not to pester their visitors.

Morgan stared out a tiny window in the house's unrelieved and stark walls. The structure was as ugly as the countryside that stretched away to desert land and rocky hills. "What do you think?" he asked Jens.

" 'Bout what?" Jens hadn't moved from the cot. He looked like a big contented bear about to hibernate for the winter. He had his eyes closed and his big hands resting on his chest.

"About Jacob Sutton?"

"Seems like a right enough fellow."

"What about that smirking son of his? Did you see the way he looked at Trish?"

"Hell, she can take care of herself. Does seem kind of a shame, though. She might take up with a guy like that . . . you know . . . just 'cause she had to." He opened one eye and peered at Morgan. Seeing the thunderous expression on Morgan's face, he chuckled silently. Yep, he had it bad, all right. Hell, any one-eyed turkey could see what was going on between them two. The guy spent half his time watching and checking to make sure the gal came through everything safe. Sure, Morgan glowered at her and was as cantankerous as they came, but it didn't fool Jens. Morgan had an itch for the gal. He'd bet his best mule on it.

In the house, Rebecca took charge of Trish. She was a petite girl, sixteen years old. Her drab dress was a miniature of her stalwart mother's—but the resemblance ended there. She wore her fair hair smoothed in a golden knot at the back of her head and intense blue eyes snapped with bubbling excitement and exuberance. Trish soon discovered there was a spontaneity about Rebecca that belied her somber surroundings. When she wasn't under the stern gaze of her mother, she chattered constantly. She asked Trish a dozen questions without waiting for a single answer as she showed Trish the way to a back room in the main house that she shared with two younger sisters. "The boys sleep in the bunkhouse," she told Trish.

The inside of the house was plain and unadorned. The rooms were furnished with crude, homemade furniture and homespun rugs and curtains. From Rebecca's chatter,

Trish learned that her parents' bedroom was just down the hall from the one Rebecca shared with her little sisters. There were nine children in the family and one growing in her mother's belly. Rebecca imparted this information with the same casual air one might discuss the weather.

She set out a basin of water for Trish and some homemade lye soap. As Trish freshened herself, Rebecca surveyed Trish's bedraggled clothes as if weighing a decision. Then she firmed her small chin and before Trish knew what was happening the vivacious girl had dragged out a battered trunk from a corner.

"They told me to get rid of these things . . . but I didn't." Rebecca's whispered tones tinkled with suppressed delight. "I just couldn't throw away these lovely things."

"Whose are they?"

"Karen Whitley's," she said simply and then at Trish's quizzical look, laughed and elaborated. "A man and woman driving a wagon showed up one night in a storm with their sick daughter. I think they were on their way to New Mexico to join some relatives near Santa Fe. Anyway, Karen was running a high temperature, coughing like nothing you ever heard. We gave her cool baths, trying to save the poor girl, but—"

Rebecca gave a shrug of her narrow shoulders. "The good Lord chose to take her home. Her folks went on to New Mexico but they left Karen's things here. Father said they weren't the proper kind of clothing for a Mormon household but I just couldn't dispose of them. And now, here you are," she said triumphantly. "The good Lord does provide!"

Trish wasn't exactly sure what that meant—whether Karen had died to provide Trish with a new wardrobe or Trish had been sent here to make use of the clothes. In any case, despite Rebecca's enthusiasm, Trish's skin crawled a little as she thought about putting on a dead girl's dress. Her squeamishness was foolish because the clothes she'd been wearing had come from missionary boxes sent to the Gunthars by their church. Undoubtedly a lot of the garments had belonged to dead people. Somehow that was different. The way Rebecca talked about Karen, Trish began to feel that she had known the unfortunate girl and that her body was still warm.

"Did you ever see anything as lovely as this?" Rebecca tenderly drew out a deep green watersilk gown. "Sometimes I just get it out and look at it," the fair girl confessed, stroking the fabric as one might touch a beloved pet. "It makes me feel like the angels of heaven are close by . . . singing." She handed it to Trish.

Trish shook her head. "You keep it, Rebecca . . . with a little mending my calico dress will hold together a little longer."

The shine went out of Rebecca's eyes and they misted with tears. She touched the fabric to her cheek. "Already it's beginning to get a musty smell. Such a shame. Oh, please," she begged. "Father won't mind if you wear it."

"Why can't you?"

"Giving in to vanity corrupts the soul," quoted Rebecca as if she had heard the quotation many times in her young life.

Unfortunately Trish knew the condition of her own soul. She sighed. A little vanity wouldn't be noticed in light of her other sins. If it gave Rebecca pleasure to see someone else wear the gown, why not?

Delighted, Rebecca dived into the trunk again and laid out a cotton shift, ruffled drawers, a stiff crinoline petticoat, a pair of white loomed hose, and shiny black shoes. Trish discarded her tattered clothing, poured water from a pitcher into a chipped washbasin sitting on a crude stand and gave herself a quick sponge bath.

Rebecca's face glowed with expectation as she handed Trish the lacy undergarments one by one, sighing delightedly as she watched Trish put them on her supple body. The silk dress went over her head with a rustling caress.

There was nothing risqué about the cut of the gown. Billowy lace ruching trimmed a rounded neckline of a tight bodice; sleeves fell demurely to lace ruffles at her wrists. An overskirt was edged with intricate rose tatting. Silver green sheens highlighted the folds of the rich fabric and rippled with changing light as Trish moved. The fit was snug, especially over the bust, but all in all, it was remarkably the right size, as were the white stockings and black shoes Rebecca knelt to put on Trish's feet.

"The minute I saw you, I knew they'd fit," Rebecca said happily. "When you stepped out of the boat, I said to myself, 'there's a girl for Karen's beautiful dress.' I'm glad I saved it. It had such a narrow escape, too. They almost buried Karen in it!"

Trish paled but Rebecca didn't notice. She made Trish turn around so she could see the skirt swirl as the stiff crinoline held it out from the floor. "Beautiful." She sighed and then began to loosen Trish's tangled braid. "I love to fool with hair," she confessed with a giggle. "Yours is such a lovely shade of reddish brown."

Trish looked at the smooth fair knot at the nape of Rebecca's slender neck. The color was that of ripened wheat. How could anyone so much at odds with her environment be so damn cheerful about it! "How long have you lived here . . . at Jacob's Ferry?"

"Nine years. My parents were called to this mission when I was eight. Brigham Young gave them the charge himself," she said proudly as she brushed out Trish's long, vibrant tresses. "The Colorado River is going to be important to our people, especially when this area is recognized as a separate Mormon state. We're ready to ferry settlers across the river. My father is good with the Navajos and they haven't tried to burn us out."

Trish's scalp suddenly began to tingle and the sensation wasn't due to Rebecca's vigorous brushing and combing.

"There have been some incidents," admitted Rebecca and she told Trish grim tales about massacres of other missionaries who had been "called" to settle the territory around the Colorado. "This is the only place above the Big Canyon where the river can be crossed. It's important that we be here," she said proudly. "Just think what would have happened to you if no one had been living here. There's not another settlement for hundreds of miles in any direction."

Her words brought a sickening lump to the pit of Trish's stomach. "Aren't there other travelers—like Karen's parents?" asked Trish, appalled. "Or army patrols?" Somebody had to take her on down the river—she had to find her father!

Rebecca thought for a moment. "About once a year we see someone, a river man or prospector. We're not anywhere close to a wagon route. Now don't you look lovely," bubbled Rebecca. "Karen would be so pleased."

A coronet of braids circled the crown of Trish's head and wispy curls dangled demurely beside both cheeks. The uplifted coiffure accented Trish's delicately molded cheeks. The gown's deep green color was reflected in her eyes, and complemented the tawny tan of her complexion.

"We mustn't be late for supper," said Rebecca as she splashed water on her face and tucked her hair back in a tight pale knot.

As Rebecca smoothed her own ugly black, hand-me-down dress, Trish visualized the young girl in a sky-blue dimity, soft and pastel against her wheat-colored hair and fair skin. Even in the ugly clothes, Rebecca was a very pretty girl.

Before they left the room, Rebecca impulsively kissed Trish's cheek. "Thank you," she said and Trish knew she was wearing the gown for both of them.

Trish's entrance into the main room of the house could not have been more dramatic if she had entered a stately, candlelit ballroom. All four men were seated at a large, crude table, Morgan, Jens, Jacob Sutton, and his son, Dirk. Mrs. Sutton was busy at the kitchen end of the room near a large, stone fireplace and was deftly dishing up food from blackened pots hanging over the fire. Trish's stomach responded to the tantalizing smells and her nose quivered with anticipation.

Rebecca had preceded Trish into the room like an attendant heralding the entrance of nobility. Feeling self-conscious in the elaborate, unfamiliar attire, Trish hesitated in the doorway, her green silk skirt and petticoat swinging around her. Then she summoned her courage, and walked stately into the room, making a ladylike entrance that would have made her mother proud. She held up her head and her shoulders back. Lantern light caught the folds of the luminous fabric and added a soft glow to the beauty of Trish's face and russet hair.

Jacob Sutton sat at the head of the table

between Jens and Morgan and his son, Dirk, at the foot. Both river men had changed clothes and washed away the river's mud. Morgan was freshly shaven and Jens had trimmed his sun-bleached, tawny beard. Dirk's sandy hair was plastered down with fresh grease and the stubble on his chin was gone.

As Trish entered the room, Jacob stopped in midspeech. Jens's round eyes widened and his mouth dropped open in a ludicrous fashion. "Well, look at Trish, would ya!"

Dirk turned around in his chair and grinned as his eyes slid from Trish's lovely face to curves and crevices of her ripening body molded by the clinging gown.

Morgan's chest constricted. God, she was beautiful! The rich beauty of her flaming hair and tanned skin was as lovely as a painting. Was this the river urchin he'd found blubbering under a hatch cover? Never in his whole life had he felt the floor give way under him as it did now as he got to his feet and held a chair out for her. He restrained an overpowering urge to bend down and kiss the sweet nape of her neck as she sat down beside him.

Dirk leaned his elbows on the table and winked at her. "I bet my little sister's got you all dolled up like that." His bold gaze lingered on the rather tight form-fitting silk bodice. "Our womenfolk don't dress to please a man's eyes. More's the pity."

"Dirk, mind your tongue," his mother ordered as she set a basket of bread on the table.

"Yes, ma'am," he said dutifully but the sparkling glint never left his eyes.

Mrs. Sutton and Rebecca began to bring food to the table. The younger children were seated at another table at the far end of the room and Trish could see places set there for Mrs. Sutton and Rebecca. She wished that she could eat with them. She was uncomfortable sitting with the men.

Morgan and Jens were looking at her strangely, shifting uncomfortably as if a complete stranger had just taken a place at the table. On her left, Dirk's legs sprawled under the table so close to hers that she could barely avoid touching them as she sat primly in her chair. She was aware of Morgan's rigid posture in the chair beside hers, and across the table Jens looked about as comfortable as a mutt cleaned up for a dog show.

Mr. Sutton cleared his throat and bowed his head as a signal that he was about to beseech the Lord's blessing upon their meal. During the prayer, Trish peered sideways at Morgan. The intensity of his expression when she had entered the room had sent her heart racing madly but he hadn't even smiled and continued to stare at her as if she'd betrayed some confidence between them.

When Jacob pronounced his final "Amen," Rebecca and her mother served each of them a rabbit stew swimming with fresh vegetables. Thick slices of sourdough bread were covered with home-churned butter and accompanied with generous slabs of goat cheese. It was all Trish could do to maintain her table manners and keep from stuffing it down like the ravenous creature she was. She concentrated on the food and left the table conversation to the men.

Jacob leveled some direct questions at Morgan. "From what you've told me the Wallace Transportation Company had concentrated their holdings on Long Island Sound and the eastern coast . . . equal to Vanderbilt and Ogden's steamboat companies."

"Yes. Earlier we had replaced our fleet of boats with new steamboats and controlled ports up the Hudson and around Long Island. Competition was fierce but we were winning and then—" Morgan stopped as if something were stuck in his throat. Trish could see muscles in his cheeks flicker as he clenched his jaw. "My father accepted Ogden's offer to buy us out. I tried to stop the sellout but I didn't own enough of the company to prevent the deal." There was anger, pain, and regret in the words and it was obvious that he felt his father had betrayed him.

"I see. So you decided to look elsewhere?"

Morgan nodded. "I was on my way to San Francisco to see if I could buy a small steamboat line on the West Coast when I encountered some Mormon leaders who expressed a great need for a waterway through this region. The possibility intrigued me. Apparently parts of the river have been traversed but a map of its entire course is not available. I was only able to find out bits and pieces about it. I can see why it is important to know exactly which parts of it are navigable."

Jacob nodded. "Our leader, Brigham Young, has formally proposed the creation of a State of Deseret. It will encompass an area that is now Utah and the territories of New Mexico and Arizona. A petition from the Church of Latter Day Saints to admit this area into the union as one state is before Congress right now. It would mean a lot to our people."

"What if Congress turns down your petition?" Morgan bluntly asked.

"We are determined to secure for ourselves our rightful land! We have been persecuted and driven farther west with each wave of violence. We will not be driven out again! If our petition is rejected, we will use arms to secure our settlements in this area."

"I see . . . then a waterway would be vital to survival?"

"And profitable for the company that dominates the Colorado," Jacob shrewdly added as if he knew Morgan had little interest in political or religious ramifications of such a venture.

"The Colorado seems ripe for plucking," Morgan said with a smile of satisfaction.

"Perhaps," answered Jacob cautiously. "There have been some attempts to run the river through the Big Canyon. A river man was picked up downstream a while back, floating on a raft . . . don't know how long he was on the river. He died from exposure and injuries. It's not an easy task you've set for yourselves."

Morgan straightened his shoulders. "I don't see why this western territory can't be connected by rivers the way the eastern states are. There is intense commerce along every major river east of the Rockies."

"That may be, but my flat-bottom scow

is the only boat for miles and it only goes from one side of the river to the other. Even small boats are in constant jeopardy. How did you find our red river behaving above?"

Jens had been listening to the conversation while he ate. At Jacob's question, he put down his fork. "Like a wild jackass drunk on loco weed. I've worked on canals around the Great Lakes. . . . I'm telling you nobody's going to get any kind of boat sailing on the river we just came down."

Trish could feel Morgan tense beside her and knew he was about to attack Jens's remarks. She swallowed a bite of bread and said quickly, "I remember hearing my father say that this was the decade that the Colorado would be opened up for trade."

Morgan's expression betrayed an astonishment that cracked his usual composure. Jens rounded his eyes and Jacob leaned forward to hear her better. Now that she had their attention, she wished she had kept her mouth shut. Still, it gave her a foolish sense of satisfaction to see that startled expression on Morgan's face.

"What is your full name, my dear?" asked Jacob with interest.

For a moment she hesitated and then with a lift of her chin, she said. "Patricia

Lynne Winters. My father has been running the Colorado for years," she bragged.

"And he was killed by Indians?" Jacob's tone apologized for touching on her bereavement.

It was fortunate that he had brought up the lie because it was on Trish's lips to say she was planning to track down her father, knowing that he would undoubtedly be somewhere along the Colorado. "Y—yes!" she stammered. Hastily she lowered her eyes, knowing that Morgan and Jens didn't believe her story about the Indian attack.

Jacob kept asking her questions and she found herself explaining how her father had left his farm in Iowa and come West with wife and infant son to the Wyoming Territory and then Colorado. "I guess he knows . . . knew . . . the Colorado River just about better than anyone." Her eyes sparkled. "He never expected me to run the same river chutes."

Morgan had listened to the exchange with astonishment. Trish's glib duplicity always amazed him. Now she had invented a story about her father being a river man.

Dirk reached out and put his hand over Trish's and squeezed it. "You're a very brave young woman. Your father would be proud of you."

The compliment made her feel warm all

over. She smiled appreciatively at him. "I hope so."

He held her hand a second longer than was necessary and when he released it, his thumb trailed over her soft palm.

"I don't understand why Mr. Sutton hasn't met your father, Trish, if he's been on the river as much as you say," Morgan challenged, irritated by the way she was reacting to Dirk's syrupy remarks. He didn't believe her new story any more than he had the last one. As far as he was concerned her "river-man father" was just another lie she told to suit her purpose.

She swung on him. "It's true . . . my father has been on the river hundreds of times!"

"Maybe he didn't come down this far," soothed Jacob, sensing her distress. "There's an overland trail that most travelers take to miss the Big Canyon." He gave Trish a reassuring smile. "And your mother . . . she was killed, too?"

The good meal sat queasily on Trish's stomach. She was certain that this righteous Mormon could see to the depths of her deceitful soul. She hid her hands in her lap as if Jacob could discern the blood of murder on them and tried to look away from his penetrating gaze, which demanded the truth. She moistened her lips but no sound would come out of her constricted throat.

"Don't look so frightened, Patricia. You are safe now," Jacob soothed. "The Lord has brought you out of the wilderness into a new sanctuary. You are without family and without a home but you have come to us on the waters, like the child Moses set adrift upon the river. This is a saint's household ready to accept another willing worker in God's kingdom."

Morgan stiffened. A surge of indefinable emotions washed over him. Logic told him that he had no right to interfere. He wasn't in any position to offer Trish anything. His own life hung precariously upon the success of a dangerous expedition that was so far *not* the answer to his dreams. More and more, it seemed that his plans to find the Colorado navigable were to end in bitter failure—and maybe in his own death. At the moment, he wasn't even in control of his own future, let alone someone else's. This godly household offered a homeless young woman a chance for a happy, productive life. What right did he have to interfere? If Jacob Sutton would take Trish in as his daughter she would be well cared for.

Very soon Jacob Sutton made it clear to everyone that he wasn't interested in a daughter—but a daughter-in-law. "I don't know the strength of your own faith, Patricia, but I look forward to explaining the beliefs of our household. We have been praying that the Lord would bring a good Christian woman into my son's life . . . someone who would fill his life with joyful thanksgiving. Perhaps you, my dear, are an answer to our prayers."

"Amen," echoed Mrs. Sutton and Rebecca sent Trish a glowing smile.

Trish fought the urge to shove back her chair and run. Neither Morgan nor Jens would look at her as she sent a frantic look around the table. Panic poured over her that was greater than any she had felt in the clutches of the river.

Dirk deliberately moved his leg under the table until his foot lifted the edge of her skirt and brushed her leg with a suggestive caress.

Eight

The next morning Dirk followed Trish to the river and insisted upon carrying the bucket of water she had drawn. Last night she had kicked him under the table for his brazen behavior, but he had only laughed.

"Don't you have your own work to do?" she demanded curtly.

He grinned at her. "Nothing important. Besides, Father wants us to become better acquainted. He thinks you'll be a good influence on me." He sidled close to her as they walked. He slipped his free arm around her waist.

She swung around and tipped the bucket up and poured water all over his front. "Gosh, I'm sorry," she said with mock horror. Then she turned and ran back to the house.

She continued to feel uncomfortable in his presence and did her best to avoid him but the whole family seemed to be in a conspiracy to throw them together.

Morgan was so engrossed in securing needed provisions for continuing the expedition that he devoted all his time and energies to that end. He wanted to buy the provisions from Jacob and be on his way but the settler was only willing to provide them in exchange for work—not money! If Morgan and Jens wanted food, ammunition, and tools, Jacob stated apologetically that they must labor for them in the fields.

Morgan did his best to change the man's mind. He had plenty of money in his belt to buy what they needed ten times over. It wasn't the work that frustrated him but the loss of time. He wanted to get back on the river as soon as possible. Jacob knew the reputation of the Big Canyon, sometimes called the Grand Canyon, which lay beyond Jacob's Ferry and he warned Morgan that he would need to start out with adequate supplies and well-caulked boats.

"He's forcing us to work like conscripted laborers," swore Morgan when Jacob would not budge from his "No work . . . no supplies."

"Reckon, that's what we are, all right," admitted Jens, unconcerned by the situation. The truth was he liked having solid earth under his gunboat feet. Farm work had been his whole life until the death of his grandmother when he had turned his back on his father's farm. He had no deep hankering to get back on the river. He only grinned good-naturedly when Jacob handed each of them a shovel and nodded toward an unfinished irrigation ditch that his four young sons were digging so they could water crops planted along a flat delta near the Paria River. Dirk had other responsibilities that kept him on horseback most of the day.

Morgan decided he had no choice in the matter. They needed ammunition and tools that Trish had dumped and he was grateful to Jacob for agreeing to sell him a good supply of corn, flour, and beans.

Jacob was a hard-nosed taskmaster. The Lord's work had to go forward—even if it took a little stubborn persuasion. From the beginning it was obvious that Jens's strong back was going to earn the most credit in Jacob's ledgers. He dug twice the distance of anybody else and enjoyed having firm rich earth under his feet instead of shifting, sandy riverbanks. His layered muscles moved in rhythm to canal songs as he hummed in rich deep tones and threw dirt from the deepening ditch. He was the first one out in the morning and the last one in at dusk.

A second person in the Sutton household

appreciated Jens as much as Jacob—his daughter, Rebecca. The young woman was enchanted by this tall, sweating giant. Her own chores would have worn out a girl twice her size, thought Trish, but Rebecca hummed as she fed the chickens, milked the goat, carried a baby sister around on her hip, and cheerfully completed her household duties. Whenever she could, she gave the baby a piece of sugared cloth to suck and then scooted down to the field to see how Jens was doing. At lunchtime it was Rebecca who eagerly filled a hamper of food to take down to the men laboring near the river.

From the first day, Trish was given her share of duties in the house. Karen's trunk had provided a simple white tunic bodice fastened in the front with tiny pearl buttons to a high collar; full sleeves ended with a gathering just below the elbow. A teal blue piping along the collar and down the front of the bodice matched a flounced skirt with several ruffles pulled to the back in a modified bustle, unsuitable for Mormon wear because of its color and elaborate style. Trish loved the luminous pearl buttons and found herself touching their smooth roundness with sensual pleasure.

Although not as elegant as the green watersilk, this day dress flattered Trish's figure and deepened the sea-blue of her eyes. She was told to wear a white morning cap over her hair which was primly held in a tight twist at the back of her neck. She was grateful for Karen's soft leather shoes, hose, and undergarments, including two petticoats starched to hide the sensuous curves of her limbs as she moved about her tasks. She put the lovely green silk back in the trunk and washed out her torn calico dress, which looked beyond mending.

Mrs. Sutton paid Trish scant personal attention. She didn't have time. Everyone labored from dawn to night in the Sutton household, waging a constant battle for self-sufficiency and survival. Trish did as she was told and the hours of tedious, backbreaking work were long and boring. Her spirits came to life only when Morgan returned from the fields at night.

Even though she sat with the women during meals after the first night, she listened to Morgan's deep resonant voice as he chatted with the other two men. She greedily clung to every word in the conversation. She watched his expression and caught his enthusiasm as he talked about the Colorado River and the hopes he had to bring trade into this area. A thousand questions stirred but she didn't dare voice them. She wanted to be a part of his dreams and share the excitement with him but she knew that he and Jens would be going on down the river very soon now . . . leaving her behind. The hopes she'd had for locating her father had faded with the isolation of Jacob's Ferry. She was stuck here, and even though Jacob Sutton was treating her like one of his daughters, he was obviously pushing her toward his son, Dirk, at every opportunity. From Rebecca, Trish learned that Dirk was the third son in the family, the older two being away in Utah. She also learned that Dirk had earned the reputation of being the black sheep of the family.

"When he goes to Yucca Springs for supplies, he stays an extra night or two," confided Rebecca. Then she whispered. "Sometimes demon whiskey takes hold of him. I smell it on his clothes when I wash them. But I don't tell Father. My brother is really a hard worker and he plays the fiddle so wonderfully that the rafters start jumping." She giggled. "He's the most fun of anybody. Father thinks he needs to find a good woman and settle down." She turned an approving smile on Trish. There was no doubt about whom she thought could work the desired change in her rebellious brother.

At night, Trish lay in her narrow, hard

bed and remembered the way Morgan's mouth had molded hers. She felt again the firm length of his body pressed against hers. Since she had never been physically aroused before by a man's masculinity, she didn't know what was happening to her when warm moisture swelled in the intimate crevices of her young body. Why was there this deep emptiness inside of her when he wasn't around? Why did she long to touch him, hear his voice, and feel rising goose bumps when she thought he might speak to her? Her aching needs and longings were a mystery to her but she knew she wanted to be in his embrace, to feel the tingling ecstasy of his lips and questing tongue and to let his hand cup the warm, soft sweetness of her breasts.

But even as she dreamed and longed for him, reality brought tears swimming into her eyes. She had never been one to feel defeated, not even when everyone and everything were at odds with her dreams, but she didn't know how to handle the emotional upheaval that now raged within her. How could she scale the thick wall he was building between them? Sometimes she caught his pensive, questioning eyes upon her. And yet, he did not make any move to change anything between them. Caught in her own lies, there was nothing she could say or do that wouldn't make everything worse. Tears eased down her cheeks and she buried her sobs in a scratchy, lumpy pillow.

In the bunkhouse, Morgan turned restlessly in his narrow bed, sleepless, plagued by nettled thoughts of his own. He wanted to be on his way. Get back on the river, marking its course, and searching for the corridor to the sea that he had been so certain lay within his grasp. But all these dreams were now tinged with an unexpected complication. Even though his rational mind mocked his feelings of responsibility toward Trish, he could not suppress them. He thought about the days and nights spent on the river—and how aware he'd been of her with every breath he drew. He remembered the tantalizing fire of her kisses and how desire had sent his blood running hot when he touched her. He tortured himself with fantasies of her passionate body under his, meeting his thrusts with a fiery passion of her own. He'd never longed for a woman like this before. There had been months when he never even thought of taking his pleasure with one. Even as he mocked himself for his weakness, every time he caught sight of her, moving about in her prim white cap and aproned dress, he could visualize the supple figure moving tantalizingly beneath the layers of cloth. The memory of each curve and plane of her body he had seen molded by wet cloth taunted him. Lying there in his bunk bed, he felt desire hardening and he wished he had taken her and then he shoved such thoughts away as pure foolishness. He wasn't going to let a river urchin arouse him enough to make a commitment he didn't intend to keep. Turning over in his bed, he centered his thoughts on the preparations that must be completed before he and Jens tackled the Big Canyon.

"Tell me everything about him," urged Rebecca, her blue eyes sparkling as the two girls walked toward the field.

At first, Trish thought she was asking about Morgan because he was the one who dominated her thoughts day and night. "Why do you want to know about Morgan?" Her tone was fringed with a jealous crispness, certain that Rebecca had fallen under his spell just as she had.

"Not Morgan. Jens! He must be the biggest, strongest man in the whole wide world. Just like Samson. I bet he could take down the roof of our house with one pull. Don't you think he could? Not that he'd do a thing like that. Anyone can see that he is the most kind . . . gentle . . . and tender man."

Trish would have thought that Jens's size alone would terrify Rebecca but apparently she was enthralled by it. "I don't know much about him. He doesn't talk about himself much."

"Tell me about his family," she pleaded as the two girls walked with a lunch basket swinging between them. "Where does he come from? Is he strong in his own religious faith? Please, Trish, tell me everything you know about him."

The "everything" that Trish knew wasn't very much. She went over in her mind the few things Jens had shared with her when she rode in his boat. He talked about the way his father had worked him like one of the animals on the farm . . . and about his nicknames, "Ox" and "Mule." She knew he could be gentle but he probably could be ruthless, too. She had seen bitterness and anger cloud those round hazel eyes. How could she put these impressions into words for this girl who had dreamy sparkles in her smile?

"He told me he was raised on a farm in Ohio and had worked around the Great Lakes."

"I knew he was a farmer." Rebecca smiled broadly under her sunbonnet. "Father says he has the Lord's touch in his hands. He knows how to make things grow. What about his faith?"

Trish searched her memory. "I think he said his grandmother had read the Bible to him," she offered. "And I don't think he has any prejudices." What more could she say? A man's faith was not something he discussed with a river rat.

As they walked over the powdery dry ground, Rebecca broke out in a song heralding the wonder of the Lord. Under their footsteps, dust came up in clouds, filling Trish's nostrils and laying a film on her well-scrubbed face. Above, the sun was an orange ball in a bleached sky, intent upon drying out the parched ground and heating the earth to a bake oven.

When the girls reached the cultivated field, Rebecca called out and waved to Jens who was clearing off some mesquite bushes near the river. He looked up at Rebecca's voice and waved back. The men always ate lunch sitting on a pile of boulders under some straggly cottonwoods that provided uncertain shade. Trish's searching gaze traveled between rows of corn as far as the river for Morgan but he was not in sight.

At Rebecca's call, Jens, her brothers, and

Jacob put down their hoes and came to get their lunch. The girls began handing out sandwiches made with thick slices of mutton and sourdough bread. Trish watched Rebecca blush prettily as she handed one to Jens.

"Thank you, kindly." His round eyes crinkled with a smile. Rebecca followed him as he walked over to one of the boulders and sat down.

Trish turned around and saw Jacob watching Rebecca and Jens with a smile on his face. Maybe he was beginning to ask the same kind of questions as Rebecca, thought Trish. Keeping the hardworking Jens at Jacob's Ferry on a permanent basis would be like finding a half-dozen laborers.

Jacob took a sandwich from the basket that Trish was holding. "Thank you, my dear. What a pleasure to have you in our household. Won't you sit a spell with me . . . so we can talk?" He guided her to a fallen tree trunk. "Now then. I hope you will not think me too forward but the annual visit of Elder Nickols is almost upon us. If there is to be a ceremony, we must prepare for it."

"Ceremony?" she echoed, her chest constricting.

He frowned apologetically. "I'm sorry. I didn't mean to startle you."

She knew what he was about to say. He was going to push her into accepting Dirk as a suitor—and a husband. From that first night, he'd looked upon her as a possible daughter-in-law. Acceptable women were a premium in this unsettled country. Every new addition to a settler's family provided another valuable worker. "I don't know what you're talking about," she answered with a dry mouth.

"Your future, my dear."

She swallowed back a sharp retort that her future was none of his business. A sense of helplessness poured over her. Morgan was going to dump her on the Suttons the same way her father had abandoned her to the Gunthars. Even though Jacob's home was a truly Christian one, she would be as firmly trapped and as hopeless as she had been before.

"We want to love and care for you, Patricia. I have given my son permission to speak to you." Jacob's weathered face crinkled with a smile. "He will be declaring himself to you and I wanted to say that—"

"No." She wouldn't listen to him. At that panic-stricken moment, she saw Morgan coming into view at the far end of the field. She bolted away from Jacob as if the devil himself was at her heels.

"Patricia, come back," Jacob called after her, obviously bewildered by her unexpected behavior.

She put her head down and ran between two rows of corn until she reached Morgan.

"What's happened? What's the matter?" he demanded as he stopped her mad flight.

She lifted frantic eyes to his frowning face. "It's Jacob," she gasped, trying to catch her breath. "He's talking about a wedding. You can't leave me here. You've got to take me with you."

"Trish," Morgan said in a firm, but gentle tone as he put his hands on her shoulders. "Jens and I will be lucky to get through the Big Canyon alive. You heard what Jacob said about what lies ahead. Other men who have tried to travel that section have never been seen again. We probably haven't seen half of what the river will throw at us. And hostile Indians live along the ridge—"

"I'm not afraid."

"If you had any sense you would be! I can't be worrying about you breaking your neck or keeping Indians from scalping that lovely crown of hair. You stay here and—"

"And become Dirk Sutton's wife!"

"That will never happen . . . unless you

want it to," he said firmly. "He can't force you to marry him, you know. Insist that Jacob accepts you as a daughter."

They began walking back toward the others. "You stay here, Trish, and if things work out the way I hope, Jacob's Ferry will be an important stopping-off place on the river. In time, you'll find someone who deserves a gal like you, Trish. Someone who can offer you a safe future, a home, and family. There are plenty of men in the world who would be lucky to have you." His eyes were pained as they looked down at her. "Please understand, Trish. I'm only thinking about what's best for you. I want to keep you safe."

"No, you want to get rid of me." Her chin quivered as she walked beside him looking straight ahead. She was agonizingly aware of his thighs and hips brushing close to hers as they walked across the uneven ground. If only he understood! She would rather die fighting the river with him than remain safely at Jacob's Ferry—but what could she say to convince him?

Jacob stood waiting for them.

"I'll talk to him," promised Morgan. "Don't worry. It'll be all right. Jacob's a kindly man. He'll accept your decision."

But will his son? Trish asked silently. She

walked over to the rock where Jens and Rebecca were sitting together eating their sandwiches, laughing and talking quietly. The intimate scene added to her rising sense of loneliness. She looked back at Morgan and Jacob talking together. She wondered if Morgan was telling Jacob the same thing he had told her . . . that the Mormon was to keep her safe until she found some young man of her choosing. But I don't want anybody else! I want you, she cried silently. If only Morgan changed his mind and decided to take her with him. The hope died as quickly as it was born. She knew that it would never happen. He'd made up his mind. He wouldn't risk her life as he was willing to risk his own.

"What's the matter, Trish?" drawled Jens. "You look like a filly with a burr under the saddle."

"Don't you want something to eat, Patricia?" asked Rebecca.

"I'm not hungry."

"What?" boomed Jens with a laugh. "Now I know something's got Trish riled up. She can be half drowned and still eat her way through three days' rations," he told Rebecca. "But she's a fisherman . . . caught us several nice messes of trout. Brave, too. Crawled right down the face of sheer cliffs, she did. Got herself nearly drowned getting us a branch from a rotten, old willow tree."

"Oh, Trish, how courageous you are," said Rebecca with sincerity shining out of those sky-blue eyes. "I could never do anything like that—"

"Oh, I bet you could," countered Jens. "I suspect you're as brave in your own way as you are pretty, Rebecca. Never seen anyone who had eyes that sparkle the way yours do."

Color washed up into Rebecca's cheeks and she lowered her eyes at the compliment. "Are you sure you won't have another sandwich?"

Jens glanced up at the sun. "Reckon it's time to get back to work. I want to get the corn all irrigated by dusk." He offered Rebecca a hand down from the rocks. "Thanks for the mighty fine lunch."

"It was . . . no bother," Rebecca said shyly. Her eyes glowed and her gaze followed him as he walked over to join Morgan and Jacob. She sighed and then turned to Trish. "Did Father tell you about the party?"

"Party—?"

Rebecca nodded and laughed gaily. "It's going to be for you, Trish. You told me that Saturday was going to be your eighteenth birthday! Don't be angry with me

for telling everyone. We want it to be a
special day for you. Our church believes in
singing and dancing and bringing joy unto
the Lord. We're hardworking saints—but
fun loving, too. A birthday . . . and a
farewell party all in one."

"Farewell?" Trish echoed in a cracked
voice.

Rebecca nodded. Her blue eyes lost their
sparkle as she sighed. "Yes, Father says the
men's work is almost done. They'll be shoving off in a few days." Then she brightened.
"But you'll be staying here with us. Oh,
Trish, isn't it amazing how the good Lord
arranges everything so wonderfully?"

Nine

All of the fuss over her birthday bewildered Trish. Her mother had never made anything of the date and she doubted if her father even remembered it. She had only mentioned it to Rebecca because she had asked her how old she was and Trish told her she would turn eighteen in a few days.

The night of the party, a festive air replaced the usual mundane, dull atmosphere at Jacob's Ferry. Tables and chairs in the main kitchen-eating room were pushed to the wall. Dirk picked up his fiddle and as his bow flashed back and forth on taut strings, Jacob patted a foot in rhythm to the rollicking music and he called, "Grab your partners for a square dance."

Every member of the family above the age of eight answered the call. Mrs. Sutton claimed Jens, and Rebecca took Morgan as a partner. Rebecca's eleven-year-old brother, Samuel, offered to show Trish how to do the steps. She laughingly agreed even though she and Teddy had attended lots of barn dances when her mother was alive.

Rhythm surged from the soles of Trish's feet to her bobbing head as floorboards, walls, and rafters vibrated with a hand-clapping, foot-stomping square dance. Jacob's deep voice was perfect as a caller and he sent the dancers spinning around the room at an exhausting pace.

Trish wore the green silk gown for the second time and fashioned her hair in a soft twist on the top of her head with long curls trailing down her back. Lantern light threaded coppery glints through the shiny strands. Her gaiety disguised an urgency building inside her. Morgan and Jens would be leaving in a few days. If she didn't change his mind tonight all would be lost.

Her courage failed the first time she saw Morgan across the room. He was a stranger fashionably dressed in deep maroon pants, white shirt, and gray frock coat. Polished boots hugged his legs and a soft silk tie matched a striped vest in gray and wine tones. She had never seen anyone attired so handsomely. Strength and determination were etched on his sun-bronzed face and her heart swelled with a wild beating as her gaze traveled the length of his handsome figure. His shoulders were broad and muscular, his waist narrow and taut and his thighs and legs firmly conditioned by the demands of the expedition. Had she really been in his arms? It seemed only an impossible dream that he had kissed and caressed her. And yet she knew how those sensuous, demanding lips felt upon her own. A spurt of desire sluiced through her young body and she was so flustered when he caught her eye across the room that she felt as if someone had bent her knees from behind. She smiled, quickly turned away and listened to his deep laughter as he exchanged banter with Jens who had donned clean work trousers and a plaid shirt for the occasion.

Trish watched Morgan dance with Rebecca and Sara Sutton. He gallantly led his partner through the steps as if he were in some glittering ballroom instead of a crudely built log house in the middle of nowhere. Like a magnet he would draw all the women to him no matter where he went, she thought, and she bit her lip to keep back a feeling of despair.

Rebecca was obviously hearing heavenly music as she danced with Jens. The pretty young girl wore a faded gray dress, her pale blond hair in its usual tight knot but the expression on her face could not be contained or subdued by religious ritual.

Her beauty overshadowed her drab attire and she looked as if she were soaring on clouds. For a big man, Jens was amazingly light on his feet and Trish knew barn dances were not foreign to him. He handled Rebecca as if she were so fragile she might break under his touch.

Trish had read his thoughts correctly. As Jens looked down at Rebecca's sweet, angelic face, he realized how much he had enjoyed being with her, seeing her bright sunny face every day, watching her move about the house and field with her light, gay step. He knew she liked him—and that was a completely new experience for him. No pretty young girl had ever pinned her affection on him before. More and more, he began to wonder what it would be like to settle down with a wonderful girl like Rebecca. Jacob seemed to accept him well enough. He didn't know anything about their religion but the good Lord probably didn't care what path you took to heaven as long as you lived a good and decent life, Jens thought as he smiled at Rebecca.

Trish danced with all of Rebecca's younger brothers. She was about to despair that Morgan was ever going to ask her to dance when he was suddenly at her elbow. "May I have the pleasure of the next dance, Patricia Winters?" he asked formally with a soft, teasing shine in his eyes.

She laughed lightly. "I thought you'd never ask." The use of her full name sounded foreign on his lips, and she much preferred "Trish," "Stowaway," or even "River Urchin." When he slipped his arm around her waist and swung her out into position, his firm touch upon her back and the possessive clasp of her hand in his drove away all of the rehearsed speeches she had prepared for such a moment.

They met, parted, spun, and glided around the room to the rhythm of a folk dance that had everyone in the family breathless. At the end of the dance, they stood for a moment in the midst of the party clamor just looking at one another. Morgan's grip tightened on her arms as if trying to steady her . . . or himself. Then he slowly let out his breath and stepped back. "Would you like some refreshment?" His voice was husky.

She nodded. Her shortness of breath was not caused by the dance they had just finished but by the caressing softness of his eyes and mouth. She let her hand rest in his as he led her over to the refreshment table.

A crock of apple juice along with john-nycakes, fresh sourdough biscuits and honey had been set out on a long crude table. There was a seed cake made with three precious eggs and an extra measure of sugar in the buttery frosting. Trish took a glass of juice from Morgan, her hand trembling with suppressed emotion. She cleared her voice, searching for words. A thick silence engulfed them.

At that moment, Rebecca brought in a birthday cake from the pantry and burst out in her high clear voice, "Happy Birthday, dear Patricia. . . ." Everyone joined in, repeating the greeting, and Trish stood there stunned. She blinked rapidly against a rising fullness.

The birthday cake would have been enough but there were even presents.

"Come sit down!" Rebecca laughingly pushed Trish into Jacob's chair by the fire. "Here open my gift first." She thrust a small box into Trish's hands and giggled with delight as Trish's trembling fingers lifted the lid. A pair of tiny emerald earrings that matched the green silk gown twinkled back at her. "They're beautiful," gasped Trish.

"Karen would be so pleased!" whispered Rebecca as she fastened them on Trish's ears.

Mrs. Sutton presented her a white apron with a lace pocket and crocheted edging, kissed her on the forehead and wished her, "A long life in the Lord's grace."

Jens gave her a small polished stone that she knew was his good-luck charm. The youngest Sutton child, a little boy of six, put a reed flute into her hands and hugged her warmly as if she already belonged in the family.

There were two new linen handkerchiefs from Morgan. "The *W* monogram can stand for Winters. I'm sure you'll put them to good use," he said with a teasing grin.

Trish had trouble handling all the emotion as she tried to thank everyone. Tears blurred her vision. She longed for this wonderful kind of family caring. The only other person who had offered her such open affection was Winnie May. She wished the motherly prostitute was here now to join in the dancing and singing. Even as the thought crossed Trish's mind, she knew that her friend would not be accepted here. Winnie didn't belong with these dedicated saints—*and neither do I!* She brushed the tears from her cheeks. Defiance had been a way of life since babyhood; she drew upon that past now. She couldn't stay here.

Trish excused herself and went into the bedroom to wash her face. As she came out, Dirk was there waiting for her. "Got a little present for you myself. Something kind of private. Just the kind of gift a fellow should give his intended."

All joy went out of the moment. Her head came up. "Then I suggest you save it for your 'intended.'"

He just gave her that infuriating grin, reached into his pocket and pulled out a blue satin garter. She knew darn well he'd taken it off some doxy.

"Hold out your leg, sweetheart, and I'll put it on."

Trish gave him a sweet smile. "Oh, you really shouldn't." Coyly, she lifted her foot off the floor, and as he stooped to slip the garter over her shoe, she kicked him not too lightly in the stomach. He doubled up and gasped for breath as she walked neatly around him and returned to the big room.

She looked around for Morgan. Time was running out. She must convince him to take her down the river. There was no question of her staying here. She had to persuade him by whatever means she could.

She asked Rebecca where Morgan was and she said she thought he'd gone out for a breath of fresh air. Jacob offered Trish another piece of cake and it was several minutes before Trish could slip out the kitchen door and look for Morgan.

Moonlight spilled on the ground like

golden liquid, softening the harsh desert terrain and creating a harmony among river, cliffs, rocks, and sky. Trish stepped off the porch and walked toward the river where the boats were moored. She searched in the shadows for that familiar breadth of shoulder, proud head, and straight carriage. The soft soles of her leather shoes whispered with each step and she lifted the rustling silk skirt so that it wouldn't skim the ground.

She could hear the river's gentle lapping and sucking. The watery counterpoints blended in a hushed melody that soothed away her tension. Breathing in deeply, she lifted her eyes to a myriad of stars, the same ones she had viewed from the depths of the river canyon.

Morgan was leaning up against some pilings at the water's edge. He straightened up as she approached. "What are you up to, Trish?" he demanded.

"I—I needed some air. I thought I'd take a walk." His tone made her testy. "Do I have to get your permission first?"

He chuckled. "Not at all. But when you come anywhere near these boats, I find myself interested in what's going on in that calculating mind of yours!"

"I'm not going to touch your precious

boats. I don't know why you don't trust me—"

He threw back his head and laughed fully. "You're unbelievable, Trish. You really are. Innocence is not an adjective that comes to mind when I think about you. You're just about the most determined, wily, foolhardy, and ingenious female I've ever met."

"I take that as a compliment, thank you," she said stiffly.

Moonlight caught her hair in rich tones like warm brandy and in the depths of her eyes silver bits sparkled at him. His searing gaze lingered on the exquisite curve of her cheekbones and he fought an impulse to trace the enticing lines of her elevated chin and slender neck. He was intensely aware of her natural vitality. Her enthusiasm for life. She didn't possess a single simpering, languid, feminine ploy that had made him so indifferent to other women. Her natural beauty constantly assaulted him. Her luminous eyes, reflecting light like silver rippling upon sea-green water were enough to send any man's senses reeling. Long, heavy lashes lay shadows upon her honey-brown cheeks and remembered desire stirred in him. "And the most intriguing and beautiful." His bantering tone thickened. "What you do to a man—" He faltered as she moved closer to him.

"And you are the most conceited, arrogant, infuriating man," she murmured, "that ever took a breath." With a fingertip she traced the hard curve of his chin.

"I take that as a compliment," he mimicked as his mouth moved to touch the finger she had near his mouth. Then he took her hand away from his face and buried a kiss in the warmth of her palm. "There's a birthday kiss."

She leaned into him and placed her hands on his chest. "I'd rather have a real one."

"Trish," he croaked huskily, looking down at her upturned face and fighting an inward battle with himself. "Good God, what a temptress you are!" His mouth found hers with an urgency that was demanding and fierce. He parted her lips and his tongue touched hers with impelling rhythm. His hands slid downward shaping her buttocks, lifting her upward, and pressing her against his rampant desire. Lord, how he wanted her! But his rigid self-discipline didn't desert him even as she molded her body against his. In the rising heat of desire, he reached up and loosened the arms she had around his neck. "Let's go for a walk," he said abruptly.

She was startled by the pace at which he led her along the sandy bank. Her own feelings were in such a whirl that she kept her silence as the brisk night air bathed her heated face and filled her nostrils with scents of piñon, dank earth, and a faint hint of desert flower perfume. They must have walked about a half mile before he began talking. It was the first time he'd shared any personal feelings and thoughts with her.

"Ever since I was big enough to sit on a pier and swing my legs over the water, I dreamed about being a part of my father's transportation company," he said in a quiet, solemn tone. "When I was just a boy, my father had a couple of vessels sailing around Long Island. They were lovely boats and I grew up on their decks, hoisting sails, and pulling rope. In a few years my father began making money and he expanded his fleet. By the time I finished my college education at Yale, my father had purchased several steamboats . . . real beauties . . . fast and dependable. The Wallace Transportation Company began to corner all the shipping trade and even beat Vanderbilt and Ogden to some of the best ports. By this time, I worked up to a full partnership—at least I thought I had. Then my father . . ." Morgan's voice was suddenly choked with emotion. "My father sold out our company without even consulting me! Everything. He called me into the office and . . ." The scene burned in Morgan's mind as if it were yesterday. He described it to Trish and heard his father's voice the way it had been that day his world shattered.

"Vanderbilt and Ogden are at each other's throats," his father had said bluntly. "I've been offered a good price to back out and leave the fight to them so I've decided to sell out."

"Not on your life!" Morgan had protested.

"Sit down, son, and listen. Railroads are going to put water transportation out of business. This is the time to make a change—!"

"Railroads! I can't abide the belching monsters!"

"I wasn't suggesting that you become an engineer, Morgan. Anyway, I've signed over every vessel we own, every freight and passenger line we have. We'll incorporate under a different name. They take possession in thirty days—"

"What in the hell about me? My vote? My share of the company? I've given everything I have to build up our monopoly!"

"On paper it's a one-man operation," reminded his father. "I gave you a limited power of attorney but the Wallace Transportation Company has always been mine." Something akin to amusement had flickered in that aging face and sharp, dark brown-black eyes. "I often wondered if you were going to demand that half of the company be put legally in your name. In any venture you should consult a lawyer and make certain you own what you think you own."

"There was never any question about it—when I came into the business, it was a father and son partnership! Lawyer, hell. I trusted you! You deliberately took advantage—"

"Exactly!" His father's voice softened. "Son, I want you to become the most successful transportation tycoon this country has ever seen. Everything I've done is for you. I've tried to give you the best. The only way you can win out over the big boys is to never let your emotions get in the way. Trust is a weakness a rising millionaire cannot afford. I hope you've learned your lesson. Now, let's forget about steamboats. Get your things out of *Milady*. She brought a nice price, by the way."

"*Milady*. You sold my boat!"

Raised eyebrows mocked him. "She's a Wallace vessel, isn't she?"

"You know that steamboat's been mine

from the first plank that was laid in her keel. I watched every fitting put in place and every rose panel secured in my quarters. We've outrun everything on the river. I love that boat—you can't have *Milady.*"

"Son, there's no place for maudlin affections in the business world. You might as well learn that right now. Hard as it is, you've got to be practical about even the smallest things. You've got to be tough. Get your stuff out of that steamboat. The new owners will take possession as soon as I can transfer ownership. We've got lots of work ahead to create some new holding companies. The future is yours, son. Don't look back."

Trish felt Morgan's hand tighten in hers as he stopped talking and stared at the flowing water rippling in the moonlight. She could feel fury surging through his body as he stared at the river, seeing a different scene. "I sailed *Milady* out into the middle of Long Island Sound. Stoked up her boilers. Locked the valves shut. Then I rowed away and watched her blow."

"You blew her up? Your own boat?" She felt something akin to a shiver go up her back.

"Yes, I blew her all to hell." His voice choked. "I loved *Milady*. She was the only thing I really felt was mine. Everything else belonged to my father. He owned and possessed everything . . . even my mother and sisters. And he tried to possess me. But my father was right—maudlin sentimentality doesn't get you anywhere. I emptied one of the company safes and headed West. I intend to show my father I don't need his damn partnership. I'll be a success in my own right."

At whatever cost, finished Trish silently. "You're his only son?"

He nodded. "I have two sisters, both older and married. My mother's dead. There's nothing to take me back East again . . . nothing. I'm going to show him I can build my own water empire . . . and nothing . . . nothing is going to stop me. Do you understand what I'm saying, Trish? I'm willing to make any sacrifice to insure that this expedition is successful. I can't afford to give in to any feelings about you or anybody else. The odds are against me. I know that now but I'm not going to give in—for any reason!"

"Please, take me with you. I don't care how dangerous it is. Don't leave me here. I'll do . . . I'll do anything you want. Anything." She threw her arms around him and kissed him with wanton fervor.

Passion was like a foaming cataract spill-

ing over them. Then he firmly pushed her
arms away. "I can't do it, Trish. You're not
going. There's too much at stake—for you
and for me."

"I'll not be a liability."

"Yes, you will. Just your presence will
work against me. I can't spend my energies
worrying about your safety. I've always kept
the compartments of my life separated—
and that's what I have to do now. It's no
good, Trish. It's not that I don't care about
you. I do! But it's going to take everything
I have to dominate this river and bend it
to my will. Don't you understand? A man
can't go back on his dreams or he's not
much of a man."

"Doesn't that apply to a woman, too?"
she asked boldly.

"No, I'm afraid not. In this case, the
decision is not yours to make. It's mine.
And I've made it. I've talked to Jacob.
He'll not pressure you to marry Dirk.
When I've finished the expedition, I'll be
back."

She searched his face. "No, you won't.
You won't come back." She had heard
words like that before. Her father had told
her the same thing."

"Promise me you'll stay here and not do
anything foolish."

"I can't promise. I'll leave here the first

chance I get. My father's not dead. That story about Indians was a lie.''

"Do tell. I can't say that I'm the least bit surprised," he said wryly. "Where is he?''

"Somewhere on the river.''

Morgan took a deep breath of relief. "Then I'll find him and send him back for you.''

Trish wanted to laugh. Her father would be as likely to come back for her as a bird would fly north for the winter. "My father is just like you. He didn't want me with him either," she said in a leaden tone. "He's following his own dream.''

"But he's your father!''

"He's a river man," she said as if that were answer enough. "His name is Benjamin Winters, and I'm going to find him.''

"Is that why you hid in our boats? You had some insane idea of finding your father?''

She was no longer afraid to trust him with her secret but she feared that she would seem less in his eyes because of what had happened. She couldn't bear to have him think of her as a murderess. "Yes," she lied in a hoarse voice.

"You've been using me to take you down the river?''

"No, it's not like that. I . . . I . . ." she stammered.

"Well, I'm afraid this is the end of the line, Trish. I'm sorry. I really am. If I find Benjamin Winters, I'll tell him you're here. And if I can, I'll come back for you and take you to him. I can't do more than that." There was a finality in his tone that defied any argument she might raise against his decision.

She knew then that she had lost. Her lower lip trembled but she kept her head high as they walked back to the house.

Ten

Two weeks later Morgan and Jens collected supplies on the bank, ready to be loaded into the hatches as soon as they had caulked the boats with pitch from piñon trees. Both men had made a decision. Jens had decided that he would honor his commitment to Morgan and continue to the mouth of the Colorado River—then he would come back. Only the possibility that he might not survive the treacherous river kept him from asking Rebecca for her hand before they left. Jens hated the thought of going back on the river but he was a man of his word. He had signed on for the whole trip and he couldn't back out on Morgan now.

As for Morgan, he had decided to bring Benjamin Winters back to Jacob's Ferry himself. He had meant it when he told Trish that he would return as soon as he had explored the river to the gulf. He knew she didn't believe him but she no longer pleaded with him to take her. She had accepted his decision but the hurt in her eyes haunted him during many a restless night.

The days following the party went by in leaden procession for Trish as she carried out her duties in the household. Her tasks were given by Mrs. Sutton in a kindly but firm way. Since there was never a shortage of work in a pioneer saint's household, every female was important to the survival and prosperity of the family.

Unfortunately, Trish did not have the proper dedication or convictions for such a role. She slipped out from under responsibilities almost as fast as they were assigned to her. The strong lye soap she made was unusable, her listless working of the butter churn never produced any worthwhile results and the clothes she pounded at the river's edge came out a shade grayer than when she started. She continually left her tasks and slipped down to the river where she could watch Morgan and Jens working on the boats. Fortunately Dirk had been sent to get some supplies at Yucca Junction nearly a hundred miles away. When he returned, she would be faced with pressure from him and Jacob to accept his proposal of marriage. Once she refused, the friendliness they had extended her would dry up and she'd have to live with a sense of guilt that she'd rejected the offer to become a member of their family.

As the days passed, Rebecca's mind was elsewhere, too, and it was no mystery to Sara why less work was being done now with three women than had previously been accomplished with two. Every night Rebecca prayed beside her bed, asking the Lord to send heavy rains that would prevent the men's immediate departure. As she went about her tasks halfheartedly, she kept her blue eyes on the sky, beseeching the good Lord to do this one little thing for her.

Trish lost all hope that she could change Morgan's mind. He was going to leave her at Jacob's Ferry and all of his promises of returning rang hollow. She had heard them from her father many times and when she was young she had waited and watched for his return, only to be disappointed time after time. Morgan had less reason for ever coming back than her father had. She lost her healthy appetite; food sat queasily on her stomach. Her features thinned out revealing delicate bone structure beneath a skin that no longer glowed with health and good spirits. Dark smudges accented eyes that sank back in her head, round and expressionless. Her usual quick and agile movements became sluggish and she was unable to give her attention to anything. She knew she must seem a dullard to the rest of the family but she didn't care. That was the problem—she didn't care about anything. She thought about her friend, Winnie May, and wondered what she would have to say about her situation. "Shaw! Things could be worse." But Trish brushed Winnie's favorite saying aside. She couldn't see how they could be worse. She was about to be forced into a way of life as rigid as an iron casting. A sense of doom settled on her and immobilized her usual spunk and defiance.

Jacob left to spend a few days helping out at a new Mormon settlement. Dirk hadn't returned with the wagonful of supplies that Jacob had promised Morgan and Trish knew he was probably having himself a wild time, drinking, gambling, and whoring. Morgan grew more impatient while Jens and Rebecca openly treasured every day's delay.

As Trish carried a basket of dirty clothes to the river's edge, she accepted the bitter truth—she would never see Morgan again once he shoved away from the crude wharf. She agreed with Jens that the Colorado River would never become navigable as a trading route. Once Morgan satisfied himself that his fortune lay elsewhere, he would go on to California as he had planned in the first place before he had become interested in the Colorado.

Trish set her pile of dirty clothes upon a rock, turned her back on them and began walking slowly along the Paria River away from that deep voice and commanding figure who had planted this deep despair within her. If she hadn't known his embrace, his kisses, heard his tender voice caressing her name, she could have absorbed another rejection. But he had changed her! Her body had betrayed her with deep longings and needs she had never known existed. His rejection had brought a strange emptiness and created a dull ache that defied description.

Listlessly, she watched a lizard run across the barren ground in front of her, hunting sanctuary in some rocks at the river's edge. She glanced up at the sky and saw clouds building along one of the distant mountain ranges. Rebecca's prayers might be answered after all . . . maybe the men would be delayed. Not that it would make much difference to her, she thought with despair. She knew that once Morgan had made up his mind, he was not a man for changing it.

Bone-deep weariness made her steps lag

until she dropped to the ground and leaned her head back against the trunk of a sturdy cottonwood. She unbuttoned several of the tiny pearl buttons at the neck of her bodice and lifted a flounce of her skirt to allow some air to slip under layers of drawers, chemise, and double petticoats. She was still wearing Karen's things but Sara and Ina were already working on darker, heavier, and more suitable garments for her.

She closed her eyes; a thick fringe of eyelashes lay on dark violet circles; her high cheekbones were void of their usually healthy luster. Her thoughts swirled in the same endless maelstrom. She had to get away. If she stole one of the gaunt work horses she could try to cross the endless stretch of desert land. She thought about it but the possibility of dying alone in a sun-parched wilderness tested her mettle and found her wanting in that kind of courage. Death, when it came, had to be quick. She hated thinking about dying with parched lips and flesh falling off her bones as her tongue hung out in agony.

If she stole one of the boats, she would have a quick death by drowning. She knew the treacherous river well enough by now to be realistic about the folly of trying to navigate it by herself. She could hide in one of the hatches again, but Morgan would make certain she was on the bank when they pulled away. No more unwanted river urchin stowed away in one of his crafts.

A distant rumbling overhead reminded her of the thunder that had vibrated between the canyon walls. She wished she were in Morgan's boat fighting the churning waters of a rapid. Even when she had been physically miserable, cold, frightened, and exhausted from constant battles with the river, there had never been any sense of despair and futility. She had been alive and happy.

Wearily, she got to her feet, reluctantly buttoned the pearl buttons to her neck, and started back toward the house. She was approaching the outbuildings when she heard hooves and saw Dirk riding through a stand of mesquite bushes and reined the horse behind one of the sheds.

So he's back, she thought, wishing she had taken a different direction back to the house. She wondered if he brought back the supplies he had been sent to get. Rebecca had been worried he would gamble away the money or spend it on drink. His rifle was still on his saddle and a saddlebag on the rump of his horse.

He didn't see Trish as he slid to the ground and threw himself down behind the shed and took a bottle out of his pocket. He took two swigs before he lowered the bottle and saw Trish trying to slip quietly around the shed.

He was on his feet in a second, blocking her path. His whiskey breath assaulted her face and he leered at her with a moist grin. "What a nice surprise. You waitin' to welcome me home. Have a drink." He stuck the bottle under her nose. "Open your mouth—"

Trish lashed out with one hand and sent the bottle sailing out of his hand. It broke on a pile of rocks, shattering the glass into a thousand pieces and spilling the raw whiskey on the ground.

Dirk's ruddy face turned an ugly shade of purple and he shoved her back against the wall of the shed. "That was my last bottle."

Trish screamed! She reached up and scratched his face with clawed fingers.

"Goddamn wildcat, I'll teach you a thing or two, you goddamn wildcat."

She screamed again as he knocked her head back against the weathered boards.

"Shut up or I'll shove my fist down your throat. Time to start training you to be my meek, little woman." He grabbed her hair and jerked her head back until she writhed in pain. He put his face close to hers. "We'll get along fine just as long as you know who's wearing the spurs. Got that?"

Trish spit in his face.

He swore, raised a clenched fist, but the blow never came.

Morgan came around the shed and grabbed Dirk by the back of his collar. He swung him around and Morgan's fist lurched out and caught him under the chin. Dirk reeled backward, stumbling and falling against his horse. The next instant Dirk had jerked his rifle off his saddle and was pointing it at Morgan.

Trish cried, "Stop!" She put herself in the line of fire.

"Get back," Morgan ordered.

"You shoot us and you'll fry in hell," she screamed at Dirk "Your father will see to that."

Her words seemed to sober Dirk. He kept the rifle leveled at Morgan but his expression changed. "Take your whore and get the hell out of here," he growled. "Now! I'll give you five minutes."

"We're not ready to leave," Morgan protested. "We haven't finished loading the boats."

"Now ain't that too bad." Dirk gave a threatening motion with his rifle. "Start walking. I'll help you get ready."

Morgan dropped his hands from Trish

and eyed the rifle in Dirk's hands. His body was poised for action. Trish's heart lodged in her throat.

"Don't even try it," smirked Dirk. "I'll blow her head off before you've taken a step. Now git. Start walking back to the house."

"Why don't you put that gun down and we'll settle this like men?" Morgan taunted, his jaw rigid and his eyes stabbing Dirk's taunting face.

"I have a better idea. You take your whore and get off our land."

"I think your father will have something to say about that," countered Morgan.

"My pa isn't here. I'm in charge."

Morgan opened his mouth and then closed it. He warned Trish with his eyes not to say anything. She knew that he wouldn't challenge Dirk as long as she was in danger.

"Start moving!" ordered Dirk. He swung up on his horse and herded them back to the crude wharf where Jens was working on one of the boats.

Jens's round eyes swung from Morgan to Trish. "What's going on?"

"You're shoving off," said Dirk from his horse, the gun leveled at them.

"You can't do this," cried Trish.

"And who's going to stop me?"

My God, what have I done, thought Trish. This was all her fault. She should have been able to handle Dirk . . . somehow. This horrible confrontation was on her shoulders.

"All right, we'll go," Morgan said angrily. "But we'll want the rest of our supplies." Only a meager stack of provisions were stacked, waiting to be loaded after they finished caulking the boats.

Rebecca had heard the commotion and at that moment came running down from the house. When she saw what was happening, she cried out, "No, Dirk. They can't go." The distraught girl pointed to the darkening sky. Her usually sunny face was bathed in anguish. "A storm's coming. The Lord's sending rain." Her prayers for a delaying storm had been answered. "Please, please don't do this. Let them stay!"

"Get back to the house, Rebecca!" her brother ordered. "Or I'll put a bullet in your sweetheart's head."

Sobbing, Rebecca turned and fled back to the house. Mrs. Sutton hurried down to the river and tried to get Dirk to put down the gun, but to no avail.

"This is men's business, Ma," he retorted.

"Your father will be angry with you."

Dirk shrugged as if that was nothing new.

"We worked and paid for the supplies you were to bring back from Yucca Springs," said Morgan in his commanding voice. "Your father is a man of honor—"

"You aren't dealing with my pa." His smile was insolent. "And I say you go . . . now!"

For a moment black fury coated Morgan's face as if he were going to challenge Dirk to shoot him. Trish's heart stopped beating. Would Dirk pull the trigger? Would he really kill Morgan to satisfy his pride?

The moment froze and then Dirk moved the barrel of his gun away from Morgan's stomach and pointed it at one of the boats. "You can leave with or without your boats," he repeated.

"No! Don't shoot," Morgan cried. "We'll go." He gave Jens a curt nod toward his boat. Then his eyes swung to Trish. "You, too."

She shook her head and faced Dirk. "I'll stay . . . do what you say . . . but give them the things they need. If you want to marry me—"

"And why would I want to marry a cast-off river strumpet," he mocked her. "I've had better offers from the whores at Yucca Springs."

Morgan glared at Dirk with his fists clenched. Trish was afraid he might try to jump for the rifle.

Rebecca came running from the house. "Wait. Wait." She thrust a bundle into Trish's arms. "You can't leave your pretty dress," she sobbed as tears flowed down her cheeks. Even in her anguish, she had thought of someone else. She hugged Trish and then grabbed Jens's hand. "God go with you."

"Rebecca . . ." Jens's voice broke on her name.

The young girl covered her face with her hands and stumbled back to the porch where Mrs. Sutton and the children had gathered.

"I'll be back, Rebecca," Jens shouted after her.

Morgan shoved Trish into the first boat, which happened to be Jens's. She sat down stiffly in the bow. Her eyes clouded with tears and sobbing protests choked her chest. It was a nightmare. It had all happened so suddenly. One minute she had been sitting innocently under a tree—and now this!

The two men shoved the boats away from the bank and began working the oars. When Trish turned her head and looked back, Dirk and his horse were fading to an indistinct image on the barren sand and the crude log buildings at Jacob's Ferry disappeared from view.

The storm Rebecca had been praying for began to rend the heavens with thunder and lightning. Forks of lighting stabbed the sky. Thunder clapped in resounding peals, booming down the canyon that lay ahead. A lowering, black lid released a blinding deluge of water from the sky.

The river's lashing, rolling tongue swept the boats into a narrowing canyon where granite walls held the rising water. Trish clung to the careening boat as Jens fought to keep it from bashing against rock-studded chutes. Rain gushed down steep crevices, spilling over cliffs, creating foaming cataracts that plunged hundreds of feet into the torrent of waters below. Trish stifled her screams as the boat rose and fell in the chaotic river.

On every side, trees growing precariously on rocky ledges were loosened in the deluge and were swirled away in an angry mass of tumbling rain and water. In the rising tumult Trish saw whole banks slide into the thickening muddy river.

Riding high in the water because of nearly empty hatches, two half-caulked boats plunged into a black inferno, completely at the mercy of a crazed river tumbling and thrashing its way into the Grand Canyon of the Colorado River.

Eleven

Storm clouds, black and insidious, captured the river. The thunderstorm for which Rebecca had been fervently praying created a deathly holocaust in the deeply cut canyons of the Colorado. Rain and fog swept into every crevice, gorge, and hollow cavern. Deafening cannon booms of thunder and flashes of heavenly artillery bounded from precipice to precipice.

Any attempts to stay on the river were suicidal. As soon as Morgan saw a widening turn, he motioned the boats ashore. He pulled in first and Jens fought the current, straining his powerful arms and back until he finally brought the craft ashore some distance below Morgan's boat.

Trish scrambled out of the boat already half filled with water. She helped Jens pull and push the boat as far up on a steep talus as they could. Jens wrapped the hawser around a huge pointed rock and lashed the rope firmly, hoping to secure the boat against rising waters that might batter it before the storm was over.

Trish was clumsily weighted down by numerous petticoats and a full skirt. If she had been standing under a foaming waterfall, she couldn't have been any wetter by the time they finished.

"Stay here." Jens's booming command was almost lost in the fury of wind, rain, and rushing water. He gave her a staying motion with his broad hand. Before she could respond he strode away, heading upstream toward the place where Morgan had beached his boat. His blond head was bent against the wind and rain, and soon his thick bulk had disappeared in the storm's lashing inferno.

A moment of utter panic overtook Trish. She was alone, lost in the fury of wind, rain, and thundering heavens sliced with lightning. All the forces of hell whipped around her. She put her hands over her ears and screams choked in her throat. The earth was rending apart. Blinded by drenched hair tumbling over her eyes, she stumbled upward away from the diabolical roaring river.

When she reached an outcropping of rocks, she crawled under a jagged sandstone shelf and lay flat on the ground in the shelter of the narrow crevice. Dank smells of mud, water, and soggy vegetation filled her nostrils as she pressed her cheek into the dirt and kept her eyes scrunched. She tried to shut out the deafening roar of rampaging waters and crashing of tumbling debris as the river charged by.

She knew safety lay in higher ground— but she didn't move. She couldn't summon any will to fight the old river. Too many warring emotions had sapped her strength. Even with her eyes clenched shut, she kept seeing the way Morgan's face had been twisted with explosive anger as he stared at the barrel of Dirk's rifle. She knew that if only the two men had been involved, Morgan might have gambled on wrestling the gun from him. When Dirk warned he would shoot Trish's head off, Morgan had backed off. It's my fault . . . my fault, she agonized. She should have handled Dirk differently. Fear and anger had made her knock away the bottle and spit in his face. She'd never dreamed her reckless actions would cause such a catastrophe. How could she ever forget how Rebecca had looked when she thrust the bundle into her arms? The memory of her distraught, heartbroken little face would torture her forever, as well as the torment on Jens's face as he cried to her, "I'll be back."

Trish sobbed and let her own anguish

sweep out in hot tears. Morgan would never forgive her. Never. As much as she had wanted to get away from Jacob's Ferry, she would have never hurt him like this. She would have sacrificed herself to spare him this catastrophe. The love she felt for him blotted out everything else—even her own unhappiness. The supplies for which the men had worked weeks had not been loaded in the boats. In his malicious anger, Dirk had sent them downriver with a fraction of what had been paid or worked for. The hatches had been fuller when they arrived at Jacob's Ferry.

If Morgan abandoned her on the river now, who could blame him? It would be better if she drowned . . . like her brother, Teddy. She didn't want to live with Morgan's hatred—she loved him! From that first moment when the hatch cover had been jerked away and she saw him—her feelings had never been the same. Even when he glared at her and infuriated her with his commanding manner, she still wanted to be with him. And when he touched her, the whole world disappeared and everything in it. In his arms she had experienced an ecstasy that had changed her forever. And when he talked about the way his father had brushed him aside, she knew his harsh exterior covered up a deep hurt. This dream of a new waterway was all his father had left him—and she had destroyed that for him. How could she live with the reproach in his eyes? She sobbed. She would rather give up and let the malicious river have her.

At first she didn't hear the din soften as the rain and wind diminished. Then a spread of sun fell on the rocks near her tearful face coaxing her to open her eyes. Like a dirty rodent she emerged from her shelter, blinking against shafts of light stabbing through thinning, misty clouds. When she stood up, the heavy weight of drenched cloth made walking difficult. She lifted her outer skirt and unfastened both petticoats and let them drop. With only wet pantaloons and a thin shift under the white bodice and blue outer skirt, she could move again.

She peered upstream in the direction she had seen Jens disappear. He was not in sight . . . nor was the other boat. Torturous thoughts that Morgan might have capsized and been swept away like the tumbling debris brought a blanching to her face.

Jens's boat had safely ridden out the storm but its oak hull had filled with water in the downpour. Looking in the aft hatch, Trish found a metal container. She stood in the middle of the boat and poured the clean rainwater over her head until her hair, face, and clothes were free of the canyon's red mud. The water was cold and it brought tingling life back into her body and restored some of her inherent resiliency.

She was on the river again!

The sun had broken through and tinted the gray sky with patches of bleached blue. All around her, cliffs shone luminous with freshly washed walls, brightened pastel lichens of pink, yellow, and green. Trish drew in deep breaths of the cleansed air. When she had finished her bailing, she sat on the hardboard seat and spread her deep russet hair to the sun for drying.

When she heard footsteps crunching on loose rock, she stiffened! Until that moment she had assumed that Morgan and Jens had no choice under the present circumstances but to take her with them. Now that conviction faded. In a breathless, suspended moment, she remembered Morgan's black glower as they shoved away from the bank and felt again Jens's cold withdrawal as if she were suddenly carrying the plague.

Her heart lurched to a stop as Jens's head appeared over the rocky talus—and then Morgan's! He was safe! All other thoughts sped from her mind and she smiled radiantly with relief. Then she sobered. She could not read their impassive expressions—

except an intuitive knowledge that they were united! Any words that had passed between them and any decisions that had been made had brought them into agreement. What was it? What had they decided? Instinctively her hands curled around the side of the boat as if she could keep them from lifting her out of it.

Morgan stopped a few feet from the boat and just looked at Trish. He could sense her agile mind working as she stared expectantly up at him. Her russet hair spread freely over her shoulders and once again her body was molded by wet, clinging cloth. Even in anger, his blood stirred hotly just looking at her. He ran a weary hand through hair hanging damply on his forehead.

"There's nothing to be done. Jens and I have talked it over . . . agreed to continue the expedition as best we can—under the terms of our original agreement." He touched his money belt. "We're not without funds. I can buy more provisions once we are out of the Big Canyon."

Her hands relaxed their hold on the boat's sides. They weren't going to dump her!

"I told Morgan that you weren't to blame, Trish," Jens said looking at the ground as the toe of his boot made a mark in the wet ground. "That Dirk's a bad one. A disgrace to his upbringing. Rebecca told me they'd always had trouble handling him."

"Why in the hell did you let yourself get in a situation like that?" Morgan flared. "I thought you had more sense than that. You just invited—"

"I didn't invite anything!" Her eyes blazed at the unjust accusation. "I didn't even know Dirk was back from Yucca Springs. I was supposed to be doing the washing . . . and I just took a little walk. He rode up and—"

"All right . . . all right. No good will come of hashing the whole thing over." It didn't set well with Morgan that he had completely misjudged the situation. He had dismissed Dirk as unimportant as long as Trish made it clear to Jacob that she didn't want to have anything to do with his son. He never realized that his father had little control over him.

Morgan avoided Trish's wounded eyes. At the moment, the shock of what had happened was too great to think clearly. Some part of his rational, well-disciplined mind took over while he held a tight rein on his emotions.

Jens looked at him expectantly, waiting. Morgan felt the weight of leadership like an iron mantle on his shoulder. If the river was as treacherous as before, getting through this Grand Canyon would be precarious under the best of circumstances. And now—? He shut his mind to the dangers that lay ahead. He cleared his throat. "Jacob told me that there's another mission, Callville," he said in a forced, even tone. "Several families there. It's somewhere on the river beyond the big canyon. But from what Jacob said, the big question is whether or not any of us will make it out of the canyon alive."

"We can make it!" Trish's exuberance was a strange contrast to the two men's desolate expressions. She longed to cradle Morgan's dark hair against her breast and infuse him with the sudden joy that his words had created. "I know we can make it!" She'd work as hard as they did, take as many chances, and show Morgan that she was willing to make any sacrifice necessary.

Her exuberant declaration brought a wry smile to his lips. He was not immune to her shining eyes, the confident jut of her chin, and the eagerness that poured out of her full lips. In spite of himself, he drew on her innocent optimism. He straightened his shoulders. "Well, let's see what supplies we have in the boats and make some plans."

Inventory of the boats took a disappointingly short time. The list of food was brief: a few sacks of dried food. Ironically there weren't any of the fresh vegetables the men had labored so hard to cultivate. "I paid him for five times that much—and we worked our asses off for nothing!" swore Morgan, staring at the pitiful stack of provisions. They had gained some canvas water bags, new rope, and tarpaulin. They had two boxes of ammunition—but no guns. The rifles had been left in the bunkhouse along with their clothes. The men had nothing to wear but the clothes on their backs. It was the loss of the guns that drew Morgan's mouth in a tight line and etched sunken lines in his cheeks. "No way to get food or protect ourselves. That blasted skunk wouldn't step out the door without his gun but he can send us into hostile, isolated country with less than a slingshot." Morgan clenched his fists as if he wished he could have rammed Dirk's rifle down his skinny throat.

Trish opened the bundle Rebecca had thrust into her arms. The green dress! Her fingers trembled as she pulled it out. At the heightened moment of her anguish, Rebecca had thought of someone else—she wanted Trish to have her precious gift. Lying on top of the dress was a small box with the tiny green earrings and the handkerchiefs Morgan had given her for her birthday. The bundle contained one more thing—Trish's faded calico dress. It had been washed, ironed, and mended with tiny, faultless stitches. Rebecca must have sewn on it at night after all her chores were done. Trish wiped her eyes again and looked up to see Morgan watching her.

"I wouldn't have hurt her for anything," Trish said. "You have to believe me." She got up and came over to him. "If I could go back and exchange myself for all the provisions left behind, I would. I never planned for this to happen." Tears brimmed at the edges of her eyes.

Morgan touched his fingers to her wet cheeks. His voice was husky. "I wanted to keep you safe. And now, I don't know whether I can."

A smile broke through her tears. "Don't worry about me. I'm more than a match for this old river."

"You're more than a match for anyone," he granted with a weak smile. "And you're going to need all that hard-necked stubbornness before we get through this."

She gave a contented laugh. He didn't hate her. He was worried about her. The realization made her heart sing.

* * *

Once more they shoved off into the swollen waters. Granite buttresses clogged the river and jagged pinnacles rising thousands of feet into the air greeted them at every turn. They barely made it past one treacherous formation before another rose in the river in front of their boats. Morgan and Jens rowed constantly to keep from hitting these rock islands head-on.

Portages were endless. The fractious river hassled them day after day until the passage of time was jumbled in Trish's mind. Some days they made good time. There was always the hope that the next bend in the river would bring them out of the canyon.

Trish wore the mended calico dress once more and put away the white bodice with its luminous pearl buttons and blue skirt in the package with the green dress and stashed the bundle in the hatch of Jens's boat. If they ever reached civilization again, she would have something to wear.

Floodwater had ruined fishing and they were subsisting on the meager rations. Jacob had warned Morgan about Shivwit Indians living along the crest of the Big Canyon. Trying to climb out would only put them in savage hands that had already tortured and killed several white men parties in that region.

True to her word, Trish worked as hard
as the men, forging for firewood, taking
care of the boats, cooking and spending
hours drying out the damp cornmeal.
She took the smallest rations that she
could. Even though she wanted to give in
to the love she felt for Morgan, she did
not force herself upon him. The three of
them were a unit and pairing off would
not strengthen the bonds among them.
Morgan made no effort to kindle the passion that had flared between them. Trish
respected his decision but she refused to
give in to the men's desolation.

Jens kept his thoughts of Rebecca to himself. The memory of her anguished face
taunted him with sleeplessness. If only he
had spoken to her of his love. Had she
heard his promise to return? Would Jacob
let him anywhere near his daughter after
what had happened? He carried his own
burden of guilt. Should he even think about
claiming such a wonderful, perfect creature
like Rebecca? Some days he wished the river
would end the pain and heartache he felt.

Although as tired and hungry as both
of the men were, Trish did her chores with
a light step and answered their growled remarks with a determined optimism. Morgan's lean face aged with an unhealthy
gauntness and Jens's beard hung loose

from sagging skin on a face that was no longer round. She didn't know that her determined cheerfulness was the only thing that put a touch of sanity in the exhausting nightmare. She spoke hopefully about the day's run and expressed confidence that they had surely weathered the worst. Without realizing it, she gave strength to Morgan and Jens to face another exhausting battle on the river.

One evening Trish came upon Jens sitting alone on a boulder staring at the river. Tears swelled up her eyes. She sat down beside him. "She'll wait for you," she said.

He shook his head. "She's too pretty . . . to wait for an oaf like me."

"Rebecca loves you, Jens. Take my word for it."

He sighed. "No offense, Trish, but sometimes your word is about as true as a bent pin." He eyed her. "Is that stuff the truth that you've been telling everyone about your pa being a river man?"

"Yes. He's somewhere along the Colorado, I know it."

"Then he's not dead?" he prodded. "That tale about your folks being killed by Indians was just a yarn."

She nodded.

He gently raised up her chin with his en-

gulfing big hand. "Come on, Trish. Why
don't you try the truth? Isn't it about time
you told me why you were hiding in my
boat like that?"

She swallowed hard and when she spoke
her voice was scarcely more than a whisper. "I killed someone."

Color washed out of his bearded face.
"Killed? What do you mean, killed."

"Murdered. I stuck a knife in a man's
gut." Once she started, Trish couldn't
staunch the flow of words. She told him
about her father and his love of the Colorado River; how Benjamin had taken her
brother, Teddy, with him on one trip and
how he had drowned when the boat capsized. "After my mother died, my father
left me with Parson Gunthar and his
wife, Gertie. The night . . . the night
that I hid in your boat," Trish said halt-
ingly, "I was taking a bath and the parson came home . . . he tried to rape
me. I stabbed him with a bread knife—
and ran. When I came upon your boats,
I climbed in and hid under the hatch
cover. I knew they'd have a posse out for
me and I had to get away from Bend
River."

"Why in God's name didn't you say something before . . . tell us the truth?"

Trish felt an unbelievable relief that

comes with confession. She raised questioning eyes to his face, hope springing in their blue-green depths. "I—I didn't think you or Morgan would understand."

"That's 'cause you lie so damn easy." Jens searched her face, his broad forehead furrowed. "Are you telling the truth now, Trish, or is this another one of your blasted stories? If you're lying again . . ."

"I'm not." She shivered just remembering that horrible night. Those lustful hands pawing her and his weight pressing down on her naked body.

"Hey, it's all right," Jens said quickly, seeing her shudder.

"I wouldn't say I'd killed someone if I hadn't."

"I guess you're right." He was silent for a moment and then there was a savage edge to his voice as he said, "I killed someone, too."

"You . . . you did?" Her eyes rounded as she searched his face. "You killed somebody," she echoed with a catch in her voice.

"Broke a man's neck like it was a chicken's. I still see his face sometimes . . . and it don't rest easy with me."

"But why?" Jens was the most even-tempered person she'd ever met.

"A woman named Dolly was the cause of it. A pretty young thing, she was. I thought I was something special to her but one night I didn't have any coins to put on her pillow and she called on some guy to throw me out. The bastard was selling her body to everyone and I couldn't stand it. I killed him with my bare hands." He brushed an agitated hand over his beard. "Wanted to kill her, too . . . for fooling me like that."

Now Trish knew why Jens had looked at her with such coldness when he thought she might be a river tramp. She remembered him saying something about a pretty gal being nothing but a barbed trap. She knew now where the bitterness had sprung from.

"Do you have nightmares, too?" she asked, suddenly feeling that her burden had lightened because she had shared it with someone who understood. "Sometimes I dream that there's a hangman's noose around my neck. I wake up with hot sweat all over me."

"A hanging is not a pretty sight. I've had a few sweaty nights myself. I kept on the run . . . until I met up with Morgan. This expedition was the best escape I could have planned. Nobody's going to be looking for me in this part of the country.

Nor you either, Trish. No posse's going to find you here." He looked at the stark canyon walls and the threatening river channel. "I guess we're getting what we deserve, Trish."

"Don't tell Morgan," she pleaded.

He grinned at her. "I won't . . . if you won't."

They shook hands and the pact was made.

The Colorado grew more treacherous every mile. Morgan had always prided himself on being in complete control of his life. Now, he was completely at the mercy of a river he had intended to tame. His dreams had been torn apart. In addition, he felt responsible for the lives of two other people and could see no way to ensure that any of them would survive. His worst fears were realized when they reached a section of continuous, treacherous rapids where there was no way to make a portage or line-down.

The chutes were deep. Waves rose and fell in a deep trough and then curved back, breaking with a crash before sweeping forward again. Sheer cliffs rose thousands of feet on both sides of the madly rushing river. Any hint of a bank had disappeared.

Trish anxiously waited as Jens and Morgan soberly assessed the situation. They sent pieces of wood down the chutes and watched their passages in order to determine the best channel. The sticks were pounded in the white-foamed surf and whirlpools and Morgan knew it was near suicide to try and put a boat through that torturous channel but he also knew that they had no choice. They could stay here and die of starvation or risk death in the devil falls.

"We'll ride the boats down," he determined in a strained voice. The frightening, heavy responsibility made his manner curt and sharp. He had been keeping his distance from Trish, allowing her to ride in Jens's boat instead of his own. Any feelings he had for her had been kept on a short leash because the life-and-death decisions he made had to be clearheaded and not influenced by emotions. Passion and desire paled beside the need to keep her alive. He would have given anything to make the run by himself without endangering the other two lives.

"It's all right," said Trish, wanting to ease the deep worried creases in his forehead. "I always wanted to ride a bucking bronco." She managed a short laugh.

Impulsively, he gave in to the urge to pull her into his arms. He planted a kiss on the top of her head and held her

tightly. He almost insisted that she ride
with him but he knew that Jens's strong
arms might be the difference between life
and death. He tried to match her confident smile as he set her away. "See you at
the bottom." Then he gave last-minute in-
structions to Jens and shoved his boat away
from the bank.

Trish watched him shoot into a trough between arching breakers of a fast-running
chute. In the next instant he was gone! Morgan and his boat had disappeared from view
into a foamy cataract as the earth fell away
in a long series of rapids.

Jens did not wait to see if Morgan's craft
had been splintered into a mass of flying
timber. "Hold on," he boomed to Trish
and committed his boat to the first plunge.

They went over the first series without
incident but there was no time to prepare
for the force of impact of the second fall.
A crash of rising water jerked the oars
from Jens's large hands as if the oars had
been matchsticks. A mass of roaring water
rose in a high wave and surged into the
boat.

Jens yelled as arching white-foamed
sprays poured over Trish with the force
of an exploding surf, sucking and pulling
at her. Her mouth and nostrils were
blocked with suffocating water! She gave

a gargled scream just as a mammoth wave like a giant hand broke her grasp on the sides of the boat and lifted her out!

Like a piece of debris the rushing current tumbled her over and over. She thrust out her arms and legs in every direction. Her lungs swelled and exploded. The river pulled her under! Her body was lacerated with fiery pain. The churning water was bottomless as an undercurrent sucked her into its depths. A moment later a revolving action tossed her back up to the surface, nearly seventy-five feet downstream from where she had been swept overboard

Trish frantically gulped in air as she broke through the surface and then a vicious undertow twisted her one way, under and up. She broke to the surface as a boat shot past her, gouged with a big hole in its side but she was unable to catch hold of it.

When hands pulled her against the current, she thought the river had grabbed her again. She lashed out, fighting. A blow to her chin brought a wave of shattering weakness—and blessed escape from the torment! When pain returned to her chest, she was on her back and rough hands were forcing water from her lungs.

Morgan turned her over. Her skin was

a whitish blue and her usually animated face was that of lifeless paste.

"Trish! Trish!" Frantically he slapped her cheeks. The imprint of his hand shown on her flaccid skin. She was still breathing but was it too late? Had the river sapped away her life before he'd dragged her from the muddy waters? Seconds before, he had been dumped from his own boat when it caught and tore between rocks. As he held on to it wedged in the river boulders, he saw Trish bob to the surface and grabbed at her. She had fought him so violently that he had struck her with his fist and then grabbed her by the hair and pulled her to shore. Had he hit her too hard?

There was little flesh on her cheekbones. Guilt that he had not given up more of his rations to her overwhelmed him. He had treated her too casually. Her tensile strength and belligerency had fooled him. He had been drawing upon her indomitable spirit without knowing it. As he cuddled her in his arms and moaned over her, he realized how fragile and small she was. He should have taken better care of her. "Trish, forgive me. I love you . . . terribly . . . terribly."

The sobbing admission startled him. He had never declared himself so passionately to a woman before. But he knew it was true. It wasn't a superficial lust that he felt for her but something deep and permanent. He loved her courage, her resiliency, and her stubborn will. Her luminous eyes and sweetly curved mouth were the most beautiful he had ever seen. He'd been such a fool. Now when she might be lost forever, he realized how much she meant to him.

It was an eternity before her damp eyelashes fluttered open and she looked up into Morgan's deep eyes, glazed with exhaustion and concern.

"Thank God," he croaked. Water poured off his face and his eyes were like those of a tortured animal. He stroked her and huskily murmured her name. She felt warm and protected even though she was shivering uncontrollably. She thought she must be dreaming.

He kissed her chilled lips, stroked back the hair from her forehead and held her protectively in his arms. Her arms were too weak to put around his neck but she lifted her head to meet his urgent kisses. Warmth flowed back into her body. For a brief moment reality was lost in a haze. It was worth any amount of pain to have him hold her like this, so loving, so warm, so caring. And then the moment was shattered when he lifted his face from hers. "Thank God, you're safe." Then he croaked, "Where's Jens?"

She knew the nightmare had just begun.

Twelve

Morgan's haunted gaze searched the river, up and down. He walked a short distance in both directions. Only a foaming cauldron met his eyes. No sign of either boat or Jens!

"Maybe he rode it down. We'll have to search downstream. Did you see him go under?" Morgan's hair was plastered wetly down on his forehead and dripped in long strands over his ears. His clothes were torn and soaked and blood oozed from jagged scratches on his face and arms.

She shook her head.

"Tell me what happened."

"I—I don't know. I heard Jens's yell just as I was swept out."

Jens's safety was more than a selfish concern for Morgan. During the months they had faced danger together, a special bond had been forged between them. He respected Jens's forthright loyalty and common sense. His steady, even temperament had helped Morgan handle each challenge that had faced them. His loss would be a heartbreaking personal tragedy

"I don't know," Trish repeated. "I don't know what happened. I heard him yell at the same moment I was swept out of the boat." Her lips trembled. "He could have gone overboard the same time I did. Maybe he had hit his head on one of the rocks and never had a chance to fight the swirling current."

"He could have been swept by me when my boat caught in the narrow chute and dumped me out," speculated Morgan with a catch in his throat. "I was trying to hold on to the side of my boat when I saw you bob to the surface. I let go to get you. I didn't see any sign of Jens. I hope that—" He didn't finish the sentence.

Tears flooded the corner of her eyes. Jens. Drowned? No, it couldn't be! A deep shudder shook her body.

Morgan put his arm around her shoulders. "Come on . . . we're going to keep walking. There's no sign of my boat caught in the rocks now. The river must have swept it on. Maybe it has beached itself below the falls. We'll have to keep moving . . ."

"No, I can't!" For the first time Trish wanted to give up. They had fought the river long enough. Her near death in the river and Jens being gone was too much. Her natural instinct to fight back deserted her. She didn't want to move. She wanted to stay where she was with Morgan's arms around her. She shook her head, her body slumped and lifeless.

Trish's collapse frightened Morgan. He had never seen her without determination and spunk. From the beginning her stubborn doggedness had inspired a reluctant admiration in him, and when they had been forced to leave Jacob's Ferry at gunpoint, she had been the one to fire their spirits and look ahead to each day's run with optimism. Without realizing it, he had come to depend upon her fighting nature. Now she trembled in his arms and his first instinct was to give in to her. Then he realized that if he did, any chances for survival were gone. He didn't have the strength to carry her. If he showed any signs of coddling, she'd never force herself to draw upon the strength and courage that had sustained her this far. He wanted to hold her in his arms and tell her how much he loved her but he choked back such declarations.

"I said we're going on." His tone was brisk and firm.

"I can't—"

"Like hell you can't!" He pulled her to her feet. "Let's go."

She wavered on unsteady legs. "You're a beast," she whimpered.

"And you're a spineless jellyfish. Look at you. You swore you could take anything a man could take. Now comes the test and you give out! Get up. We're going on. We've got to find my boat. That's what's important now."

Anger brought some color back into Trish's face. He cared more about his damn boat than he cared about her!

Morgan saw a glint in her eyes replace the dullness of shock. He put his arm around her waist, but she jerked away. "I don't need your help!"

"Well, you'd better keep up!" he warned as he hid a smile.

Every step she took was agony. She wanted to collapse on the warm bank and forget about walking and thinking and remembering. She wanted oblivion to coat the ache and pain that assaulted her mind and body. The river had claimed Jens in a watery grave like her brother, Teddy. She was sure of it. What would happen now? They had lost everything, food, ropes, and all the meager supplies they had brought from Jacob's Ferry. Even the bundle with the green watersilk dress, her earrings, the blue skirt and white blouse with the lovely pearl buttons, everything had been lost in the hatch of Jens's boat. Even the handkerchiefs Morgan had given her for her birthday. It was this loss that childishly brought tears streaming down her face. His caresses and endearments when she regained consciousness must have been an illusion. There was no sign of that love and tenderness now. He was just as he'd always been, hard, domineering, and commanding.

Morgan was aware of the dagger looks she was sending him. There would be time later to put things right between them. If he showed any signs of tenderness now, she would collapse. She needed all her stubborn doggedness to stay alive. Dear God, what was he going to do? This was the nightmare he'd been fighting all the way, the reason he wanted her to remain safely at Jacob's Ferry. He had been willing to gamble his life, but not hers.

As they made their laborious way downstream, he searched the river, his gaze covering every rock island, collection of driftwood, and swirling eddy as if he expected to find a body caught in the debris. There was no sign of his boat, and the hope that by some miracle Jens had beached his craft dimmed as they trudged along the sandy bank.

When they came to a straight stretch in the river, Morgan stopped, his eyes riveted ahead, searching for some sign of a boat or a thick-shouldered man.

The river was empty.

Still, he wouldn't let her stop. Unless they found one of the boats, all would be lost. They staggered forward until darkness overtook them. Shadows as somber as their spirits finally ended their fruitless trek along the river.

When they came to a scrimshaw of depressions in the canyon walls, carved through the centuries by relentless wind and water, Morgan pulled her away from the river and they labored upward until they reached one of the cavelike pockets.

With a grateful sob, Trish slumped down and pressed her wet cheek against the gritty hardness of the rock floor. Her clothes were still damp from her near-drowning and she shivered uncontrollably. She didn't even raise her head when Morgan left her there and disappeared in the shadows outside. He was mad, she thought. How could he continue to search in the dark?

But in a few minutes, he was back with his arms loaded with dry wood. He reached into his buttoned pocket where he had saved a small metal box, a penknife, and a small comb from being swept away in the river. Matches! Trish couldn't believe it when he soon had a fire roaring at the cave's entrance.

"Come closer to the fire."

She heard him but she could not move. Every ounce of reserve strength had been depleted. Her head was still bursting with the roar of the river and water pressure ringing in her ears.

He swung her up in his arms, carried her to the fire, and held her in the curve of his body. Even with the warmth of the fire, she shivered in the circle of his arms. "Why didn't . . . you let me drown?" she sobbed. "It would be over by now . . . all over. . . ."

"I don't know," he answered in a thoughtful tone. "I guess I wasn't thinking too clearly."

She thought he was teasing—but how could she be sure? He must be having second thoughts about letting go of his boat to save her. "I would rather drown . . . than starve to death."

"I might have known you were thinking about food."

"Poor Jens. It shouldn't have been him. He didn't deserve it—"

"Haven't you heard? The Devil protects his own. Guess that's why the river spit the two of us back." Guilt had been weighing heavily on Morgan all day. Revenge against his father seemed childish and inconsequential in this life-and-death situation. In truth, he had sacrificed himself and two other people to further his own selfish ambition. He kept his morbid fears to himself and said briskly, "Let's hold off mourning Jens until we find out what's happened. He may have ridden the rapids down."

"But he would have stopped and waited for us."

"Not if he lost his oars and couldn't beach the boat. If he's still alive—"

Her head went up. She searched his face. "Do you think that's what happened?"

"I said, it might have. A runaway boat could carry him a long distance before snagging up. And my boat may be hung up somewhere downstream. At least, that's what I'm hoping. If we find it, and it hasn't broken up completely, we can empty the hatches or maybe even repair it." The last was said without conviction for his penknife was the only tool left.

"But if we don't find your boat or Jens, how are we going to get out of this horrid canyon?"

"Build a raft." He knew such a thing wasn't possible but he lied to raise her spirits. She was coming around. By tomorrow she would be herself again.

"A raft—on this river!" She knew then that he hadn't really meant any of the things he had been saying. He didn't expect to find his boat nor Jens. A runaway boat would be dashed to bits in the first spillover. Jens would have pulled up if he were still alive and in control of his craft. They had walked far enough downstream to find him if . . . if . . . She swallowed back a hard lump in her throat. He was dead and Morgan knew it. She was angry with him for lying to her. "I'm not stupid. Don't talk to me about building a raft!"

"Jacob said some fellow had made it through on a raft. Remember, the first night at the dinner table? He said the guy had made it through the Big Canyon to Callville—"

"And had died from injuries and exposure," finished Trish. She knew all this talk about a raft was only a defense. He couldn't face the truth. The expedition was over! He might as well accept it. The mighty Colorado River was never going to be the waterway he had been dreaming about. At that moment, if Trish could have made his dream come true—whatever the personal cost, she would have gladly done it. The disaster that had engulfed them was her fault. From the moment she had hidden in the boat at Bend River, she had doomed the expedition. Without her, they would have passed through Jacob's Ferry without incident. If Jens were dead and she and Morgan died here in the Big Canyon, she was the one who had brought them to it. She began to cry.

It took all of Morgan's willpower not to let himself go. If he gave in, all would be lost. He buried his face in the thickness of her hair. He'd never come so close to crying in his whole life. "We'd better get some sleep," he whispered gruffly to hide his feelings. "We've got a lot of walking to do tomorrow. I don't intend to drag you every inch of the way. Sleep while you can."

Trish could feel the rise and fall of his exhausted breathing as she lay beside him. His sunken cheeks were still caked with blood and she could see bruises on his body where his torn shirt had been pulled free from his belt. She was confused, bewildered, and heartsick. She was ready to fall apart and he didn't care. Even though he had saved her life, he continued to treat her with a detached briskness that bewildered her. At this moment when she needed his arms around her, he was falling fast asleep. She heard his deep breath-

ing change into a light snoring. How could
he sleep like that? She was so keyed up
and emotionally distraught, she wondered
if she would ever sleep again.

When the fire began to die down, she
slipped away from his prone figure and
threw more wood on it. She thought the
noise and movement would wake him up—
but it didn't. She sat back down beside him,
stared beyond the fire at the black night
outside. The wind had come up and
moaned through crevices in the vaulting
cliffs. She could hear the relentless river as
it maintained its counterpoint of lapping,
gushing, and sucking. Some of the night
noises sounded like wild shrieks and
thumping feet. Scary thoughts about massacres and Indian torture made her scalp
tingle. She knew that their fire could be
seen clearly for some distance as it blazed
in the opening of their cave. Suddenly she
was terrified. She turned and touched Morgan's shoulder, wanting his reassurance that
they were safe.

At her touch, he groaned and turned
over on his back. As he shifted his position, his shirt and pants separated and she
could see a leather money belt strapped
around his lean waist. She had been aware
of it the first morning she had seen him
washing and shaving in a stream. She had

also seen him take bills out of it to pay Jacob. Money. The knowledge of it suddenly became a reality.

For some reason she remembered Winnie May and the petticoat she sometimes wore. The garment jangled when she walked because of the silver coins she had sewn in the hem. Trish had been intrigued by Winnie's portable bank even though she'd never had any money of her own in Bend River. Once she had stolen a coin from the church collection to buy a ribbon at Stubbens Mercantile and Feed Store. In truth, Trish never thought much about having lots of money—until that moment.

Her speculative gaze went to Morgan's profile. In sleep, he was more handsome than ever despite the gauntness of his face. Long black eyelashes lay on tanned cheeks and the beard that he had grown added to his bold, vigorous profile. Love for him poured over her like a whirlpool and with it came despair. How he must hate her for jeopardizing his expedition. And she couldn't blame him after what her presence had cost him. In spite of everything, gentleman that he was, he would take responsibility for her as long as he must, but Trish knew that would end once they reached civilization again.

Tears dribbled down her cheeks as she stared at him.

Then her eyes fell to the belt once more. She pushed away the thought at first. But she had lived by one precept since childhood: survival depended upon her own strength and wits. Her agile mind leaped ahead. If they successfully reached Callville, Morgan would most likely dump her there. She was certain that his responsibility toward her would end the moment they reached civilization again. What would she do then? Without money she would be as helpless as she'd been in Jacob's Ferry. Homeless, dependent on whatever favors people would bestow upon her. She knew what Winnie May had gone through when her trapper threw her out on her own. Trish shuddered at the thought. What would her friend tell her to do? She could almost hear Winnie's admonition, "You have to look out for yourself, young'un. Don't expect no man to do it. Shaw, they'll let you down every time."

With money she could continue her search to find her father. Winnie May's imagined advice was right. She shouldn't depend upon Morgan. Hadn't life taught her that she couldn't depend upon anyone? Yes, she had to look out for herself. There was no one else to do it.

The decision made, Trish gingerly reached out a hand, letting the tips of her fingers lightly undo the fastening on Morgan's money belt. She held her breath and watched his face for a flicker of his eyelids. His breathing continued to be deep. She swallowed and ever so carefully eased her fingers inside the belt.

He groaned!

She froze! The pounding of her heart alone was surely loud enough to wake him, she thought in panic. With shallow breaths caught in her throat, she watched and waited—but he didn't wake up. Her deft fingers touched a wad of bills. She quickly drew them out and clutched them in her sweaty hand.

She'd done it. Then she almost put them back. She stared at the money, more than she'd ever seen in her life, and realized that it would buy her a wagon and a horse so she could follow the trail of her father. She closed her fists over the money. It was only a wad of paper but somehow it strengthened her.

Firming her chin, she closed the money belt and eased Morgan's shirt down over it. Every second, she expected those shadowed eyes to flash open with an accusing glare. She trembled to think what his anger would be like. When he continued to sleep deeply, Trish let out the breath she'd been holding. The belt still had money in it, she reasoned, praying he wouldn't notice how much flatter it was.

Now what? She looked at the mass of bills, several hundred dollars' worth. She pulled up the edge of her faded calico dress. Breaking a thread from the hem that Rebecca had so carefully stitched, Trish made a small opening and stuffed the money inside—just like Winnie's bank. Since Trish couldn't sew up the small opening, she eased the bills around to the back of her skirt where they wouldn't work themselves out.

The deed was done! She lay down against Morgan's side. If they made it out of the canyon, she would never see him again. He belonged to another world. What would he want with a river rat? She fell asleep with tears on her cheeks.

Sun spilled into the opening of the cave when Morgan nudged her awake with his foot and handed her a breakfast of cactus pulp and some vile-looking purple seeds. The sight of her tearstained cheeks and shadowed eyes almost dissolved his determination not to pull her into his arms and give in to the need to love and caress her.

"Eat up," he ordered briskly. "We should have been on the move an hour ago."

Trish glared at him. "Yes, sir!" she snapped. He looked refreshed and in command of the situation—which should have reassured her but it only made her feel resentful because she felt so awful. He had the bad manners to watch her gag on the offering that he expected her to swallow.

"Don't tell me I finally found something you won't eat?" he chided. His own stomach had twisted with nausea at the unpalatable stuff but he knew that she needed some nourishment. He laughed openly at the faces she made. She met the challenge by swallowing the awful-tasting stuff and then covered her mouth as if her stomach threatened to reject the so-called food.

"Come on. I've found a small stream of fresh water breaking through a crack in the canyon wall."

They drank freely and washed the sour taste out of their mouth with water cupped in their hands. Trish scrubbed her face, got the tangles out of her hair with Morgan's pocket comb, and smoothed out her skirt— then she remembered the money!

She must have gasped because Morgan stiffened. "What's the matter?" he demanded.

"Nothing, I . . . I just ache all over. Can't we rest today?"

"Exercise is the best thing for stiffness. Besides, we might find Jens just around the next bend. Wouldn't you rather ride in a boat?" he bribed with a mocking curve of his mouth.

The Colorado roared in their ears, licked at their feet, and maliciously withheld any sign of man or boat. Morgan was convinced that if they could just walk far enough, they would come upon the wreckage of his boat. Surely around the next curve they would find it caught in one of the rocky traps . . . or piled up on some logs . . . or swept into a quiet eddy. He knew that if they gave up hope, there would be nothing left.

They survived on agave plants, roots, and cactus pulp. Instead of appeasing Trish's hunger cramps, the unpalatable food made them worse. They fell asleep exhausted every night and each day her strength slipped away in slow starvation. Even the indomitable Morgan slowed his pace and she saw his dogged, driving spirit begin to deteriorate.

There were times when she sat by the fire with flickering light bathing her hair and face that he wanted to forget everything and spend his dwindling strength just holding her. He had to keep his eyes away from her supple body revealed so tauntingly by her thin dress. There were times when a spurt of sexual desire would overtake him as he listened to her rhythmic breathing and felt her body stretched out only inches from his. He promised himself that if they survived, he would declare himself and make love to her tenderly, passionately, with all the pent-up emotion that stirred within him.

The distance they covered each day became less and less. Sometimes when Morgan would wearily signal a rest, Trish would look back and could still see the place of their last stop. Their progress in the choked canyon was so labored that they spent most of their time going up and down over huge masses of tumbled rock and their forward movement was so pitiful it brought tears to her eyes.

Once they found a tiny wounded quail-like bird and Morgan killed it with a rock and they feasted on the miserable tiny carcass. Every time Morgan pulled her to her feet after a brief rest, she wanted to bury her head against his chest and pour out her feelings for him. There were times when she caught a soft tenderness in his sunken eyes and she wondered if it were possible that he really cared for her. When he bathed her face in cool water and teased her about having freckles on her nose, she felt a stirring of the physical attraction that had been between them from the beginning but he never acted upon it. He held her hand, sometimes put his arm around her, and lay beside her at night, and yet, he kept a distance between them. He would never forgive her for what had happened.

Once when she fell to her knees, exhausted, she begged him to go on without her. If he were alone, he could make it. "I'm only holding you back," she sobbed. "I can't go any farther." He pulled her to her feet, scolded her, and half carried her until some strength came back into her legs.

The gorge was black and narrow with perpendicular cliffs rising in pinnacles, pillars, and colossal arches and bridges. As Trish bent her head backward and stared up at the distant rim of the mammoth canyon, a red glare like a bank of heat descended upon her. She had the sensation of being buried alive in the depths of the earth.

She took to plodding along after Morgan without looking up from the ground. And then one noon when the sun was almost directly overhead, he halted so suddenly that she ran right into his back.

"Wh—?" she gasped.

"Shh—" He grabbed her and shoved her down upon the bank, flattening himself beside her. "Just ahead," he whispered. "Cultivation along the river . . . must be Indians."

Trish's mouth went as dry as the dusty ground on which she pressed her cheek. Dear God, no! She was too exhausted to meet any new dangers. Only Morgan's rigid form beside her kept her from shrieking hysterically.

After a minute or two, he slowly raised his head. He motioned for silence as his intense gaze traveled over the green vegetation near the river's bank. "Can't see anybody," he whispered. "It looks like a cornfield . . . have to get closer. Come on."

"No," she whispered hoarsely. "I can't . . ."

Ignoring her protests, he pulled her toward a clump of mesquite bushes. She pressed against him like his shadow, not wanting him to get an inch away from her. They squatted on their haunches and peered through the thorny branches. It was a cultivated field, all right, extending up a fairly wide canyon fed by a small stream. The plot of land was rich in corn and squash.

At the sight of the fresh vegetables, Trish forgot about her paralyzing fear. Bravery might lie in most people's hearts but without question it was Trish's stomach that instantly began to secrete courage. "What'll we do?" she hissed.

Morgan didn't answer. From his expression, she knew he was trying to examine all the information he had. If the Indians were Navajo, there was a slight chance that they might be friendly. If they were Shivwits, they would kill and torture any intruders in their territory. Not knowing for certain which tribe was cultivating land in this deep canyon, they sure as hell couldn't take a chance on making themselves visible, though. He turned and whispered in Trish's ear, "How are you at stealing?"

The heavy skirt she wore, trailing in the dirt with stolen money mocked his question. She had lived in fear that first day that he would look in his money belt and find part of his wealth gone. Now, she swallowed hard and nodded.

"Good. We'll try for the first rows. You take the squash and I'll grab some corn. Don't take more than you can carry and run fast! Understand?"

She nodded again, her heart suddenly skipping around like a lopsided top.

"If someone sees us—throw everything

down and run like hell! It's a gamble. Do you want to take it?'' He searched her face and waited as if the decision was hers.

"I'm hungry," she said simply.

He gave her a weary grin. "Then let's get something to eat." Peering through the bushes, he said, "I'll go first. If you hear anything, stay hidden. If not—" He left the sentence unfinished.

She watched as he moved stealthily around the bushes, then spurted across the open ground. He reached the first row of corn and was instantly obscured by green leaves and stalks as he crouched down in them.

Without waiting another second, Trish bounded like a jackrabbit toward a row of propped-up vines where bumpy squash hung in profusion. She spread out her skirt. Holding the edge of it with one trembling hand, she loaded her lap with the yellow plump vegetable. When she tried to stand and could barely straighten her back, she knew she had taken too many.

"Come on!" hissed Morgan, already running in a low crouch away from some cornstalks he had stripped.

She refused to lighten her load. With her skirt pulled up in front cupping the squash in its folds, her legs were free to move. And move they did! She expected wild shrieks like war drums to be raised as they raced away from the field, but all she heard was her gasping breath and pounding heartbeat.

When they made it around a bend in the river, out of sight of the cultivated field, Trish slowed down. The weight of the squash shot pain into her arched back. She had been too greedy. The load of squash was breaking her in two.

"Keep running," lashed Morgan.

"I—can't!" She stumbled and almost fell. "It hurts—"

"So does Indian torture!" he reminded her grimly.

Stubbornly she refused to dump any of her burden as she kept going. Finally pain and exhaustion won. If a dozen warriors had been dogging her heels, she doubted if she could have stumbled one step farther. She sat down on the ground. Stolen squash scattered on the ground beside her.

Morgan came back to her crumpled figure. His own chest moved in labored jerks as he gasped for his next breath. "We've . . . got to . . . get out of sight," he panted.

His eyes searched the terrain ahead. A narrow recess went back into the canyon wall. Hardy Joshua trees grew at the entrance, probably fed by water trickling through the crevice.

"Come on." Lightly he nudged her with a foot. Both of his arms were clutching numerous ears of corn to his chest. "We'll hide in there." He nodded toward the narrow, nearly hidden ravine. "Then we'll eat!"

He had spoken the magic word. Eat!

Groaning, Trish lumbered to her feet and loaded up her skirt again. Food! Real food!

She followed Morgan through the trees and into a chasm that extended away from the river. He deposited his load and helped her to the ground.

"I told you not to take too much," he scolded but there was an appreciative glint in his eyes that she had not seen for a long time. "Now for a fire."

"Is it safe?"

Morgan glanced around in every direction. "The smoke will go straight up and be lost before it reaches very far. Better to have one during the day than at night with Indians this close."

The fire he built was small. He laid the vegetables on rocks licked by the flames. Before the squash and ears of corn were half done, they began eating them. No telling how many Trish would have consumed if Morgan hadn't stopped her.

"Easy does it, urchin. You don't want to make yourself sick. Besides, we'll have to put ourselves on rations . . ."

"Always the captain," she mocked, but with a smile. She knew he was right. Even his briskness could not hide the grin that reached his eyes. She licked corn juice from her fingers and then laughed aloud.

Morgan laughed back at her and thought the smear of corn juice all over her face was the prettiest thing he had ever seen.

Thirteen

After they had eaten, they lay back on the ground and slept as afternoon shadows stretched across the small cleft in the canyon. When Morgan awoke, he sat up and looked at Trish curled with her head resting on one arm and her supple legs showing under the edge of her tattered skirt. Her lips curved sweetly and long lashes rested on her shadowed cheeks. Relaxed facial muscles gave her a sweet, angelic look. He smiled to himself, knowing that the impression was deceptive. She was a tough, unrelenting, brave, and the most exasperating female he had ever met. And he loved her. When he had pulled her from the water and held her listless body in his arms, he knew how much. He let his eyes feast on the warm curves of her body and his blood began to stir hotly within him. She had one arm raised over her head and the outline of her breasts stretching the faded cotton dress tantalized him. He bent over and nuzzled her ear with his lips.

She stirred, sighing heavily. Then she opened her eyes and looked at him. For a moment she couldn't remember what had happened and then her full stomach reassured her. "Is it time to eat again?" she asked with a hopeful grin.

"Always thinking about food," he teased but he was glad to see that the dull glaze had left her eyes. He knew that the stolen food was just a temporary stay of hunger but for the moment, it was reassuring to see Trish with a hint of her smile on her lips. "Are you still hungry?"

His soft, caressing look confused her. "Yes," she said but she wasn't thinking about food at all.

Morgan reached out and handed her another ear of corn still warm in the gray ashes of the fire. He laughed deep in his chest, a self-mocking kind of laugh.

"What's so . . . funny?" she asked as she sat up.

"I was thinking what my father would say about this half-raw meal covered with ashes. He'd never believe it was the best food I ever ate. He wouldn't understand any of this."

"You really hate him, don't you?" The question just came out and she was sorry when the expression on Morgan's face changed. She had ruined the moment with a painful question. Why had she spoiled this first sign of tenderness? For a moment, she had thought he was about to kiss her.

"He taught me that sentimentality clouds the judgment. I don't think there was ever any real affection between us."

"Is that why you're afraid?"

His dark eyebrows lifted. "Afraid? Afraid of what?"

"Caring. I think you hate your father and yet you want to be just like him." Trish hadn't meant to accuse him like that. It just came out. She couldn't resist trying to make a dent in his insufferable self-control and self-discipline. He had the faults of his own strengths. The same traits that made him strong and proud could cause his own downfall. "You won't let anyone get close to you, will you?"

"You can't let emotions rule your life," he said flatly.

"Why not?" A full stomach had made her reckless.

"My father was right. It's a sign of weakness. Strong men think logically and don't give way to their emotions."

"The way you did that day you saw Jens and me playing in the water?" she taunted.

He flushed. "I admit I overreacted. A case in point. I should have handled the matter in a calm, rational way. Instead I let my feelings cloud my judgment. Thank heavens, Jens was sensible and didn't take offense. I should have known I could trust him."

"But not me!" She flared.

He raised an eyebrow. "And what reason have I ever had for trusting a conniving stowaway who threw out our valuable supplies, tried to blackmail me with my own compass—"

"I told you I was sorry about that. Are you some kind of elephant that you never forget?" she snapped.

"You should have told us the truth that you were trying to find your father instead of all those lies about Indians."

Trish didn't say anything for a moment. Then she sighed. "The truth has never worked for me. Even my mother never believed me when I told her something wasn't my fault. I always got blamed for it. She always believed my brother, Teddy. He'd be the guilty one and I'd get switched for it." Emotion filled her voice. "My mother never liked me."

"Nonsense. You probably were a handful from the moment you howled your first breath. Undoubtedly, she tried to give you the discipline you needed," he reasoned. "I've wanted to warm your backside more than once, myself." His eyes traveled over Trish's tangled hair burnished copper in the sun and then lingered on full breasts ripening under the thin cloth of her faded bodice. He sighed "You're quite a challenge, Patricia Lynne Winters. Do you know that your eyes glow like greenish gems when you're angry?"

A softness in his voice encouraged her to raise hopeful eyes to his eyes. "Were you really going to leave me at Jacob's Ferry?"

"Yes. I thought it was the safest place for you. But I was wrong." His jaw tightened. "If I had realized that Jacob had a son of a bitch for a son—"

"What would you have done?"

"I'd never have left you there." He loved the way color had washed back into her cheeks. She'd better hurry up and eat that ear of corn, he thought. In another minute he was going to kiss her until she was breathless and quivering in his arms.

"I'd have gotten away somehow and searched for my father."

"If it's true that he's a river man—"

"He is!" she flared at his skeptical tone. He was just preaching to her about telling the truth. When she did, he didn't believe her!

"Have you thought about how he is going to react when he finds himself with a grown daughter on his hands? That may be the last thing he wants . . . assuming, of course, that he is still alive."

Trish wasn't at all certain how welcome her father would make her. Deep down she knew that for years she had been building a myth around Benjamin Winters. Pretending that he was a devoted, loving father had helped combat a lost, displaced feeling. As long as she could cling to him, she belonged to someone! But what if he turned his back on her as he had always done? What then?

"It'll be all right," she said aloud as if trying to convince herself.

"What if he's dead?"

"Then I'll build a new life for myself, somewhere—"

For a moment he wondered if she would reject the love he was about to offer. He knew how stubborn she could be. Her pride had been hurt because he admitted that he had intended to leave her behind. Maybe she would fling any declarations of love back in his face. Uneasiness made him tart. "Just as easy as that! Without friends or money. An unattached, simple female—"

"I'm not simple. And I have money!" Her eyes rounded in horror the instant that the angry retort was out. "I mean—I'll get some!" she stammered hastily, trying to cover up a disastrous slip.

Morgan stared at her without blinking for a long, long minute. His eyes narrowed into a hard line.

Trish held her breath, praying that he would ignore her outburst. Please God let him consider her words as so much wild boasting. But even as the frantic prayers swirled frantically, he deliberately began pulling up his shirt.

She watched in horrified silence!

He loosened the fastening on his money belt and reached into the flattened pocket. For a moment, he looked as if she had kicked him in the stomach. "You took my money."

"No . . . no . . ."

"You goddamn, little thief!"

She wanted to tell him why she'd done it but his black rising anger frightened her. How could she explain that she was afraid he would leave her penniless in Callville the way he had intended to do at Jacob's Ferry? The lies rushed out. "I—I don't know what you're talking about. You . . . you must have lost some of your money . . . when . . . when you fell in the river," she stammered. "The catch must have come open. That's what—"

"You stole it." He couldn't believe the raw fury that surged through his veins. He wanted to strangle her.

"I don't have your money! Let me go—!"

His fingers bit into her shoulders as he shook her. "Where is it?"

"I don't have it—"

"Give it to me or I'll tear off your clothes and find it—"

"Don't you dare—"

"Give it to me!"

"No, I—"

With a vicious jerk, he shredded the front of her bodice and the thin chemise that covered her breasts. Rose-tipped nipples contracted in the sudden swish of air upon her bare skin. He had expected to find the bills in the cleft of her breasts.

"Are you satisfied?" she gasped, trying to cover her nakedness with one arm. If only she could bluff him—the money would be safe in the hem of her skirt. "You can see now that I don't have it. You must have lost the money out of your belt somehow." Fear made her lash out at him. "Just like you to blame someone else for your own carelessness."

Morgan's eyes narrowed as if he were squinting against the sun. "We'll see."

Before she could react, his hand grabbed the cloth at her waist and tore away the skirt of her thin dress. Since she had already abandoned her petticoats and stockings, she stood before him in a pair of ruffled drawers from Karen's trunk.

Morgan's searing gaze traveled from her round, frightened eyes, over her bare shoulders, lingering brazenly on pink nipples and the hugging hands trying to conceal them. Then he eyed the tie string at her waist. "Well, do I take them off, or do you give me my money?"

"How dare you . . . treat me like this?" She tried to step away from him. "Don't you dare touch me!"

"Take them off!"

"No—"

He grabbed the top string of her drawers—

"Wait. Don't tear them! Morgan, please, you have to understand . . ."

"Take them off!"

His eyes were hot coals burning into hers. With trembling fingers, she loosened the fastening, letting the undergarment drop to the ground.

For a moment he couldn't move. Her breasts and hips were molded like an exquisite female statue, smooth, hauntingly lovely, beguiling the eye and arousing the

senses. Her maidenhair was the same russet color as her copper brown tresses. She
had never looked so lovely or desirable.

Trish saw his caressing gaze. Her emotions were exploding—fear, embarrassment,
anger, and hope. She had outwitted him!
The money was safely on the ground, still
in the hem of her skirt. She would find
some way to put it back. He would never
know.

An apology seemed to waver on his lips
as he felt the empty drawers and then
something in her eyes made him hesitate.
His gaze hotly swept from her face, dip-
ping to her smooth pelvis and slender legs
and then came back to penetrate those
eyes looking at him so fearfully. Very deliberately, as if something in her expression told him she had tricked him, he
reached down and picked up her torn
clothes.

She knew then that he was still not convinced. As casually as she could, she held
out her hands to take the clothes from
him. "If you don't mind, I'll take those—"

Morgan's mouth curved into a mocking
smile. "I don't think so."

He had seen the way her gaze darted to
the bundle in his hand. Watching her eyes
widen, he slowly began to slip the dress
through his searching fingers. He stopped

when his hand touched a thickness in the hem. Trish felt the ground dip under her.

"What have we here? Not the missing money, surely?" he mocked. "You wouldn't lie to me like that . . . not an honest, truthful lady like yourself?" There was disappointment and bitterness in his tone. He pulled out the stolen bills. "However did they get in the hem of your dress, my love, when I lost them in the river? Isn't that what you said?"

"You have to understand . . ." she pleaded.

"I understand completely," he growled. "And it's time you understood a few things." He reached out and jerked her naked body against him, pinning her arms helpless at her side.

"Please, I'm sorry . . ."

The rest of her plea was lost as his mouth captured hers. The kiss was a savage one. Passion, revenge, and anger surged within him. He cupped Trish's bare buttocks and pressed her against him. As he felt her body quivering against his, he forgot about money, about lies, about everything. His anger was lost in a love that had grown within him and desire surged through his body like molten fire. This was his woman. Nothing mattered except that he held her in his arms. A sudden rush of happiness sluiced though his veins.

Trish felt a hardening surge of desire in his loins. She gasped for breath as his kisses bruised her lips, his hands touched her breasts and sent spirals of sensations into the warm crevices of her body. She mistook his passion for anger.

"No—" she struggled, "not like this!" She had dreamed that someday she would be his but he couldn't take her like this— not out of hateful revenge. He'd never told her that he loved her . . . that she would be his forever . . . that she would never be lonely again. She writhed in his embrace as he kissed her with parted lips, his demands harsh and compelling as he worked her mouth and sent his tongue darting in a rhythmic quest. His demanding kisses fired deep longings within Trish, sapping her strength until she was clinging to him and willingly sank to the ground with him.

When her mouth was soft and pliable, his kisses trailed down the sweet crevice of her breasts. Her naked body was fired by his touch as his hands and lips stroked her and found their way into the soft triangle of maidenhair between her legs. His fingers and the palm of his hand created an ecstasy of sensation that eased away all stiffness from her limbs. He took a lover's pleasure in his domination of her senses, his hands and mouth creating spiraling sensations from her breasts down into the warm, intimate crevices of her body.

"I love you," she murmured, lost in a sensuous maelstrom of desire she hadn't thought possible. Like a banked fire, desire radiated in incredible zeniths. Dominated by his rhythmic caresses, she clung to him. When the moment came that he swept her legs apart, she raised her hips to meet his thrust.

Bewildered and frightened, she cried out. She pressed her hands against his chest, pushing him away, but his body suffused with desire. Sweat shone on his brow and his mouth was half open and tense as his heavy breathing mingled with sounds from her own constricted breath. Her heart leaped with stark terror and a demanding hunger she didn't understand.

She whimpered and then the rhythmic thrusting within her mounted into an excruciating crescendo. She gasped his name as her body exploded in wild sensation and she quivered with fulfillment.

As he slipped from her, he delighted in the knowledge that he was the first. The thought of someone else having her had always brought raw fury coursing through

him and now he knew. She was a virgin.
She had lain in his arms only. What a fool
he'd been.

"Trish—"

She moved out of his arms. "Don't." She
managed to get to her feet while he remained half sitting on the ground as if too
stunned to move. With a sob, she picked up
her torn clothing and fled behind a mound
of nearby rocks and mesquite bushes.

Morgan watched as her sculptured back,
thighs, and legs, lovely and supple in their
nymphlike nakedness disappeared from
view. She acted as if she hated him for
what had happened. He had forgotten all
about the money. The outrage he had felt
had completely disappeared as he had
been swept up in the act of kissing, caressing, and loving her. Then he cursed himself. He had held back all this time, only
to let his anger fuel his passion. No wonder she had run from him. The pain that
shot into his eyes was the same kind that
had been there when he had brought
about the destruction of his beloved boat,
Milady.

Fourteen

Trish's thoughts were as shaky as her emotions as she tied her torn dress as best she could, grateful that at least her drawers were in one piece. Winnie had been wrong! The mating of a man and woman was not an indifferent happening. There was nothing casual about giving yourself to a man. The union had unleashed sensations she had never imagined. How had such indescribable ecstasy lain dormant in her body, waiting for a man's domination? Her cheeks burned with embarrassment. How could she have responded to Morgan that way? Clinging. Moaning. Delighting in every caress. She blushed to think about it. Even now her body floated in a tingling, wonderful sensation. If only Morgan had said he loved her! Tears flowed down her cheeks. She knew she had destroyed any feeling he had for her by stealing his money. He had every right to be furious with her. She shouldn't have done it but he had refused to even listen to her. Instead he had taken her in rage and not in love. "I hate him . . . I hate him," she sobbed.

Her fingers shook as she braided her hair. How could she ever look at him again? She bit her lip, feeling a scarlet flush mount into her face. She'd never known a man's body before. It was bewildering and frightening. What would happen between them now? She covered her face with her hands. How could she keep him from taking her anytime he pleased? There was no place to run. No Jens to be a buffer between them. Her train of thought was suddenly cut off. She stiffened and listened.

Footsteps.

Her breath quickened. Someone was moving up the narrow chasm from the river. Dear God! Indians?

Her heart stopped. Smoke from the fire must have alerted them, after all. She stuffed her fists against her mouth to keep from screaming. Morgan—she had to warn him! But there was no time. A faint swish of air told her someone had moved by the rocks and mesquite bushes that concealed her.

She closed her eyes tightly and didn't move a muscle.

A long moment passed and then she heard Morgan's loud cry. They've killed him! My God, they've killed him! Her body twitched in a trembling spasm. Only a moment ago she had been thinking of hatred and revenge. Now the love she had been struggling to deny swept over her. Her shoulders shook convulsively. What should she do? Shock paralyzed her.

Morgan dead . . . Jens drowned . . . and her life in the torturing hands of merciless Indians. "Please, God . . . don't let them find me. Please, not savages . . . !" Her prayer was cut short by the murmur of voices.

Her head came up as her ears strained to catch the sounds. Talking! She couldn't make out the words—but it was no heathen tongue. The voices were speaking English!

Even before she reached them, her ears had transmitted recognition of the booming voice. Jens. It was Jens!

She bounded out of her hiding place, crying with joy. The two men were hugging and slapping each other on the back.

"Jens . . . Jens," she cried, rushing at him. Laughing, the big man swung her into his arms, lifted her off the ground and gave her a bear hug.

"I can't believe it's you," she sobbed, cried, and laughed all at the same time.

"Don't reckon you'd mistake me for anybody else," he teased.

"You're alive . . . alive."

"I'm just as surprised as you are," he admitted wryly with a shake of his curly mane. His clothes were intact but his coloring was unnaturally pale and his eyes were dull as if slightly out of focus. "What's left of my boat is downstream . . . about a day's hike from here. Is that food I see or have I really died and gone to heaven?"

"It's food." Trish laughed.

Morgan fished out some baked corn and squash from the gray ashes and Jens greedily devoured the vegetables.

"What happened?" asked Morgan.

Jens talked with his mouth full. "Damn breaker took the oars right out of my hands. One of them swung around and bashed in the side of my head. See . . ." He drew back strands of sun-streaked matted hair. An ugly wound, bruised and swollen, rose on his skull just above his ear.

Trish winced just looking at it. "Oh, Jens . . ."

"I was knocked out but somehow my legs got caught under the seat of the boat and I rode it over the rapids and several miles downstream. I don't know how long I was out. When I came to, I was crumpled up in the bottom of the boat and luckily, it had caught in one of those rock islands near the bank. Her bow was completely gone."

Morgan's face blanched. He'd been praying Jens's boat had remained in one piece. Now he knew the worst. Both boats were gone.

"What did you do then?" asked Trish, still unable to believe all three of them were sitting there, talking like always.

"I didn't do much of anything. I was too weak and dizzy to move. Must have lost consciousness a dozen times. Sometimes when I came to, it was night and sometimes the sun would be blazing down on me. Yesterday, I began moving around a little. The stern hatch was sticking out of the water so I was able to get at some dry food." He ran a thick hand over his face. "It's my eyes . . . they don't work right . . . guess it's that blow on the head."

"How awful." Trish touched his thick arm. "Oh, Jens, I'm glad the river didn't get you."

His grin parted a beard wet with corn juice. "That makes two of us." He squinted at Trish and his slow gaze took in her torn dress tied together with knots. "Looks like the old river didn't treat you too kindly either."

Trish managed to keep her expression natural as she nodded. "A breaker lifted me out of the boat . . . swept me downstream." Let Jens think she had torn her clothes in the river.

Morgan refused to meet her eyes. If she hadn't known better she might have thought that he was the one who was embarrassed. Only that didn't make sense. There was no room in his life for sentimentality. He had told her that himself just minutes before he'd found out she'd stolen his money.

Morgan was aware of Trish's scathing and damning eyes upon him. He swore silently. The shock that she'd stolen from him and brazenly lied about it had kindled his unbridled fury. But once she trembled in his arms, responding to his kisses and caresses, everything else had been forgotten. There had been nothing but love in his heart when he had taken her, but she'd never believe that. He should have declared himself to her, revealed his feelings for her, but his stiffnecked pride had kept him silent. Now it was too late. She cowered close to Jens as if she feared he would reach out and touch her. The realization that she was afraid of him made him sick. He wanted to gently stroke and reassure her but he knew he would have to wait until she began to trust him again. Right now, he had best leave her alone and keep his distance.

"How did you find us?" he asked Jens. "I thought we were hidden from anyone following the river?"

"The smell. Roasting ears! I didn't know who was cooking them but I decided I'd take a chance . . . bash in a few Indian heads if I had to. I just followed my nose."

"Damn, I didn't even think about that."

"This morning I started walking upstream. I knew you hadn't come down as far as my boat or you would have seen it." Jens nodded at a piece of canvas tied in a three-cornered knapsack. "Didn't bring much with me . . . not much of anything left in the hatch." Then he gave Trish his broad smile and untied the canvas. "Brought this, though." He tossed Rebecca's package into Trish's lap. "Looks like you might be needing something else to wear—not that I'm complaining about the view," he teased as his hazel gaze touched her bare legs and the skimpy fabric stretched over her breasts.

Trish's eyes misted. Thank heavens it was her old calico dress that Morgan had savagely ripped off of her. The lovely green silk, the green earrings, the white bodice with its white pearl buttons from throat to waist and the matching teal blue flounced skirt were all in the package. The dead Karen's clothes. Trish's vision blurred as she fingered them for they brought back memories of the fair-haired girl.

"Here now," chided Jens. "I save your package and only get tears for my effort."

"Thank you," she choked and took the clothes back into the bushes to change.

When she returned to the campfire wearing the teal blue skirt and white bodice, the men were still talking about the devil falls that had taken away their boats. Morgan was questioning Jens in detail about the condition of his boat.

"It's not salvageable," answered Jens. "What about yours?"

"The side was gouged with a big hole. We might have been able to attach some new timbers if—"

"If he hadn't been foolish enough to let go of it and fish me out of the river instead," finished Trish tartly.

Morgan didn't rise to the bait. He knew it was too soon to beg her forgiveness. She was hurt, bewildered, and angry. And so vulnerable! He wanted to draw her into his arms and bury his face in the hollow of her sweet neck. His chest tightened.

Even the thinness of her face could not mar the finely chiseled bone structure of her face and the habitual saucy jut of her chin. And she was his! No other man had touched her. A strange joy swept through him.

Trish misread the glint in his eyes. She took her place beside Jens, daring Morgan to make a move toward her. "We're mighty glad you're back, Jens," she said with a double meaning that wasn't lost on Morgan.

Jens seemed oblivious to the tension radiating between them. "We had made good progress through the canyon before the accident," he said, wiping corn juice from his mouth. "I don't think we should be more than a few days from breaking out of it."

"God, I hope so," breathed Morgan.

"Isn't Callville supposed to be somewhere close to the river . . . just beyond the Big Canyon?" Jens asked.

Morgan shrugged. "Jacob admitted he didn't know much about land west of the canyon. He couldn't even tell me which direction we should head once we reach open ground."

"Wouldn't hurt none if we had a map, would it?" said Jens with a wry smile. "Guess we'll have to make one of our own."

"If we still had our boats," said Morgan thoughtfully, "I'd say we should stay with the river even after we leave the canyon behind. But on foot . . . it might be shorter to cut across land. The damn river doubles back on itself so much that we could waste precious time keeping on its bank. We know that Fort Yuma lies south."

Jens stretched and stood up. "Well, guess there ain't any big need to settle everything right now."

Morgan glanced up at the sky. "Gets dark early in the canyon. If you feel like it, Jens, I think we should head downstream before nightfall. Put a little more distance between us and that Indian camp. What do you think?"

"Sure. Give me a few minutes in the bushes. After that good meal, I'm ready for anything—"

Then he stumbled on a rock that obviously had not been in his vision. As he caught himself Trish cried out and sprung to his side. "I'm all right." Jens waved her away.

Trish turned on Morgan. "Can't you see he's hurt! Something's wrong with his eyes."

"It's that crack he took on his skull. As it heals, his vision will probably come back."

"Why can't you show a little compassion? The man's suffered a head injury."

"We can't stay here and wait for it to mend."

"Surely one night isn't too much to ask."

"If Jens followed his nose, so can an Indian. Collect the rest of the food," he ordered in his martinet tone. "Get Jens's knapsack and pack it as full as you can."

"Yes, sir . . . Captain." She gave a mock salute and flounced away.

Everything was going to be as before, she thought, relieved and yet strangely disappointed. She knew men could mate and forget it as easily as they forgot their last meal. Winnie May had filled her in on the appetites of men. They were different, she had told Trish. They could make love to a woman and never get their emotions in a tangle. Trish bit her lip, unable to keep her feelings safely detached. Even though she would carry love for him to her grave, she could tell that Morgan had already put aside what had happened between them.

"Ready?" Morgan asked her, his eyes searching her face as if seeking more than answer to his superficial question.

"Ready." Her voice was even. "Let's go."

Jens came back and they started down the river just as long shadows from a fading sun enveloped the bottom of the canyon.

Fifteen

The brutal majesty of the Colorado mocked them as they inched their way through the deep chasm in the earth. They squinted against cliffs hotly absorbing heat from a relentless sun. From morning till night, intense white sunlight stabbed their eyes and brought thrusts of pain pounding in their heads. Radiating rocks blazed scarlet, vermilion, shimmering oranges and yellows. The canyon maliciously held the piercing heat and changed dark sheltered caverns and crevices into banked ovens. Temperatures rose into the hundreds and the deep canyon became a smoldering furnace.

As always they were short of food. Despite Morgan's frugal rationing, the supply of stolen vegetables soon disappeared. They had not come to any more Indian gardens along the river so they were back to gagging on roots, seeds, cactus pulp and drinking life-sustaining fresh water trickling over steamy rocks. Animal life was scarce in the lower canyon and without guns, they couldn't bring down the few they saw. Once Jens pointed out some bear tracks in soft mud.

"Bears!" gasped Trish. If the animals were hungry, they might stalk human flesh. The huge paw print made them wary of exploring any of the nearby caverns.

Morgan kept them moving. His relentless determination refused to waver even as they trudged wearily along without food, guns, or a reliable map that might indicate in some vague fashion where they were. He was always driving, always commanding, exacting the last dram of strength each day. He seemed more rigid than ever as if any indications of weakness or caring on his part would doom them all.

Jens hunched his thick frame as he shuffled along. They were all relieved that his eyesight seemed to be improving. Morgan had probably been right that he was recovering from a cracked skull, thought Trish.

Their senses were so dulled that when the landscape finally began to soften with new vegetation, the change failed to arouse them immediately. A variety of ferns appeared near tiny plunging waterfalls and red monkey flowers hugged shady crevices, dotting the bleached sandy ground with color. In their weariness and misery, the exhausted travelers failed to realize that these plants heralded their exit from the Big Canyon.

Even when the river spread out into open land on both sides, the welcomed view brought no shouts of joy. They were out of the Grand Canyon but their victory seemed hollow! As far as they could see, endless miles of brush-covered prairie lay ahead stretching across an endless horizon.

The moment of decision had come. Should they continue to follow the river in its rambling pattern as it turned north?

Morgan didn't think so. He knew that eventually the Colorado ran south into the Gulf of California. It seemed to him that following the river in its northern direction would only make them double back on their tracks when it veered in its southern direction. The sun's position would keep them moving west across the desert land until they found the river again.

Morgan explained his reasoning. He took a stick and drew a map in the dirt. "According to Jacob, we could lose several days following the river in a northwest direction when one day's hike straight across the land would bring us to the river again as it turns south."

Jens shrugged his slumped shoulders and

rested his head in one of his mammoth hands. His head hurt too much to make any kind of decision. Surprisingly enough, Morgan turned to Trish. "What do you think?"

Her usual obstinacy barged to the front. "I think we ought to stay with the river."

"Why?"

Her reason was a selfish one and not based on any logical deductions. She didn't want to take a chance of missing her father by leaving the Colorado. If he were still alive, he wouldn't be far from the banks of his beloved river. "If we follow the river, we'll get to some settlement eventually."

"Eventually. That's the word that worries me. Eventually may be too late. We don't know how far the river wanders north. I think walking directly west is our best bet. According to Jacob, Callville lies west of the Big Canyon. One day's walk could bring us to the settlement."

"I think we should follow the river," Trish stubbornly repeated.

"What do you think, Jens?"

"It's up to you, Captain," he said wearily. His jowls sagged from lack of flesh in his usually round face.

Morgan knew they were taking a calculated risk and that responsibility was his as he led them away from the river. He also knew that they were using up the last of their reserves, both physically and mentally. They had to find Callville—and soon. He avoided Trish's accusing eyes as they filled the one water bag that Jens had rescued from his boat. They left the river and picked their way through mesquite thickets, cactus, catclaw bushes, and sagebrush.

They learned later that they had unwittingly headed right into territory inhabited by four different Indian tribes. On these prairies, Havasupai, Yumans, Yavapai, and Mohave tribes constantly warred with each other and together they fought the ever-encroaching white man invading this region. The Mohaves and the Yumans fiercely battled United States Cavalry that had detachments riding out of Fort Yuma, and as Morgan learned soon enough, the welcome mat was not out for three renegade river travelers even if they were half starved and unarmed.

Heat from the desert sun was fierce, parching their nostrils, thickening their tongues and sucking moisture from their taut skin. Even Trish's tanned complexion was burnt and her lips cracked. She was constantly begging for sips of water.

They were stumbling forward with their heads down the second day out of the canyon when they flushed out two little Indian boys who had been squatting and stirring sticks in some tall rushes.

"Kawah! Kawah!"

The savage cry curdled Trish's blood.

"Back!" shouted Morgan. "Run!" He grabbed Trish's arm and shoved her back the way they had come. Their flight ended abruptly when suddenly they were surrounded by Indians rising out of the high thickets.

Trish screamed! Morgan and Jens froze as a human stockade of Indians, shoulder to shoulder, began to tighten a circle around them. The savages held weapons—spears, clubs, and a few were pointing army muskets.

Trish's heart stopped! Then pounded in a runaway speed. She'd never come so close to fainting in her life.

The ghoulish savages that surrounded them were short of stature and looked deformed to Trish with their thick arms, bowed legs, and protruding stomachs. Scraps of loincloths were their only piece of clothing and mud was thickly plastered all over their bare torsos. Dull, black hair hung loose on some of the savages; others had theirs weirdly braided or twisted in mud curls around small sticks. Their faces—smeared with red, blue, and black paint—were hideous masks with no expression in their black eyes. Morgan's arm went around Trish as she trembled in raw terror.

The Indians stopped a few feet away and seemed hesitant to move in any closer. Trish waited for a spear or bullet to pierce her heart. As the agonizing wait went on, she became aware that it was Jens's hugeness that had captured their attention. Every pair of eyes was centered on him. His head towered several heads above the tallest of the savages. His curly, bleached hair and beard made him look like a blond giant.

Morgan became aware of their fascination and hissed to Jens. "Smile . . . do something friendly . . . act important."

Jens shot a bewildering glance at Morgan. How did anyone act friendly and important with two dozen weapons threatening instant death? Swallowing hard on the lump of fear caught in his throat, Jens tried. He parted his broad mouth in a wide, false, stiff smile. Then he slowly made an exaggerated bow.

"Good," whispered Morgan. "Hold out your hands, palms up!"

Jens made the gesture.

None of the savages moved or changed expressions.

"What are they going to do?" whispered Trish.

"Quiet!" whispered Morgan.

They waited.

At last an aging Indian with stringy, gray hair raised a bony hand. He had a hawklike nose and cheekbones so prominent that they made his black eyes look sunken. His skin was like wrinkled bronze parchment and his visage was carved rock, hard, enduring, and without expression. He must be the chief, thought Jens, and centered his stiff smile on this old man.

Trish didn't know whether the chief's raised hand was an order to kill them or an acceptance of Jens's friendly overtures. The circle of Indians became a flowing wall of bodies, forcing the captives to move forward. Trish cried out as she was roughly pushed forward in front of the moving mass. Morgan grabbed her arm or she might have stumbled and been trampled.

"Steady," he whispered.

"Where are they taking us?"

"Probably to their camp." He dared not think of the torture that might await them there.

Even before they reached the Indian camp, Trish smelled it! A malodorous stench nearly took her breath away. Raw excretions, decaying carrion, green pools of stagnant water and other odors that defied identification gagged her. The Indian camp was a pathetic collection of mud and stick shelters, crude, dirty, and ugly.

Dogs ran everywhere. Several lean bitches dumped puppies off their tits as they stood up and yapped at the visitors. Trish saw to her horror that other plump dogs were being cooked on spits over the fires, trussed like lambs for roasting. Animal offal squished underfoot as they walked and the stench of decaying raw garbage rose in an odious miasma. Gagging, she put her hand up to cover her nose.

Morgan jerked it down. "For godsake, don't insult them! You'll get us all killed!"

She clenched her mouth shut tightly. She was certain she was going to vomit. Bile came up into her throat. She shot a look at Jens, walking on the other side of her. He was walking straighter than he had for days, keeping his head up and stretching his stature to the last quarter of an inch. A ridiculous frozen smile was pasted on his lips and unblinking round eyes took in the camp as they were escorted through it.

Trish swallowed back rising bile and tried to ignore the stench filling her nostrils. She didn't want to be killed—or tortured! There had been massacres of wagon trains near Bend River and she had heard stories of Indian atrocities, captives burned alive, their skin stripped off, impalings that defied belief! These horrors came flooding back as the savages drove them like cattle into their camp.

Squaws and naked children were everywhere; some staring from doorways of flat-roofed huts covered with sagebrush. These crude dwellings were built so low even these Indians of small stature were forced to sit or lie down when inside. All of the women were bare to the waist, exposing dangling brown breasts, and wearing skirts of grass or dyed bark. Wide necklaces of seeds, shells, and stones choked their thick necks. Some younger women were nursing babies and Trish saw children as old as five years standing and sucking on their mothers' breasts. The women's expressions were all the same; solemn, withdrawn, embodying a cold stare that sent shivers up Trish's back.

"What are they going to do to us?" choked Trish, her voice rising.

Morgan tightened his grip on her hand but didn't say anything. There was a whiteness around his own lips. He had been remembering accounts of Indian torture and feared they could expect nothing less from this tribe.

The old man who had been walking at

the front of the procession finally stopped at what must have been the center of the squalor. A large communal fire sent out a sickening bank of heat but he didn't seem to notice as he took a position nearby.

"They're going to roast us alive," gasped Trish.

The old chief kept his eyes glued on Jens. With great ritual, he finally stretched out a bony arm and curved his withered hand in an inviting gesture.

"What does he want?" whispered Jens as he made another elaborate bow.

"I think he wants you to give him something," said Morgan. "Some kind of a gift!"

"What do we have?" Jens stalled, bowing again. The canvas knapsack he had been carrying was nearly empty.

Morgan reached into his pocket and brought out his pocket knife. It was plain without any shiny metal or stones but he didn't have anything else. He slipped it to Jens. "Give it to him unopened. An open blade might give offense."

Jens's huge jaw worked into an uneasy smile as he lifted his mammoth arm and held out the knife as an offering.

The old man nodded for a young boy to go get it and bring it back to him.

When the knife was in his withered hand,

the old man turned it over and over. He frowned and it looked as if the aging chief was going to refuse the knife. Its dull casing held no interest for him. The small boy, probably a grandson, thought Morgan, exchanged a few words with him. In response, the old man handed the knife to him. Quickly the youngster pulled out the largest blade and then gave it back.

The old man took the knife and then began walking slowly toward the prisoners, the knife extended menacingly in front of him. His eyes were not fixed on Jens now—but on Trish! The knife was leveled at her throat.

Morgan stiffened. Fear lurched like a hard knot in his chest. He knew that some tribes delighted in torturing females. Morgan's eyes searched the withered face and the knife. What was the old man going to do? Good Lord, was he going to try out the knife on Trish's neck? Morgan knew the savage could slit her neck as easily as he gutted a rabbit. The man's gaze was fixed on her white bodice.

"Stay calm, Trish. Don't move," Morgan whispered. If she lost her nerve, all might be lost.

Wedged in tightly between the two men, she watched the slow approach of the Indian, her eyes fixed on the knife's sharp point like a victim mesmerized by the arch of a deadly cobra. She felt Morgan stiffen but he made no effort to stop the Indian's approach. Neither did Jens. They weren't going to lift a finger to protect her. She shot Morgan a bewildered, pleading look.

"Steady. Steady!" He squeezed her hand. She closed her eyes and waited.

The knife touched the high collar of her white bodice. She felt a light tug on the fabric and heard a soft ping as a pearl button fell away. And another, and another. The old man collected the pearl buttons he was deftly cutting off from the front of her bodice.

Relief hinged Trish's knees and she nearly buckled to the ground before the old chief had finished. Morgan's grip on her arm held her up. The chief stepped back, holding a dozen pearl buttons in his hand and leaving her bodice gaping open. She instinctively clutched the opening to hide her bare breasts from view— which was foolishness in view of the half-naked women all around her.

Looking at the pearl buttons in his hand, the Indian's expression softened like cracks in tanned leather. He was pleased with the gift! He raised his gnarled hand and motioned for Jens to follow him. Although Morgan and Trish were not included in the gesture, they followed Jens and the chief to a thatch-roofed structure open on four sides to offer shade and a movement of air. The old man sat down and motioned Jens and Morgan to sit but gave a rejecting wave of his hand toward Trish.

At the chief's guttural command, two Indians pulled her away and motioned her to sit outside in the sun, just behind Morgan and Jens. She opened her mouth to protest but Morgan's eyes warned her not to make a scene. Jens, Morgan, several other Indians including the small boy sat down on their haunches in front of the wizened, old chief.

He waved his skinny arms and several squaws brought bowls of the steaming mixture to the men. They began to eat. Trish couldn't tell from Morgan's and Jens's expressions whether the food was tasty or vile. She wanted to laugh as Morgan made a big production out of rubbing his stomach and belching loudly. Her fright ebbed away as her stomach rumbled with emptiness. She was hungry, too. After all, the pearl buttons had been hers, she thought indignantly. She was the one who had experienced the mental torture of nearly getting her throat slit. Morgan and Jens were acting as if she didn't exist. She was tempted to give their squatting rumps a firm kick to remind them of her presence.

Suddenly, Trish felt a jab in her back. A young girl, bare to the waist, with breasts just beginning to form had kicked her lightly with her foot. She wore a wide shell necklace around a broad neck and her ears had been pierced to hold some kind of an animal's tooth. To Trish's utter amazement she spoke one clear word of English. "Come" and motioned Trish to follow.

As if the festivities of the capture were over, only a few women and children remained around the communal fire. Large, soft containers, which looked like the stomachs of large animals hung on sticks and Trish watched the squaws drop hot rocks into them to make the mixture boil. No dogs were being roasted on this fire, thank God. Her stomach lost its queasy feeling and as usual the smell of food began to revive her. She tied her bodice in a knot and waited for the food to be served. The girl had led her to another structure similar to the one the men were using, open on four sides with a flat stick and mud roof giving shade from the relentless sun. Here women and children were eating and Trish was handed a crude clay bowl filled with the same bubbling mixture that had been served to the men.

"Thank you," Trish said, watching the girl's round face for a sign of comprehension. There was none. Her bland expression did not change.

Cautiously Trish raised the bowl to her lips, gingerly taking only a sip of the food despite urges from her empty stomach. Her nostrils quivered from the pungent odor but it was aromatic compared to other smells in the camps. The taste was flat, unfamiliar but eatable. She learned later that the Havasupai ate everything from prairie rodents, dogs, and field mice to deer and grasshoppers. She ignored mysterious greasy bits floating in the mixture and drained her bowl. If they had offered a second helping, she would have taken it.

When the young girl came by again, Trish handed her the dish and said hopefully, "English? . . . you speak English?"

Without smiling she nodded. "Little."

"Who taught you . . . to speak . . . English?" stammered Trish. Communication was a miracle Trish had always taken for granted before but in the midst of these savages, it was more beautiful than finding Coronado's cities of gold.

"Father Ryan . . . from California."

A priest! "Where is he?" Trish gasped in a rush. An Irish priest! Thank God!

"Gone . . . many moons." She held her hand down to show how small she had been at the time.

Trish's exuberance died. Three or four years ago. It was surprising the girl had remembered any English at all. "What's your name?" Trish asked, clinging to this human contact.

"Shapai."

As if to verify the name, an Indian woman called, "Shapai" and motioned the girl away. Her mother's black eyes scolded her daughter and Trish read her expression. "Time was not to be spent with the white woman!"

Father Ryan. Trish had heard about priests penetrating the Southwest, exploring and establishing missions. The parson had always spoken of them in derogatory terms. He raved that the Catholics and Mormons were only making it more difficult to bring the unbelievers into the true Protestant faith. Trish had never had much interest in conflicting religious doctrines and now she blessed the Catholic father for having been here. They could probably thank him for the civilized treatment they had received so far.

This gratitude was driven from her mind

when the woman who had called the young girl away put Trish to work at an odious task. Squatting down beside Trish, the squaw handed her a piece of deer hide and a clay pot filled with a revolting, grayish substance with a rancid odor that looked like some animal's brains.

With grunts, the Indian demonstrated what she expected Trish to do. Taking a handful of the slimy stuff, she threw it on the leather; then rubbed it in briskly like a tanning lotion. Unsmiling, she handed the bowl to Trish and grunted again.

Gingerly with her nose wrinkled, Trish put her hand in the foul mixture and mimicked the squaw's action—but only in a halfhearted way.

The squaw made a guttural sound. Then she raised her broad hand and cuffed the side of Trish's head. Then the squaw grabbed Trish's hand and forced it down on the leather, showing her that she had to put some pressure in her movement.

Morgan had been watching from his place in the chief's lean-to. He had seen Trish led away and had relaxed when he saw that she had been given something to eat. He didn't know what was going on between Trish and the squaw but he prayed that Trish held her temper. The squaws would delight in stripping off her clothes and whipping her with cutting switches. He stiffened when he saw the Indian hit her on the side of her head.

Trish's ears rang from the blow. With tears in her smarting eyes, she took another handful of the gray slime and tried again. This time the Indian woman seemed satisfied. With another grunt the squaw returned to her work skinning some small rodents—undoubtedly in preparation for the evening meal. She kept her eyes on Trish and grunted a warning whenever she slowed down. Morgan drew in a breath of relief as he saw Trish go back to her task.

Once, when Shapai went by with a load of firewood, Trish nodded toward the odious stuff in her hand. "What is this?"

"Brains."

Raw, spoiled brains! Trish's stomach turned over from the thought. She was covered with them. The awful, slimy stuff coated her arms, cheeks, hands and bare skin showing at her midriff; her hair was sticky where she had brushed it back.

"Brains . . . make skin . . . soft . . . white," said the girl.

Her mother called Shapai away. Trish took another handful of the warm, putrid brains and blinked back tears filling her eyes. The torturous days in the canyon without food had depleted her energies. Every muscle in her weary arms protested the vigorous rubbing that her Indian captor demanded. Trish had shirked plenty of work in Bend River and during her stay at the Suttons, but she knew her behavior in those situations would only bring frowns or scoldings. In an Indian camp, she wouldn't be chastised with words but action. Visions of hands being cut off and tongues jerked out kept her working even though every movement became pure agony.

She could see the shelter where Morgan and Jens still sat, smoking and talking with the chief and some younger Indians. Apparently the small boy was acting as some kind of interpreter. It didn't help Trish's disposition any to know she was being treated like a slave while Morgan and Jens basked in the chief's favor.

A short time later, she looked up, brushing the hair from her eyes, and saw that they were gone. Fatigue and pain was instantly replaced by fear! Where were they? Had the Indians sent the two white men on their way, leaving her here—or had they designed some kind of a ruse to kill them? Their show of friendliness could have been some trickery of a savage mind. Morgan and Jens had been fed and then—?

Her thoughts ran wild! Morgan? What would they do to him? If they were going to die, she wanted to be with him. It was his force of will that had brought them out of the canyon alive. Tears filled her eyes and she tried to brush them away but only succeeded in smearing more of the foul brains on her face.

"The men? Where are the men?" she asked Shapai when the girl passed by.

The Indian girl did not answer. Her silence fueled Trish's fears.

Shapai's mother finally came and took away the leather that had become soft and white under Trish's labors. Trish slumped down, vowing that she couldn't lift her arms once more even if they had whipped her. The mettle of this conviction was shortly tested. She couldn't believe it when the squaw returned with pestle and mortar and a basket of corn to be ground. Late-afternoon shadows had eased under the low roof but the day's work was not done.

Trish shook her head. "Tired. Tired." Instantly the squaw's broad hand batted Trish's head back and forth with sharp blows like it was a disjointed ball. Then she thrust an ear of corn into Trish's hands. The squaw stood over her until Trish had ground the kernels into meal.

By the time the evening meal was ready, Trish was physically exhausted and filled with growing anxiety. She had not seen

Jens and Morgan since early afternoon. Where were they?

Then her fears were suddenly and unexpectedly alleviated. Jens appeared with a pretty young Indian girl who bowed her dark head and followed several subservient steps behind him. She was fully mature, with firm breasts and smooth thighs and supple legs that moved under strips of bark barely covering her nakedness. The couple disappeared into one of the stick huts.

Trish gaped, hot color eased into her cheeks. She knew exactly what was going on. Jens had been given a woman to bed. Where was Morgan? Gone to his own shelter with his own Indian girl? Trish felt a new kind of sickening in the pit of her stomach.

It was almost dark when Shapai touched Trish's shoulder and motioned for her to follow. She led her to one of the stick huts which she learned later was called wickiup. It was located a short distance from the one she had seen Jens enter with his female companion. The hut was empty except for some dried grass on the floor.

Trish's fatigue was only a part of her total degradation. She had been in the camp less than one day and already she smelled as foul as any of them. She lay down on the dried grass and stared up at the mud and stick roof. Twilight filtered into the small enclosure like a gray haze. She was alone in a miserable hovel with putrid brains and gritty cornmeal all over her.

·   She winced as she stretched out her weary body, trying to shut out a tormenting picture of Morgan taking his pleasure with another woman. Without his protection she would be callously treated like an animal, worked until she couldn't move, then ruthlessly destroyed.

She could hear dogs outside yipping and baying as they ran freely, sniffing out garbage and gnawing at discarded animal carcass. Trish closed her eyes and the only sound she heard was a loud sobbing coming from her own throat.

Sixteen

"What are you caterwauling about?"
Morgan demanded good-naturedly a few
minutes later as he slipped into the wickiup and lowered himself beside her. "My
God, Trish, you stink—!"

His blunt remark instantly diluted her
joy at seeing him and starched her anger.
"Get out," she hissed. "Go . . . go back
to your Indian concubine!"

"What in the hell you talking about?
I've been down to the pasture with the
chief, looking over their horses. Mostly Indian ponies but they have a couple of
army horses that interest me. I'm betting
they killed the soldiers who rode them.
What've you got all over you, for crissake!"

"Brains. In one day, they made a filthy
slave out of me!"

Morgan's nostrils quivered with the on-
slaught of rancid brains but he managed
a teasing grin. She looked so forlorn, so
miserable, that he wanted to hold her

close, filthy clothes and all. "Nobody can make anything out of you—and you know it! It's exasperating as hell sometimes but you're nobody's putty, that's for damn certain. Jens and I were proud of you today. I'm not sure either of us would have acted that well with a knife at our throats."

"You were going to let him kill me."

"No, I wasn't . . . I saw the old man's eyes fixed on those pearls as he walked toward you. I should have thought of them myself. Damn, I'd give a thousand dollars for a handful of trinkets right now. The old chief seems a little nervous about keeping the army horses. He says they showed up without riders, but who knows? I think I could trade for them—if I had anything to trade."

"You think . . . they killed the soldiers?"

"Hard to tell. They sure as hell aren't going to admit to ambushing a patrol."

"Then the army is close by!" Hope brought a surge of life into her listless tone and she sat up, searching Morgan's face.

"I don't know about close but I think the Havasupai chief is afraid that a U.S. cavalry patrol will find the horses and burn this camp in retaliation. As far as I can gather, the chief's had the horses for a couple of months and no army has shown up yet. If we only had something to trade for those horses," he pondered. "Tobacco . . . jewelry . . ." Suddenly, his arms tightened around her. "I'd forgotten. Your earrings. They're still in the pack with your green dress, aren't they?"

"I don't know if they're real stones . . . or just glass."

"Doesn't matter . . . if the chief likes them."

"Will they let us go . . . if he likes the earrings?"

Morgan didn't answer. Even when they had been fighting rapids, making portages and lining-down, he never once had lied about the situation. When they committed themselves to those devil falls, he had been honest about their chances for survival. Now, he said evenly, "I doubt it."

She swallowed back her fear. "Will they keep us captive?" She told him abut Shapai and Father Ryan who had taught some of the young ones English.

"Yes, I know. The chief's grandson has been acting as interpreter for us. I'm trying to find out as much about this particular Indian tribe as I can. None of them are alike, you know. The boy had some interesting things to say."

Pure joy raced through Trish's veins. Morgan had been talking to the chief's grandson! He hadn't been with an Indian woman after all. He was here with her. She suddenly felt like laughing; her tears had dried up; she listened carefully to everything Morgan had to say.

"The Havasupai are an interesting tribe. They believe in visions. In fact, their whole life seems to be regulated by them. Someone not long ago had a vision . . . about giants!"

"Jens—!" she gasped.

"Right. They took one look at him and decided that the vision had come true. And that's what worries me. You see, they believe he's some kind of a god and are treating him that way."

"He's with an Indian girl. I saw them go in a wickiup together."

Morgan's smile was knowing. "Who knows, Jens may enjoy his royal status too much to want to leave. He seems to be able to adjust to whatever environment or situation he's in. No doubt he would have been contented living at Jacob's Ferry . . . probably would have married Rebecca and turned out to be a damn good Mormon." He chuckled. "He might even become a polygamist."

"He would not! Jens would never be a polygamist! He's too—too fine for that!"

His eyes twinkled at her. "What a child

you are, Trish. You have such a mixed-up, contradictory set of mores and values that there's no rhyme or reason to your right and wrong ethics. You operate strictly on expediency."

"What's that?" she demanded, certain that the term was degrading.

"It means you do whatever suits you at the moment. What's right and wrong changes whenever it's convenient."

The criticism hurt and angered her. "At least I'm different from you," she snapped. "You're a bastard all the time."

His chest shook with laughter. "True. They offered me a girl, you know. Aren't you grateful I told them that you were my woman?" His tone was mocking. "My slave."

"I'm not your woman! Your slave. I'm not your anything! How dare you tell him that?" she snapped, forgetting that a minute ago she was ready to throw her arms around his neck.

"Shhh! Use your head, my love. You don't think an unattached, white female is given a wickiup of her own, do you? You'd be out sleeping with the dogs. By now the chief would have turned you over to the women to cut off your hair and divide up your clothes."

"You don't know what they did to me

today—you were too busy belching food and smoking with the chief. While I . . . I was cuffed around and forced to—" Her voice broke.

"I kept my eyes on you—and I was proud of the way you held up. I know it wasn't easy." His voice was as tender as she had ever heard it. "Sure, they worked you. That's a woman's role."

"While men sit around and act important! It's unfair!"

"I'm sorry, Trish, but I'm afraid you're stuck with needing the protection of a male—no matter how much you resent it. You ought to be thankful that I told the chief you were my property. Even though it galls you to admit it, you're better off with me."

She managed to match his even tone. "All right, but that doesn't mean—"

"That I can hold you close like this?" He pulled her against him. "Now if you scream and protest, the chief might think I lied. We wouldn't want that, would we?" He hadn't moved any closer to her but his tone was suddenly husky and the way he was looking at her sent her emotions whirling.

She managed to stiffen trembling lips and whisper, "Are you going to . . . ?" Her voice faltered.

His dark eyes were warm and soft, caressing and reassuring. "Yes, I'm going to make love to you. The way it should have been the first time. But first I'm going to get you out of those filthy clothes and give you a bath. I'll be back in a minute."

He was gone before she could protest. Give her a bath? Make love to her? This was the first time she'd heard the word "love" leave his lips. And he'd never looked at her with such tenderness, such an expression of caring. It was bewildering. She had never been less attractive in her whole life. She didn't know whether to cry or laugh.

When Morgan returned he was lugging a stomachlike bag filled with water. He was gentle, yet purposefully as he poured water over her hair and dried the long, red-brown tresses with his own shirt. He lightly washed away the grime on her face and dust from her long eyelashes. "Beautiful eyes . . . always weaving a devilish spell," he murmured as he used the cloth to gently bathe her tear-streaked cheeks and wash along the sweet curve of her neck and cupped breasts. She watched his expression but his thoughts were closed to her as he dampened one of his handkerchiefs and washed her naked body as if it were a fragile art object that needed his attention. She made no protests. This gentle cosseting was new to her. She must be dreaming, she thought. She felt treasured.

The cool water was wonderful. It brought back memories of early-morning dips in a clear stream and the feel of cool rain upon her face. Her spirits rose as her skin tingled from the brush of the soft linen cloth all over her body.

A woman's figure was not new to him but Morgan had never felt such deep, rich pleasure as he gently washed Trish's enticing nakedness. All of the perfumed, silken-clad females who had enticed him to their beds could not compare to the natural beauty of her supple body. She did not need any feminine artifices to arouse his virility. Her breasts, her thighs, her legs were visions of loveliness and his male member responded with hardening promptness. Never had a woman appealed to him on so many levels. Morgan drew a long, unsteady breath as his hands followed the sweet lines and curves of her body.

"Trish," he said huskily. "I'm sorry about the last time. Now . . . now I want to show you how it should have been."

He bent his head until his lips were poised above hers, a tantalizing distance from her mouth. He waited until she raised her mouth in willing acceptance. He kissed her then, softly at first, and then with more demanding pressure, working her lips until all stiffness had disappeared and her mouth clung warmly to his.

Their breaths mingled and she felt her will slipping away under an hypnotic attraction that made her weak and giddy. His lips tasted the fresh sweetness of her face, kissed her eyelids and sent his lips slithering down the curve of her neck into the warm crevice of her breasts. His hands explored their fullness. He cupped and caressed them as his mouth fastened upon the pink nipples that budded under his flickering tongue.

All of the humiliation and degradation of the day faded away under his caresses. Trish forgot everything as he performed a loving ritual that made her feel fresh and desirable again. As his hands skillfully moved over her smooth hips and thighs, her own desire rose. With teasing deliberateness he moved his hand between her legs, exploding points of sensation until a husky gasp escaped from her lips. Every stroke and caress heightened the zenith of desire.

The endearments he had flung about so easily with other women had no place in the bewildering emotion that made him willing to give his life for her without regret. His usual glibness while making love deserted him. His emotions were too deep. Too all consuming. He took her slowly and with a caring that was foreign to him.

Trish's desire rose in radiating waves, sweeping at high tide, rising and falling with commanding, relentless force as the delicious hunger within her body grew. Words of love escaped from her own lips as she clung to him. "Love you . . . love you . . ."

When her body was soft and pliable, arching against his, he separated her legs with one of his own. For a moment he let his weight lie upon hers as if waiting for some resistance or struggle against his rising hardness. His answer came with fingers pressed urgently into his back and his name breathed on her warm, moist lips as she willed him to fill her with exquisite, throbbing pleasure. She surrendered herself completely to him, nothing held back.

His face above her was laced with hunger and desire as his heavy-lidded eyes bored into hers. Her passionate ardor was the most compelling he had ever known as he took command of her body with rising thrusts. He withheld his own coming until she gasped and her body shivered with the explosion of ecstasy as he took her possessively for the second time . . . this time not in anger, but commitment and love.

Seventeen

Sun was coming through the mud-caked slats of the wickiup when Trish stretched languidly the next morning. Unfamiliar sounds suddenly alerted her: dogs yelping, foreign voices and speech, and strange noises that she had not heard before. Reality swept back. She sat up.

Where was Morgan? All night he had been beside her, touching and caressing her and bringing up flashes of desire that could be quenched only by his possessive domination. A touch of fear sped through her. Where had he gone? Had someone whisked him away while she slept?

She bit her lip as she quickly reached for her foul-smelling clothes. They were gone except for Karen's underdrawers that tied under the knees. In place of her blouse and skirt, there was a plain leather tunic that fell to her knees. A soft pair of moccasins had replaced her shoes. Morgan must have traded for them, she thought.

Some squaw must have liked the green earrings.

Before she had finished dressing, she heard drums. The rhythmic, frantic beat was accompanied by wild screeching. Trish's fingers trembled as she secured her hair in a hastily plaited braid. The Indian noises sounded ominous. With no thought to her own safety, she pulled back an animal hide covering the doorway and darted out into the midst of Indians milling about in the alley in front of the mud structures. Indian men, squaws, and children were collecting in the center of the camp.

With her heart pounding almost as loud as the drums, Trish hurried to the communal fire. Several dozen warriors wearing feathers, paint decorating their bodies, and bones rattling at their waists were screeching, hopping, and pounding their feet in rhythm with vibrating drums. They carried willow bows about six feet long and arrows with feathered flint tips.

Trish's heartbeat quickened. The warlike dance was ominous. What was happening? Fear caught in her throat. Then her frantic eyes spied Morgan and Jens seated in the midst of the braves surrounding the chief. Knowing that she couldn't rush up to him and demand to know what was going on, she moved slowly toward the shelter where they sat.

Morgan saw her and he moved his head slightly, motioning for her to stay back. Jens's congenial expression seemed unruffled, his hazel eyes rounded as he watched the Indian ceremony. Whatever was happening it did not seem to be a threat to the two men, thought Trish, relief sending a weakness through her limbs.

Morgan watched Trish ease quietly to the ground in the midst of other women and children and drew a sigh of relief. When he had awakened at dawn, she was sleeping soundly. The night of passion had left her relaxed and her mouth was slightly open and her thick lashes motionless on her cheeks. His heart was filled with the poignant need to keep her safe. He didn't know how he was going to do it. He slipped away to talk to Jens, intending to come back before she awakened.

Unfortunately, the chief had other ideas. As soon as Morgan reached Jens's wickiup, both white men were escorted to the chief's hut to watch this pagan ceremony, which seemed to go on forever. Was it a war dance? The ritual initiating the killing of captives? Were they preparing some kind of test for Jens? If he failed, would they all be killed? These anxious thoughts raced through Morgan's head as he kept his expression bland and watched the dancing, whooping savages. When the ceremony was finally over, the chief's grandson began translating the old Indian's word to Morgan and Jens.

From a distance, Trish watched anxiously as Morgan smiled broadly at the chief but the hardening of his jaw and the tense flicker of muscles in his cheeks were not harmonious with his curved lips. Jens looked stunned as if everyone had suddenly taken leave of their senses. He started to protest but Morgan's sharp, warning look made him close his mouth and swallow hard.

At last, the old man gave a nod of dismissal and Morgan rose, left the shelter and came toward Trish in a slow, deliberate walk that showed no sign of any inner tension. With his eyes he motioned her to follow behind him and he led her back to the wickiup where they had spent the night.

"What is it? What's happening?" she demanded the minute they were inside. "Was that a war dance? Is the army coming?"

"No such luck. The chief's ordered out a hunting party."

"A hunting party?" echoed Trish, trying to understand what that would mean to their chances of escaping.

"All of that yelling and dancing is supposed to convince the spirits to grant them a good hunt."

She leaned back on her heels as they crouched in the hut. "Does that mean the men of the camp will be gone?" she asked hopefully. "That might be perfect! We'll have a much better chance of getting away—"

"You don't understand," Morgan cut her off with his former briskness. "Jens and I are going with them. We don't have any choice. They think Jens is some kind of god sent to lead them on a successful hunt. If they didn't, they wouldn't bother to keep us alive."

"But you said you were going to trade my earrings for the horses." Raw fear made her sound pettish.

"I know what I said. The chief didn't think much of your earrings. You've seen the big things the women have stuck in their split ears. He shook his head when I offered him yours. Too small. We've got nothing more to offer—except ourselves. I'm hoping that if the hunting is good, he'll be persuaded to let us have the army horses anyway. You'll have to stay here—"

"No. I'm going with you."

He looked into her wide, beseeching eyes. "You can't. I won't let you. You'll be safe here. The chief has promised. It's your precious skin I'm trying to save." Then his expression softened and he drew out a small blue-green stone that was hanging from a circular piece of leather. He put it around her neck. "It's the same color as your eyes."

She touched the smooth stone and tears filled her eyes.

He thought of all the expensive gifts he'd given other women but the rubies and diamonds hadn't meant anything to him. The crudely polished rock was in some strange way an expression of his love. "The Havasupai believe it is a magic stone . . . with the power of the sky and water in it. It will keep you safe."

"Please, please, don't leave me . . ." The words had a familiar ring to them. She threw herself into his arms the way she had at Jacob's Ferry. "Take me with you."

"A hunt is no place for a white woman, my love," he said firmly. The squaws are used like pack animals. They work from dawn to dusk and serve the men's needs at night. I couldn't stand it and I'd get us both killed trying to protect you. I can't chance it."

Panic made her lash out at him. "You get to be the Great White Hunter and Jens is treated like a giant God. And what do I get? The chance to wallow in filth and break my arms and back?"

"The work won't be anything you can't handle. We don't have any choice."

"Yes. We do!"

"What?"

"Escape. We can steal food and horses and—!"

He grabbed her shoulders and shook her. "You little fool! Promise me you won't try any insane thing like that. I've told you—we've got to be careful. Any false move and it's all over. My God! You try stealing and they'll strip the skin from your bones and roast you over one of their fires."

She tried to jerk away.

His eyes were wintry as he held her in his firm grasp. He knew how stubborn and willful she could be when she set her mind to something. "Promise me, you'll do just as they say. A little work isn't going to hurt you. Use your head, Trish—or you may not have one by the time we get back."

She looked into his eyes. "I can stand anything if we're together. I don't care how hard they work me."

"We're going back in the canyon. I can't put you through that again. You don't have the strength. You'd give out under such demanding work and be beaten for your weakness." It wasn't only the work, he thought, keeping his worries to himself. If the hunt was bad, he and Jens might be killed in retaliation. If Trish stayed here, there was a chance the army would eventually find her. "You have to understand—"

"I understand better than you think," she snapped, hating herself for the fear that had lurched through her. She knew there was a chance that he might never return. If he died she wanted to be with him.

"For once in your life, Trish, take some advice without lifting that stubborn chin of yours. This is no time for any of your lying, deceitful tricks." Raw fear made him harsh.

"Is that what you think of me?" Where was the lover who had stroked and murmured soft endearments in her ears? "You could take me with you . . . if you really wanted to." She let the accusation hang, waiting for him to deny it.

The way he clamped his jaw shut and didn't speak, she knew it was true. He had chosen not to take her! She knew he was just trying to look out for her welfare but being safe when he was risking his life made her eyes pinpoints of fire. She wanted to be with him and Jens no matter what hap-

pened. The three of them had survived
death together many times. She belonged
with them. She wouldn't be left behind because it was safer. She jutted her chin. "You
told the chief I was your woman . . . your
slave, didn't you?"

"Trish—"

"I'm going," she said with quiet determination.

"No, you're not."

She gave him a smile that didn't reach
her eyes. "We'll see about that." She
ducked out of the hut, ignoring his infuriated swearing. She wasn't going to
give up. She'd talk to Jens. He had influence enough to include her in the
hunting party.

She saw him surrounded by painted Indians who were leading horses from a pasture. He had the reins of one of the army
mounts in his huge hand and looked at her
in surprise as she flew across the ground to
him.

"What's the matter, Trish?"

She was out of breath and gasped, "Morgan says I have to stay here. He won't let
me go on the hunt. I can't stay here alone.
Please talk to him."

Jens frowned. "I'm not sure I should go
against Morgan. He doesn't want to see
you come to any harm, Trish." His round

eyes teased her in his gentle way. "Besides, it's the Havasupais who will need protection while you're around."

"I'm going, Jens," she said with a steel firmness in her voice. "If you and Morgan don't want to claim me, I'll trail along behind with the other squaws. I don't think either of you want to make a fuss about leaving me behind. Might not set too well with the chief if his blond god has a fight with a woman."

"You wouldn't do that, Trish," he said, but he looked worried.

"I hope you've talked some sense into her," said Morgan as he joined them. "She's so damn stubborn, she won't listen."

"I don't think she's going to listen to me," confessed Jens.

"Trish, please be reasonable," Morgan said gently but firmly. If he weakened and let her go with him, the hunt might kill her. The long trek through the canyon had taken its toll. She had been surviving on inner resources for much too long. Physically she was depleted. And if he and Jens were killed, she would be killed, too. No, he wouldn't give in. Anger always strengthened her and he saw that dogged courage rising in her now as she glared at him.

"It's because I care for you more than my own life that I won't let you come."

"She's threatening to throw a fuss if we don't take her along," warned Jens. "Knowing Trish she'll get her way in the end. Might as well give in now, Morgan, and save ourselves a hullabaloo."

Trish flashed him a grateful smile. "It's settled then."

Morgan swore.

With a triumphant lift of her head, she walked between the two men back to the center of the camp. Morgan knew that he and Jens were to ride the army mounts, the braves on Indian ponies, but Trish would have to walk with the rest of the women. There was nothing he could do to make it easier on her.

An hour later the procession began to move. Squaws going with the party followed behind the horsemen, carrying provisions like pack animals. Even the pretty Indian girl who had shared Jens's tent walked behind the men filed in a single line toward the Big Canyon.

The giant white god was to be granted all earthly pleasures during the trip, thought Trish as she trudged with the other women, carrying a sack of dried corn on her back. She fixed her gaze upon Morgan's tall, straight figure as he rode ahead on the army mount. Even though her weary worn body was already protesting the heat and tired muscles, she took strength from the knowledge that he was close and tonight she would share his bed.

As the hours passed it was all Morgan could do not to keep from turning around to see if Trish was keeping up. He knew her well enough by now to know that she covered fright with open defiance—and that's what worried him. She was impulsive, stubborn, and willful. If she lost her temper, god only knew what the savages would do to her.

As the red cliffs of the canyon came closer and closer, he felt the river reaching out for him, and suffered a strange illusion that they had never left it.

Eighteen

The hunting area of the Havasupai was restricted by unfriendly Indians tribes on all sides. They dared not hunt along the top of the canyons for fear of encountering the Shivwits nor could they hunt west and south because of the Mohaves. The mouth of the canyon where the Colorado River emerged from choked canyons offered some small wild game that could be brought down with bows and arrows. The Havasupai hunters usually had to content themselves with such prey—but a vision had told them that the Great Spirit was sending them a giant who would bring down bigger and more ferocious prey.

Morgan was deeply worried. If the hunt went badly, it didn't take any great stretch of the imagination to know what would happen. The superstitious Indians would turn on Jens as a false vision and they'd be lucky if they didn't strip the flesh from their

bones. And now he had Trish to worry
about.

The first night the hunting party camped
on the flat ground outside the canyon. As
Morgan had expected all of the work was
put in the squaws' hands. The women
skinned warm small game, freshly killed,
and cooked the evening meal over the fires
that they built and tended. Morgan saw
Trish collecting firewood and was relieved
to see that she seemed to have weathered
the day's hike with her usually dogged stubbornness.

All day long he had ridden easily in the
army saddle, constantly keeping his eye on
her, wanting to swing her up beside him.
A painted Indian brave rode in front of
him, and one behind, keeping him sandwiched in between them. Every time he saw
her russet head lowered as she trudged
along like an animal of burden, he had the
urge to strangle someone with his bare
hands and rush to her side.

At nightfall, the young Indian maiden,
Namaqua, made Jens's bed ready for him
with rushes and a woven rug, but Trish
was not allowed near Morgan. She was
kept with a small group of women who
did not have men to serve. Morgan protested as strongly as he dared but there
was nothing he could do. His guards re-

fused to bring Trish to him. His temper flared but he kept his expression placid. He knew that staying alive depended upon his staying in the savages good graces. There was no choice. He had to meekly submit to their dictates and he only prayed that Trish would do the same.

The next morning, the Havasupai chief led the hunting party into the mouth of the Big Canyon. Once again the river roared like a penned-up beast. As they entered the mighty canyon that choked the Colorado River into a raging tumult, Morgan and Jens exchanged worried looks. They had traversed the entire Big Canyon along the river and had not encountered anything but bear tracks. How far into the canyon were the Havasupai planning to go?

They got their answer when the chief held up his withered hand and directed the riders away from the river. The party was forced to navigate sandstone shelves scarcely wide enough to accommodate the four feet of the animals they were riding. In single file they ascended higher and higher on a narrow path, the men on horseback, the women trudging behind.

"Good God!" swore Morgan, wondering what kind of game the chief hoped to find high above the river where every loosened

rock tumbled eighteen hundred feet downward to the bottom of the cavern.

They made a perilous climb upward
creeping along ledges that fell away thousands of feet to the canyon below until
they reached a high plateau. The chief
motioned toward a dry water hole where
rains had collected earlier. The parched
earth around the sunken indentation was
cracked and dry now because there had
been no precipitation for weeks. The chief
raised his scrawny arm and pointed. A
huge animal's tracks had been pressed into
the earth when the dirt was wet.

Morgan and Jens looked at each other.
Now they knew. The Havasupai had
brought them here to kill a mammoth
bear.

"With what? Our bare hands?" Jens
asked Morgan.

"The great white hunter can work his
godlike power," Morgan answered wryly.

"Crissake, Morgan," Jens swore. "A fire-
fly's got more magic in his tail than I have.
When the chief finds out his vision is so
much poppycock—" He swallowed. "We've
got to get away . . ."

"With guards watching our movement
day and night? Hell, we've got about as
much chance of escaping as that wild goat

we had for supper. And now there's Trish to think about."

"How's she holding up?"

"How in the hell would I know. They won't let me close to her. She should have stayed back at the camp. With most of the braves gone on the hunt, she would have been safe and not treated like a mule."

"What are we going to do?" Jens looked for direction from Morgan as if the command were still in his hands.

Morgan's eyebrows met in a deep frown. "A couple of the braves are toting army rifles. They probably got them the same time they acquired the horses—by foul means, no doubt. I haven't seen them shoot at any game with them. When the time comes you tell the chief that the white man's firearms were meant for the bear. We'll have a fighting chance to bring it down before it mauls us to death."

That night they camped in a high cavern deep in the side of a cliff. The site reminded Morgan of the deserted Indian ruins. He tried to imagine building a whole village adobe brick by adobe brick, large enough to house a whole tribe. He remembered the day he and Trish had wandered up and down ladders and quipped about the pictographs drawn on the walls.

He was able to exchange a few words

with Trish that night as she carried water around to the men. He was pleased with the way she kept her back straight and her head up as she moved through the camp. When she came to him, she offered him the pouch of water and then gave him a smile that sent his heart dancing.

"How you doing?" he asked, his throat tight. She wore the green-blue stone around her neck and looked small and fragile in the Indian garb.

"I'm not complaining."

No, she wouldn't give him the satisfaction of saying "I told you so."

"Are you getting enough to eat?"

Her smile broadened. "My stomach has already surrendered to the enemy. Fresh game every night and plenty of hot corn-meal. The squaws make sure there's plenty to share among the women."

Morgan made a pretense of drinking slowly. As quickly as Morgan could he told Trish about the bear. He could feel the eyes of his guards watching the exchange between him and the white woman. They were probably suspicious that they were planning an escape. "They expect Jens to bring in the kill."

Her eyes widened. "How is Jens going to bring down a bear?"

The two Indian hunters moved closer to Morgan and motioned Trish away.

"Don't worry," Morgan said quickly, silently cursing the painted faces that glared like masks at him.

One of the Indians gave Trish a shove. She turned on him, her eyes pinpoints of fury. For a moment it looked as if she were going to throw the rest of the water in his face.

"Stay calm," Morgan ordered, struggling to hold his own anger in check. He watched her tighten her lips, then toss her head in her usual belligerent fashion and stalk away. He let out a long slow breath of relief, fighting the urge to swing a clenched fist at the two guards who prevented him from keeping her at his side.

The next few days, lowering clouds hung around crags, jagged pinnacles and sheer walls of the canyon. As the hunting party straggled down one rocky steppe and up another high above the river, man and beast hunched against gusty winds and driving rain. Morgan and Jens didn't know where they were going. As the rain fell, tiny rills of water formed high above them and then grew into lashing waterfalls, pouring down the walls in innumerable cascades, and finally adding their wild roar to the plunging river. Footing became slippery and precarious as they went single file along narrow shelves where one false foot would send man and beast over the side for thousands of feet.

For a week they had hunted for more bear tracks and found none. The restless braves were beginning to grumble. Morgan and Jens could feel their hostility rising. Something had better happen soon, thought Morgan, or the Havasupai would brand their new god as impostor and take their revenge.

The chief led them to another large cavern hollowed out of the side of a cliff where they had protection from the rain. The squaws quickly dispersed to light fires and soon the huge cavern was filled with rising smoke and the smell of roasted meat. Small animals they killed were cooked every day to keep the hunting party's stomachs full.

Trish seemed to be thriving on the steady meat diet, thought Morgan. And even though she walked with heavy burdens on her back, she was more nimble of foot than any of the squaws and he quit worrying that she wouldn't be able to navigate the treacherous rocky shelves. She had kept up with him and Jens on the river and now she easily kept up with the hunting party.

Morgan had to admit to himself that he was glad that she was here. He'd rather worry about her at close range than be tortured by thoughts of what might be happening to her back at camp. He had been offered a woman but had turned down the hospitable gesture.

"I'm getting worried," Jens said anxiously as the two men sat together, listening to the rain pour over the opening of the cavern. "No sign of any goddamn bear. If one's still around, he's holed up somewhere. We haven't got a coon's chance of finding him in these hole-pitted cliffs."

Morgan nodded. "The rain isn't helping. Washes away any tracks that might still be around."

"Bows and arrows sure as hell aren't going to help much." Jens sighed. "I never liked hunting. Wouldn't even set any rabbit snares on the farm." He shook his woolly head. "They sure as hell picked the wrong guy for their hunting god. I don't know nothing about tracking. My little gal, Namaqua, says the chief is only going to give us a couple more days."

"We got to think of something." Morgan set his mouth in a hard line.

"Yes. But what? We ain't got much chance of a bear strolling in here."

For a moment Morgan didn't speak. Then his dark eyes took on a glint of thoughtfulness. An idea began to stir.

Morgan approached the old chief the next morning. "Giant white god had vision last night . . . we must go down to the river." Morgan spoke slowly so the young boy could relay the message to his grandfather.

"Bear is there?" the wizened Indian chief queried as his dark eyes fixed on Morgan.

"Bear will come." Morgan's voice was firm and dogmatic. "White god says it is so."

The chief looked from Morgan to Jens and back again. The leathery expression did not reveal his thoughts. Finally he nodded and spoke rapidly in his own tongue. Immediately everyone around him moved. They started packing up.

Jens muttered at Morgan, almost under his breath. "Where in hell did you get all the vision stuff? And why in God's name are we going down to the river?"

"You said the bear wasn't going to find us here."

"Yes, but—"

"Well, then we've got to find him. Remember that time we saw tracks along the river?"

"Yes, but with this rain, there's water every place. He's not going to amble down to the water to get a drink."

"No, but maybe he'll amble down for something else. Come on. They're waiting for you at the head of the line. Watch your footing. We don't want our great white god to slip and fall off the side of a cliff." Morgan gave him a wry smile.

"I hope to hell you know what you're doing."

"We'll find out. At least we have a chance. Crawling all over these cliffs is not doing us any good."

The rains had brought down large quantities of mud that had slithered over narrow passages and made them slippery and treacherous. A dizzy path led downward from the high steppe where they had found the cavern. Sunlight on the stark high rocks blinded them and Morgan gave his horse its head, hoping the creature would find sure footing in the plunge downward. He almost wished he could dismount and press against the inside of the cliff like the women were doing. There was no room on the shelf to turn around. If it ran out, they would have open air in front of them and no place to go.

He had begun to question the wisdom of his idea. At most, it had a hundred-to-one chance of working. Desperation had made it seem promising last night but in the stark daylight of reality, he knew that he had probably put them in more jeopardy than if they'd followed the chief's preference to stay high in the cliffs where a bear's lair might be found.

Below them, the gorged river fed from heavy rains during the night rolled and roared and boiled. Black granite walls held the river in a rocky chute and the sight and sound of it was enough to bring pallor into the faces of Morgan and Jens.

The trail held and when they finally emerged out of one of the narrow canyons and reached the water's edge, Morgan instructed Jens to motion downstream. "We want to camp just below the place where we found the bear paws up above," said Morgan and gave Jens a nod when they had reached a widening curve in the river.

"What now?" hissed Jens with a stiff smile on his face.

"Tell the chief you want several freshly killed jackrabbits. We're going to spread blood all over the place. Up and down the river . . ."

Jens's eyes widened and then stroked his beard in a knowing way. "You aiming to bait him?"

"Right. He won't come down to the river for water but I bet the smell of fresh blood and meat might be a little tempting. Let's just hope he's close enough to catch the tantalizing smell.

It became apparent to everyone that the chief's patience was at an end. If the bear didn't show up soon, he would sacrifice the white captives to the Great Spirit for he would know that Jens was not the giant god of their visions. This sentence hung over their heads as they waited for the bear to take their bait.

At the bottom vaulting canyon walls loomed darkly in the moonlight, Morgan hunched down behind some rocks, waiting and praying that the smell of fresh blood would bring the animal out of his hiding. For several yards up and down the river, they had spread a blood trail leading to the hunks of fresh meat piled enticingly within view of the two army guns, which the chief had agreed to let the white men use. Four braves with arrows ready in their bows flanked Morgan and Jens, and they kept a fruitless vigil for several nights.

The rifle felt good in Morgan's hands. He knew that once the chief's patience gave out, the gun would be taken from him. Before the chief called off the hunt and pronounced a death sentence upon them, they would have to make a break for it. The chances of success were minimal but with two rifles they stood a better chance of escaping than if they waited until they were defenseless again. Morgan prayed that it wouldn't come to that. He prayed that the damn bear would show up.

The river's constant roar vibrated in his ears. Shadows played upon the water, rocks, barren slopes as a full moon shone down into the canyon. Thank God, for its fullness, Morgan thought. They should be able to see a dark form moving into view even if they didn't hear the bear's approach. He kept his eyes fixed on the bait of raw meat and waited.

Morgan's thoughts wandered to Trish and the anxiety that was always with him about her safety. She was such a contradiction . . . so brave and foolhardy and at the same time vulnerable and fearful. Half of her belligerent bravado was a cover-up for a deep sense of helplessness. Even though Trish would not open up to him about what had happened to send her fleeing down the river, he knew it had been something traumatic. Whatever it was, she was fearful that it would turn him against her. She would learn to trust him but it would take time. The life-and-death struggle in the canyon had wiped away all superficial pretenses. No ordinary woman would ever satisfy him now. Shallow, simpering females had no place in his life after he had known a passionate, courageous woman who could fire all his senses. She was—

Suddenly his thoughts were brought back to the roaring river and the spot where the bait lay. Movement! Morgan flexed his stiff fingers and positioned them against the trigger of his army rifle. Something was after the meat. He blinked. Was he hallucinating? He stiffened as a dark form moved between him and the meat.

Before he could determine whether or not it was the bear, several arrows whizzed over his head. Morgan swore. The braves had tried to bring the animal down with arrows and only one of them had pierced the bear's leg.

Morgan stepped out into view, straining to see in the wavering shadows.

With a loud roar, the creature raised up on two feet. A black bear nearly eight feet tall! Wounded in the thigh and ready to charge.

Jens fired but only hit the bear's shoulder. Enraged, the wild creature opened its mouth and bared its fangs.

Morgan took aim as the bear was ready to pounce at the two of them standing out in the open. He pulled the trigger. For a moment, Morgan didn't know whether his bullet had been any more effective than the other three. The bear finished his lunge and then the wild, ferocious creature crumpled almost at Morgan's feet. Blood trickled out of a small round wound in his head. He had shot him in the middle of the forehead. Morgan looked into the bear's glazed eyes and slack mouth.

"Yahoo! We did it! We did it!" Jens pounded Morgan on the back, laughing and whooping and hugging him. Morgan's knees were suddenly too weak to hold him and he sat down on a rock. It was a miracle that he wasn't being mauled to death by mammoth sharp claws and pointed fangs. Stepping out in front of the enraged bear was suicidal. Only desperation would have made him do it.

A triumphant Indian chant and the beat of drums began a clamor in Morgan's head that sent relief surging through him. But the moment of victory was short-lived. A more immediate, perilous challenge faced him. How were they going to escape when the triumphant bear hunt had only tightened the manacles of captivity?

Nineteen

Even at the height of celebration when the animal was triumphantly skinned by the warriors and the meat cut into manageable chunks by the squaws, Morgan and Jens were closely guarded. The hope that the Indian warriors would leave the rifles in their hands came to naught. Their chances of escaping became narrower and narrower as the hunting party began its trek out of the canyon. Morgan feared that once they reached the Havasupai camp, their chances of slipping away would greatly diminish. He lay awake at night, tense and waiting, watching the sentries standing guard. If he'd been alone, he might have managed some deception that would have let him slip beyond the bounds of the camp but any scheme had to include Jens and his guards—and then there was Trish to worry about. He had asked that she be brought to him as part of the celebration but had been refused. Unlike Jens, who was granted the company of Namaqua.

Trish had watched as the pretty young woman trailed after Jens and she remembered how Rebecca had dogged his footsteps. She couldn't see why the Mormon girl had set her sights on Jens instead of Morgan but she was grateful that it was Jens who was enjoying all the feminine attention. She would have been scratching somebody's eyes out if Morgan had been in Jens's place.

She lay on her thin pallet and stared up at the stars. Her thoughts sped ahead—not in the same vein as Morgan's. She was glad that the hunt was over and they would be back at the Indian camp soon. Then she and Morgan could be together. At that moment, that was as far ahead as her thoughts would take her. She could tell from Morgan's tense expression that he was worried about what lay ahead. They had exchanged a few words at breakfast time and he had warned her that she might have to act without hesitation if he gave the word.

Every day's hike brought them closer to the camp. Morgan's frustration grew. Finally he admitted defeat as the odorous smells of the Indian village welcomed them back. Trish threw down her bundles and was heading for the wickiup that had been given Morgan when she was stopped by Shapai's mother and another squaw. Sandwiched between them, she was taken to a shelter full of Indian women who were sitting quietly as if in some kind of trance.

Trish shook her head and made pantomime gestures but they roughly shoved her down on a pallet of reeds. When Shapai came by the enclosure, Trish called to her.

"Why am I here? Why can't I go to my white man?"

"Time for cleansing," said the young girl. "Time for visions. All women stay here seven moons."

Tears welled up in Trish's eyes. She had endured the humiliation of being treated like a pack animal, worked until her body was lacerated with muscle pain and her hands nothing but a patchwork of scratches. She'd suffered all daily abuses and lonely nights with resigned acceptance because she knew at the end of the hunt, she would be back in Morgan's arms again. And now, because of some weird Indian ritual of absolution, they would be kept apart for another seven days and nights.

The women's retreat was carefully guarded and Morgan was not allowed anywhere near it. With every passing day, his anxiety grew. They couldn't put any escape plan into action until Trish was allowed to rejoin him.

"I think Namaqua might help us," said Jens in his quiet, matter-of-fact way. "She won't be having much more to do with me from now on."

"What in the hell you talking about? What happened?"

"She thinks she's with child. A kind of honor, I guess." He looked embarrassed.

"How do you know it's yours?"

"She'd never lain with a man before. It's mine, all right. She's really happy about it but she warned me that once the chief knows she's with child, he won't be inclined to keep me alive. He'll have his own giant. The Havasupai will have another vision that demands my death."

Morgan swore and the lines in his face deepened.

"I think Namaqua will help us get away. She . . . she doesn't want to see me killed."

Morgan's mind began to work at a furious pace. "All right, the first night Trish is back, we'll make our move." He lowered his voice. "This is what I think we ought to do."

* * *

The night was overcast. Only feeble shafts of light came through thick swatches of clouds moving fleetingly across the heavens. Namaqua was only a quick moving shadow as she slipped among the Indian ponies. Quietly she removed the hobbles from the front feet of the two army horses and put leather straps around their necks. Walking between them, she slowly maneuvered the horses into the possessive shadows of some nearby mesquite bushes.

At the same moment, Jens was cutting a hole in the back of his wickiup, spreading the mud and sticks apart until the opening was wide enough for a man to slip through.

Across the alley, Morgan was doing the same thing. Trish had only been returned to him earlier in the evening and he barely had time to explain the escape plan. He helped Trish through the opening and handed her a leather pouch containing hoarded food and the green silk dress that he knew Trish would not want to leave behind. Once outside, they pressed up against the back of the wickiup. If a hue and cry were raised immediately, they would never make it to the tall rushes where Namaqua was supposed to be waiting with their mounts. Morgan and Trish were to meet Jens there.

No sounds except the usual nighttime noises.

Morgan nodded his head, signaling Trish to move.

She spurted across the bare ground to the cover of bushes and reeds. Morgan remained pressed up against the wickiup, hiding in its shadow.

Damn! Before Morgan could move, a dog came bounding toward him. Morgan smothered a curse. If the mutt started barking all would be lost.

Morgan stayed where he was, pressed against the rough slats of the hut, frozen as the dog snooped around his legs.

Knowing that every minute lost could jeopardize their escape, Morgan stooped down, reaching out his hand, whispering reassurance to the mongrel as he scratched his neck. The dog wagged its tail. At that moment the clouds suddenly parted and man and dog were clearly visible. Anyone looking in that direction could not fail to see them, Morgan thought with a lurch of panic.

He straightened up. If he started running the mutt would run after him. The sounds would alert someone. He couldn't just stand there forever. Trish waited in the bushes. Namaqua waited with the horses.

And Jens was already sleathily making his way to the point of rendezvous.

As if in answer to Morgan's prayer, a dog barked somewhere else in the camp and the mutt turned and ran off as if some bitch's whelp had summoned him. Morgan waited until a whale-shaped cloud had moved across the moon's face and then he darted across the clearing to join Trish who was hunkered down in the bushes.

"Come on." He grabbed her hand and they made their way through swampy ground and through thick stands of rushes until they reached the place where the ground dried out and a patch of corn had been planted.

Jens was there—but Namaqua wasn't.

Should they wait—or get away as fast as they could? What if Namaqua had changed her mind, or been caught, or played them for a fool by promising to steal the mounts when she had no intention of helping them escape?

Morgan searched Jens's face. He knew the girl. It was his decision. Jens's large mouth formed the word, "Wait."

Five minutes.

Ten minutes.

Still she did not come.

"Wait," said Jens again with tight lips.

Another five minutes.

The muffled sound of hooves finally reached their ears. Namaqua appeared with the two mounts, coming from a direction that was opposite from the camp. She must have been afraid to come directly to this spot and had taken a roundabout way to avoid detection.

Morgan was weak with relief.

Jens smile was broad as he took the reins from her. She only gave him a nod and disappeared into the night.

Morgan swung Trish up on the horse and took his place behind her. Namaqua had fitted the horses with a crude halter but they had to ride bareback. The well-trained animals moved out in a quick step.

They headed back toward the main channel of the river.

Trish smothered a smile. Apparently Morgan had decided that it was safer to stay with the river, as she had wanted to do in the first place. She leaned back against Morgan, delighting in the way his arms encased her waist as he held the reins. There would be no Indian warriors to keep them apart that night. They were making good time when she felt a brush of rain on her face and remembered the heavy downpours in the canyon and wondered if they would be less devastating out in open country.

Morgan was hoping that their pursuers might not expect them to turn back to the river. This time they would follow it no matter how far it meandered northwest before turning south.

As dawn began to absorb the shadows of night, he could see that storm clouds were gathering in the heavens above and the scattered raindrops were beginning to thicken. Rain would obliterate their tracks which might be a blessing, he thought, but at the same time a fear arose that their flight might be slowed.

They heard the Colorado River before they reached it. The water's roar had never sounded so lovely in Trish's ears. In the open flat country, the river spread out and rolled with a leisurely pace. Raindrops sent rippling rings across its surface.

"We've got to find shelter." Morgan nodded toward an outcropping of rocks forming a low hill a short distance away from the river. They reined the two mounts in that direction. In a few minutes, they had dismounted in a protected gully, sheltered by Joshua trees. A small pool of water lay cradled by worn sandstone rocks. The horses began to drink and feed upon some stands of grass growing nearby.

"We'd better eat and be ready to ride when the storm passes." Morgan and Jens had been hoarding food for the seven days they'd been waiting for Trish. If their lives hadn't been in jeopardy every minute that passed, Trish would have delighted in the kind of impromptu picnic.

As they ate, they expected the heavens to open up any moment but the light scattering of rain stopped and the dark clouds moved on. For once, nature was being kind to them.

They were about ready to mount up again when they heard horses' hooves—lots of them.

"Down." Morgan gave Trish a shove to the ground. Then he and Jens dashed for the horses who were tethered at the edge of the pool. They brought them back into the Joshua trees but Morgan knew that the straggling branches offered inadequate screening. Anyone looking in their direction would see them.

Morgan's eyes widened as he peered ahead. His breath caught. Suddenly his heart was beating so loudly in his ears, he couldn't hear anything else. He blinked furiously. The mirage did not disappear.

"What is it?" hissed Trish.

Jens raised his head and he muttered, "I'll be damned."

Trish looked up. Coming across the open prairie was a black line of uniformed horsemen—with a United States flag flapping in the lead. With cries as loud as any war whoops, the three fugitives ran out of their hiding place. Waving their arms, they ran toward the U.S. Cavalry.

The commanding officer held up his hand and stopped the column. When they reached his side, Morgan quickly identified himself and explained that they had escaped from the Havasupai.

The officer doffed his hat. "Lieutenant James Williams, at your service, sir. United States Cavalry out of Fort Yuma."

"We've been riding a couple of army mounts, probably taken from your men."

He nodded. "A detail was ambushed and several men were lost. I am happy to see that your party escaped unharmed." His glance went to Trish who was giving him such a radiant smile that he felt his face grow warm. "We'll be happy to see you safely on your way."

Impulsively Trish said, "I'm looking for my father—"

"Is he an army man?" asked the lieutenant.

"No, but I know he'll be somewhere

along the Colorado. He sent me letters from Fort Yuma."

"What's his name?"

"Winters. Benjamin Winters."

Lieutenant Williams's round face broke in a smile. "He's a pilot for the Southwest Navigation Company. They have three steamboats plying the Colorado River from the Gulf of California to three hundred miles north."

Trish couldn't bring herself to look at Morgan. His dream was already a reality . . . and in the hands of someone else, including her father.

Twenty

Fort Yuma perched on a high bluff across the river from a makeshift town called Colorado City. This was the only settlement near the mouth of the river in the Gulf of California and it owed its existence to the military garrison that the U.S. government had established to keep the Colorado River open and the neighboring Indians under control. One muddy main street was wide enough to turn around a twenty mule team, and the rest of the town consisted of haphazard clusters of adobe and crude wooden buildings. Void of any paint or decoration, these flat-roofed, drab structures looked ready to dry up and blow away like uprooted tumbleweeds rolling across Indian country.

A crude ferryboat, several barges, and one stern-paddle riverboat were nosed up to the wharf at Colorado City on the evening the detachment of soldiers arrived with Trish, Morgan, and Jens.

"You're in luck," Lieutenant Williams

told Trish, pointing to the riverboat. "That's the *Excursion.* Your pa should be aboard, getting ready for his next run up the river."

"Are you sure?" Trish questioned, unable to believe that her father was the pilot of the biggest boat she had ever seen. It loomed in the water like a white three-storied house with lantern light blazing from portholes on the main deck.

"Yes, ma'am. Benjamin Winters is pilot of the *Excursion,* all right. Has the reputation of being the best captain on the river. Knows every sandbar and snag, he does. There's no worry about getting places on schedule when he's at the wheel." He gave her a tip of his hat. "Now, I'd best be on my way and get my men back to the fort."

"Thank you very much," Trish said with a sincere smile. "I'm terribly grateful."

"Glad to be of service." He turned to Morgan and Jens. "Good luck to you."

"And to you," Morgan said, shaking his hand.

"Mighty grateful to the U.S. Cavalry," added Jens with a grateful nod of his head.

The officer left them at the wharf and then led his men toward the waiting ferry boat that would take them across the river to the army base.

"I'll bet your pa will be happy to see

you, Trish," said Jens as they approached the riverboat.

Trish's mouth was suddenly dry. Would he? If he had wanted her to join him, he could have come back to Bend River after her. He might be furious about her intrusion into his life. Now that she was about to realize her dream, she was frightened.

Morgan took her arm. "Come on. You're not getting cold feet, are you?"

"What's the matter, Trish?" Jens asked as shadows flitted across her face. He had seen this gal meet dangers without a glint of fear in her eyes. If he hadn't known better, he would have thought she was plain scared. "Aren't you eager to see your old man?"

"Of course, she is," answered Morgan in a reassuring tone.

As Trish's eyes went to his face, she remembered his words. "Have you thought about how your father is going to react when he finds himself with a grown daughter on his hands? That may be the last thing he wants."

She swallowed hard. "Maybe I shouldn't just walk in on him," she hedged.

"Why not?" asked Jens.

Trish didn't answer. What if her father already knew about Parson Gunthar? Maybe someone had informed him that his daughter was on the run from a posse? What if the law was watching and waiting for her to contact him? Bend River was a long way from here but notices of wanted criminals were passed from one settlement to another. As these thoughts skimmed across Trish's mind, her face drained of color.

Morgan kept a firm grip on her arm as if he knew she was about to bolt in the opposite direction. "Hey, steady, gal. What's the matter? Could it be that you're about to be caught up in another one of your lies?" he teased.

Her mouth was suddenly dry. "I don't know what you mean."

"Could it be that Benjamin Winters isn't your father at all?"

"Don't be stupid. Why would I lie about that?"

He sighed. "God only knows."

She pulled her arm away. "Benjamin Winters is my father."

"Then it's time you said hello," he insisted.

She might as well go through with it. Morgan wouldn't be satisfied until she proved to him that everything she had said about her father was true. "All right, come on, I'll introduce you." She'd always thought Morgan and her father would get along fine since they were both river men.

As they approached the gangplank of the *Excursion,* laughter and voices floated out from the riverboat's large common room. It was ablaze with lantern light as they mounted the gangplank. Obviously, a party of some sort was in progress.

"Looks like somebody's having a shindig," Jens commented as they reached the main deck of the boat. Through an open door they could see an array of army uniforms.

A rather portly, gray-haired officer was facing the door and when he saw a fiery-haired, white young woman in Indian garb standing in the doorway, he choked on his drink. He wiped his gray mustache with his hand and set down his glass. His bushy eyebrows matted and his wide-eyed stare went from Trish to Morgan and Jens who were standing behind her.

Trish sent Morgan a questioning look as the officer started toward the door. Was he going to throw them off the boat? Morgan quickly stepped in front of Trish. Even in his worn clothes, Morgan presented a posture that bespoke authority and good breeding. His steady eyes made an appraisal of the officer as if the man was the one who needed to identify himself and not the three renegades standing in the doorway.

The officer's forehead furrowed in puzzlement and then he said briskly, "This is a private party."

"We are looking for Benjamin Winters," answered Morgan smoothly.

Trish frantically looked past him for some sight of her father. He was nowhere in sight.

Then Morgan introduced himself. "Morgan Wallace from New York's Wallace Transportation Company. These are my companions, Jens Larsen and Patricia Lynne Winters."

Obviously the name meant something to the officer and he responded quickly, "Major Hamilton, commander of the U.S. garrison at Fort Yuma."

Morgan held out his hand. "A pleasure to meet you, sir."

"But I don't understand," the major said, trying to reconcile Morgan's identity with his dishelved appearance.

Morgan explained succinctly that the three of them had been rescued by the U.S. Cavalry and brought to Colorado City. "Miss Winters is looking for her father. We were told he's the pilot of the *Excursion*."

The officer's gray eyes swept over Trish, her lithe figure clothed in Indian garb and a stone the color of her eyes hanging around her neck. He frowned. "Ben never mentioned he had a daughter."

Trish's stomach took a sinking plunge but she kept her gaze steady. Even if her father had not talked about her, he couldn't have forgotten completely about her existence. In any case, she was about to remind him that he had a grown daughter who had made her own way down the Colorado. "Where is he?"

"Up in his quarters behind the wheelhouse, I imagine. He joined us in a few drinks and then retired early. Shall I send a man up to get him?"

"No," she said quickly. "I want to surprise him." Her head came up. "How do I get to the wheelhouse?"

"Just take the center ladder to the upper deck. Ask him to join us for a celebration drink."

"I'll go with you," said Morgan.

She shook her head. "I'd rather see him alone."

"Are you sure?" He could tell she was taut as a bowline. He didn't know the reason but if Ben Winters didn't treat her right, he'd find himself in the river with a bruised chin, Morgan silently vowed. "I'll be here if you need me."

She nodded and turned away.

The major smiled at Morgan and Jens. "May I offer you gentleman some refreshment? I'm most interested in hearing about your captivity. The government is eager for any information you can give us about the Big Canyon. There is an appropriation in Congress for exploration of the Colorado River. Your insight will be most helpful."

Trish didn't hear Morgan's reply as she left them and mounted a center ladder leading upward. Her thoughts raced ahead. She wished she'd waited to see him. She should have changed into the green dress that she had guarded so jealously. He was going to be shocked enough without seeing her dressed like an Indian squaw. Then she brushed such a minor concern away. She was here, whole of body, and sharp of mind. She had survived a thousand perils to see him. Surely he'd be proud of her.

On the top deck, she glimpsed a huge wheel inside a windowed room where her father must stand when piloting the boat. She knocked on a small door just beyond it, timidly at first and then summoning her courage, she gave it a demanding pound with her fist.

The next instant, the door opened and her father stood there. He was still dressed but obviously had been asleep in a big chair sitting beside a narrow bunk bed. He blinked at the apparition standing in the doorway and then brushed his hand over his eyes to clear his vision.

"Hello, Papa." She controlled the trembling of her lips and gave her russet braid a defiant flip.

"Trish?" he croaked. "Trish, is that you?" Was this young woman clothed like a squaw really his daughter?

"Yes, it's me." She wanted to throw herself in his arms but he didn't make any move to touch her.

"But what? How?" He was too stunned to utter more than fractured questions.

"May I come in?"

He backed away from the door and she walked into the small room filled with bare comforts, meager belongings. She saw nothing personal to show that he was anything more than a man whose life began and ended on the river. There was no hint of the wife and son he'd brought from Iowa, nor the daughter he had left over two years ago in Bend River.

Ben stood in the middle of the floor, utterly bewildered. "I can't believe it. You . . . here?" He stared at Trish as if he expected to wake up any moment from this incredible dream. "How did you come? Wagon train?"

"No, I came down the river."

"But you couldn't have! I know that

river. It's suicide to run that river. Heaven knows, I tried hard enough to come down here, but gave up and came overland."

She faced him. "It's the truth. All the time we were on the river, I thought . . . I thought." She struggled to keep the bravado in her voice, and failed. "I thought you might want to see me again."

Something in her voice broke through the shock he had experienced when he first saw her. He held out his arms to her then, stammering some befuddled assurances that he was too surprised to know what to say.

She laid her head against his chest. "Oh, Papa. I've missed you so."

He stroked her hair. "I've missed you, too. But why would the parson—?"

"He died," said Trish quickly, pulling away and holding her breath as she studied her father's expression. He didn't know. Word hadn't traveled to this remote spot about his murder. For the moment she was safe.

She sat down on the edge of his bunk and told Ben about the two men who had stopped in Bend River. She made it sound as if the two explorers had willingly brought her down the river with them. She made light of their capture by the Havasupai. "A detachment of cavalry brought us to Colorado City. And here I am." Her eyes glowed with victory. "I knew you would be near the river somewhere."

Her smile brought pain to his chest as he was reminded of the family he had lost. And with the memory came a wash of guilt mingled with new worry. He couldn't take her with him on a riverboat that transported soldiers and drifters up and down the muddy river. The drinking, swearing, gambling and whoring made the *Excursion* no place for a decent young woman, let alone his daughter.

He shook his head and said bluntly, "I can't keep you here . . . we'll have to find some nice family to take you in."

Trish just smiled at him. It wasn't the time to tell him about Morgan. She was certain that he would want to speak to her father and declare his intentions in a proper fashion.

"We'll talk about that later." She bounded to her feet. "Come on, Papa. There's somebody I want you to meet. Morgan and Jens are downstairs. You'll want to thank them for bringing me safely down the river."

Ben scowled. His daughter in the company of two river men for God knew how long? It made his blood boil just to think about it. What had Trish let herself in for?

He'd left her with Parson Gunthar to keep her out of the clutches of such men.

"They're talking with Major Hamilton," she told him as she waited impatiently for Ben to smooth his hair and put on his seaman's jacket and pilot's cap. "You'll like both of them. Jens is a farmer from Iowa . . . a big hulk of a man, but gentle as they come. And Morgan . . . well, you'll see for yourself that he's the most intelligent, handsome man you've ever met."

Ben only grunted.

Trish took his arm as they entered the common room together. It was all coming true. As Rebecca had said, it was amazing how the good Lord arranged everything so wonderfully.

Morgan and Jens were standing in the middle of a circle of men pressing close and listening to the conversation with Major Hamilton. Trish could hear both Morgan's and Jens's voices rising and falling in excited tones. Whatever was being said had generated an excitement that was almost palatable. She tried to press forward and get their attention but her father was reluctant to intrude.

Trish waited impatiently for several minutes, growing more furious with a conversation that excluded her participation. She

could have answered some of the questions
as fully as either of the two men. Then a
cold chill went through her as the conversation turned to offers made by Major
Hamilton, which included Jens and Morgan in new exciting explorations proposed
by the government. "We'll be needing
scouts—"

"I'll sign on as a scout," interrupted
Jens. "Especially if I can join any detail
going overland to Jacob's Ferry. There's a
family there that will be needing some protection if Indians are as restless as you
say."

"Your knowledge of the area would be
invaluable, Mr. Larsen. The army can use
men like you." His eyes passed appreciatively over Jens's impressive stature. Would
you be ready to leave in a few days."

Jens grinned. "Reckon I could be ready
to leave by mornin'."

"How about you, Mr. Wallace? I hope
you will offer your service to Lieutenant
Ives who is in charge of the government's
exploration of the Colorado. He's super-
vising the assembling of a riverboat downstream at the gulf. The craft was recently
shipped from Philadelphia. A joint command might even be arranged."

"What kind of craft?" Morgan asked. "I
can't imagine any boat built for eastern

waters surviving one day on the Colorado."

"All the more reason for you to share your valuable knowledge, Mr. Wallace."

"If you think it would serve a good purpose, I'd be happy to talk with Lieutenant Ives."

"Excellent. We'll set up a meeting at the Gulf of California where he is overseeing work on the government craft. Now, I imagine both you and Mr. Larsen are weary from your travels and are ready to turn in for the night. I suggest that you accompany me back to quarters. I'm honored to offer you accommodations at Fort Yuma. We should implement our plans as quickly as possible."

Trish's spirits had turned into leaden weights as she listened to the conversation. The eagerness in Morgan's voice dissolved any hope that he would turn his back on the river once and for all. Obviously he wanted to educate the government explorers and share his findings with them. As for Jens, he couldn't wait to get back to Jacob's Ferry. In less than an hour, both men had already found new challenges and new paths to follow.

And where does that leave me?

As the men dispersed, Morgan looked across the room and saw Trish and Ben watching him. She had her arm through her father's so all must have gone well, Morgan thought with relief. He knew how important it was to Trish to be loved and accepted by her father. Everything was going to work out well. While he spent a few days with the army, the two of them would have a chance to get reacquainted.

He smiled and offered his hand to her father. "Benjamin Winters? I'm glad to meet you, sir. Your daughter has told me a great deal about you. You should be very proud of her. She suffered a great deal of hardship to reach your side."

Ben did not return Morgan's smile. "Why in hell did you expose her to such danger? I lost my son to the Colorado and it's no credit to you that I didn't lose my daughter. Why didn't you leave her in Bend River with Parson Gunthar and his wife?"

To Morgan's credit, he kept his expression neutral. "I'm sure that Trish will explain everything to you."

"It is you who has some explaining to do. My daughter had no business traveling in the company of two river men." Ben looked ready to thrust his fist into Morgan's face.

Trish held on to her father's arm. "I told you, Papa. It was my decision." She sent Morgan a warning glance not to in-

dicate that there had been anything intimate between them. Ben was fired up to
defend her honor. She needed some time
to explain the situation to him.

Jens came up at that moment and Trish
introduced him. The scowl deepened on
Ben's face as Jens began telling him what
a wonderful daughter he had and how
much he was going to miss her.

"Why don't you stay here?" Trish said
brightly. "I know that there must be empty
staterooms—"

Jens shook his head. "Can't. I've promised the major to be ready to leave with
the first detail heading back toward Jacob's
Ferry."

"And I've promised to spend a couple
of days talking to some men involved with
a proposed exploration of the river and
Big Canyon. It's important that the government have as much information as possible. You understand, don't you, Trish?"

Her eyes met his without flinching. "I
understand completely." She turned to her
father. "Will you excuse us a few minutes,
Papa, while I bid my friends goodbye?"

The three of them walked out of the
lighted room and stood together at the
railing. The boat moved restlessly in its
mooring and the moon sent shadows darting across the water.

"Well, I guess this it it," said Jens, his deep voice suddenly husky.

She bit her lip to hold back tears. Her voice wavered as she said, "I'm glad you're going back to Rebecca. I know she'll make you happy. She's a sweet, wonderful person who always thinks about the happiness of others." Impulsively, Trish took off the necklace with the blue-green stone. Without looking at Morgan, she handed it to Jens. "Please give this to her . . . as a token of my love."

"Are you sure?"

"Yes. And tell her I've kept the green dress safe. And whenever I wear it, I'll be thinking of her."

Jens gave a swipe at his eyes and then turned away, leaving Trish and Morgan alone.

"How did things go with your father?" Morgan asked quietly.

"All right."

"He seemed ready to knock my head off."

"Don't go," Trish said, looking up into his face. "Stay here . . . on the boat with me."

"I think it's better if you and your father have a couple of days alone," he said softly. "You need a chance to talk . . . get acquainted again. I know how important his love is to you . . ."

"Not as important as *your* love," she said flatly.

He took her arm and moved her into the shadow of the paddle wheel. His mouth descended upon hers in a kiss that sent fiery spirals all the way to the tips of her toes. "Be patient, love," he murmured. "I'll do my duty to the army and then we'll make our own plans."

"What if . . . what if you can't resist getting involved . . . with this government exploration?"

Morgan didn't get a chance to answer because Major Hamilton and Ben came out on deck. The lovers drew apart and Morgan led her back into the light of the common room.

"Oh, there you are," said the major. "Shall we go, Mr. Wallace?"

There was nothing for Morgan to do but nod and then turn to Trish's father. "Goodbye, sir," he said formally to Ben. "I would enjoy a tour of the *Excursion* sometime."

Ben's expression softened a mite. "She's a fine boat. The best thing on the river."

Jens appeared from the direction of the bow where he'd been dreaming about the pretty, blue-eyed girl who would soon be in his arms.

"Bye, Trish." He gave her a bear hug. "Take care of yourself."

Morgan ignored her father and kissed Trish's forehead. "I'll see you in a couple of days. Keep safe."

Ben growled. "You can depend on that. Good night, Mr. Wallace."

Twenty-one

All night the big steamboat swayed slightly in its mooring in a soothing motion. Light from an outside lantern came softly through a porthole and made a mellow splash on the wide planking and thick-timbered walls. Trish drew in a tantalizing odor of soaked timbers, grease, oil, rope, and canvas.

Gently rocked by the motion of the water, she stretched out on the bed and found it strange after sleeping on the ground for so long. A stubborn line narrowed her lips. She knew her vulnerability, her lack of resources. She feared that Morgan would get swept up in the excitement of the new exploration of the river and his life would veer off in another direction without her. As new, exciting challenges filled his life, his feelings for her could lessen and then finally fade away. She had heard the excitement in his voice when talking about a joint command of the government craft. Morgan . . . Morgan. She clutched a lumpy pillow that smelled of musty feathers. Why hadn't he stayed with her? He could have faced her father. But he had chosen to leave her on the *Excursion* without declaring his intentions to her or her father. He had said he would be coming back in a couple of days. Why didn't she believe him?

She pounded the pillow angrily. All right. She knew better than to depend upon anyone but herself. Morgan could walk away from her but Benjamin Winters was going to have a daughter whether he wanted one or not. She fell asleep with the haunting fear that if she failed to make a place for herself in her father's life, she'd find herself abandoned once again.

In the bright light of morning, she saw that her cabin was simply furnished, a narrow bunk, small wash stand with pitcher and basin, a narrow wardrobe of stained oak and one straight-back chair with a cane seat. Compared to a wickiup, it was sumptuous! Outside the small porthole was the river, changing every day and bringing new delights. She would love living on the river. Her spirits rose as she dressed in her Indian garb, eased herself quietly out of the cabin and cautiously looked up and down the narrow deck.

No one was in sight.

She let out a breath of relief. With an exuberance that sent her pulse racing, she walked around the *Excursion*'s three decks, skimmed up and down ladders, and peered over railings at the water from every angle and delighted in every corner of the steamboat.

A huge stern paddle wheel took her breath away. She had never seen anything like it with its huge paddles that would rise and fall as the wheel turned, filling and emptying, propelling the boat forward. Her father's quarters were on the top hurricane deck with the wheelhouse; passengers' cabins on the second next to a common room where meals were served. Next to it was a small galley where someone was shoving pots and pans around on a wood-burning stove.

She peeked into the common room. The same Chinaman who had been serving drinks last night was cooking breakfast. Dressed in white with a long, black queue swinging down his back, he pounded something so vigorously with a long knife that his head bobbed.

Trish ducked back and scurried away, bounding down another ladder to the boiler deck. If she had seen a steam whistle, she would have been tempted to give it a tug. As she sped around a corner on the lower deck she ran smack into a glowering, red-headed little man, nearly knocking him off his bandied legs.

"Who in tarnation are you?" His speech, laced with a Scottish burr, was harmonious with unruly shocks of carrot hair and dobbles of freckles all over his scowling face. He reminded Trish of a pugnacious mutt growling at anyone who dared to invade his territory.

"Who in tarnation wants to know?" she challenged just as pugnaciously with a toss of her braid.

They both stood their ground, glaring at each other and then an appreciative grin lit the Scotsman's face. "Scotty McPherson, you little varmint!"

"Trish Winters . . . you old goat!" She laughed broadly.

"Well, I'll be. Ben's daughter!" He chuckled, peering at her under bushy carrot eyebrows. "Thought he left you some place in Colorado."

"He did . . . but . . . I came down the river. Arrived last night."

"Well, well . . . reckon Ben was a mite surprised to see you."

"Yes, he was," Trish agreed in a dry voice. Then she brightened. "I want to see everything. The *Excursion* is going to be my new home," she announced with dogged conviction.

The Scotsman frowned, matting his thick red eyebrows together. "It's a pretty lass, you are. Too pretty to be living on the river. You don't know Big Mud when she gets in one of her moods."

Trish laughed. "The Colorado doesn't have anything left to show me." If she's tame enough to take steamboats, she's tame enough to make a home for me."

Scotty kept shaking his head in disbelief when she told him about coming down the river with its devil rapids and raging currents. "Spunky, that's what ye be. Well, come along. I show you the most important place on the boat—my engine room!"

Trish thought Scotty's engine room was a terrible little place, smelly, grease-splattered and dirty with oil droppings, and crowded with stacks of wood and a black boiler ready to be fired up when orders rang down from the wheelhouse. At first Trish had to force herself to respond to his enthusiasm but Scotty soon caught her up in his love of steam. The power was a living thing, he told her, the heartbeat of the boat, and soon Trish was responding to his poetic descriptions of moving valves and thundering pipes.

She was sorry when he led her outside

again and showed her the cargo deck
where stiltlike pillars held up an upper
deck, leaving an open space underneath
for the stacking of cargo. They walked
around barrels, boxes, and sacks filled with
flour, sugar, iron bars, tools, nails, and
cotton goods. Everything seemed to be
tumbled in messy heaps and unorganized
piles. Scotty had told her that all of it was
to be delivered at different stops of the
river.

"How on earth do you find what you
want? How do you know what goes where?"

"Nosy little lass, ain't ye?" Her questions
came at him like birds diving at scattered
seed. Superficial explanations didn't satisfy
her. She kept picking at him for more information. "The mud clerk takes care of
that."

"Mud clerk?" repeated Trish. "Why is
he called that?"

"Don't rightly know. He handles bills of
lading. Stacks the cargo so it comes off in
order. Next stop is Ehrenberg, then Hardy-
ville. On the way back we'll pick up passengers going down to catch a schooner in the
gulf. Always have army aboard, too, coming
and going from Fort Yuma."

Trish heard the whinny of a horse and
raised her eyebrows questioningly.

"Yep, livestock, too." Scotty motioned her

over to the railing. "See that—?" He pointed a greasy finger at a flatboat snubbed up to the side of the wharf. "That's a broadhorn. We'll pull it loaded with horses, cows, mules, anything needing a ride up or down the river. Takes a skillful pilot like Ben to keep her from getting hung up on a sandbar. Ain't many as good as he is, lass . . . best captain on the river."

"Where's the rest of the crew? Or do you run this whole boat all by yourself?" she asked with a teasing green sparkle in her eyes.

"Don't be spreading it around—but that I do!" he cackled. "When those lazy yahoos start showing up after a night in Colorado City, ye'll be believing every word I'm a tellin' ye.

As if to verify his words, an unshaven, blurry-eyed fellow shuffled aboard on two daddy longlegs followed by some other equally disreputable-looking roustabouts. The men looked Trish over with blurry eyes and then said something lewd in smirking whispers.

Uncomfortably under their scrutiny, she said quickly, "Guess I'd better get back to my cabin, Scotty. Thanks for the tour."

Scotty stared after her, muttering to himself. "Wonder why Ben's been mum about a daughter like that? Never talked about anybody but his dead son." The little man shook his moppy head and headed for the engine room.

Just as Trish reached the passenger deck, she saw her father standing in front of her cabin about to knock on her door. He hadn't shaved, his eyes were bloodshot, and an unhealthy pallor spoke of a sleepless night. His pilot's hat sat askew on his thick salt-and-pepper hair. He seemed shorter in stature than she remembered him in Bend River but maybe that was because she had been with Jens and Morgan too long—or maybe she had grown up and lost her childhood perspective of him.

"Want to talk to you, Trish," he said as she greeted him. She followed him into the common room. "Breakfast, Ching Joe," he ordered as they sat down at a table.

The Chinaman bustled around them, filling two mugs with hot, strong coffee and placing a pitcher of thick cream and hot molasses beside her. In another minute he set a huge stack of flapjacks in front of her. Even her father's dour mood could not destroy Trish's ravenous appetite, much to Ching Joe's delight as he kept filling her plate.

"Missy, eat good," he said happily.

Ben drank the coffee but almost ignored his food.

"I love the *Excursion,* Papa," said Trish, trying to ease his scowl. "Scotty's been showing me around. I can see why you're proud of her."

This time the subject didn't kindle any fire in Ben's half-lidded eyes. He continued to stare at his plate and stab a fork aimlessly at his pancakes.

Undaunted, Trish chattered easily about what a wonderful life it would be to be on the river all the time. She took a deep breath. "This boat is the best home a girl could ever have!"

Ben's head came up as if she had shot him. Coffee spilled over the side of his mug as he set it down. "She's no place for a woman! Spent all night thinking about it. Got to find a place for you some place else."

Food choked in Trish's throat. "No!"

"Can't keep you around here," he went on as if he hadn't heard her. He wasn't even looking at her ashen expression or the sudden trembling of her lips. "Your ma has some kin back in Ohio. I've decided to send you back there. They'll take you in . . . even if they still hate my guts for bringing Nancy out here and all."

"Please, Papa. Please don't send me away—"

He stared at some point beyond his daughter. "Your ma shouldn't have come out here. I told her to stay back on the farm. But no! She cried, begged. And I gave in. Brought her out here. Killed her it did!" His voice broke in an anguished sob. "She'd still be alive if she had let me go. A river man has no business with a woman hanging around his neck. I told her so thousands of times. But she'd never go back home where she belonged."

Trish couldn't move. It was going to happen all over again! Her father was going to dump her as fast as he could. Trish's lips had gone cold and her skin contracted as if fighting a sudden chill. She clenched her hands so tightly in her lap that sharp fingernails bit into her flesh but she didn't feel them. She fixed desperate eyes on her father as she gathered her wits to do battle.

"Mama wanted to be with you," she said as evenly as she could. "She loved you very much . . . even when Teddy died," she said quietly, holding her emotions under tight rein.

Her father's anguished eyes met hers. "I never wanted to hurt her. The first time I saw her was at a barn dance." The memory eased away some of the age lines that had been there an instant before. "Light as a butterfly, she was, turning and spinning . . . the belle of the ball. Couldn't believe that she had eyes for me." He smiled wanly.

A sob caught in Trish's throat as she listened to her father relive that night when he took pretty Nancy home in a surrey and asked if he could come courting. Trish's mother had never talked to her about her own youth, about falling in love, or being married. Trish hung on every word. It was an insight into her parents' relationship that she had never had.

"It was wrong . . . all wrong from the beginning. Your mother was a lady. Come from good blood, she did. Should have married that skinny-faced lawyer who was after her. I was farming then. We tried to make it go but it was no use. My heart wasn't in it, tied to a dry land farm. I couldn't take any more of it. I tried. God, how I tried." His tortured eyes raked Trish's face as if she had denied his words. "Good God, I was dying on that farm. I had to come West."

"Yes, Papa, I understand. And Mama did, too. I know she did."

"I tried to leave her with her folks. But no, she had to come with me!" He lowered his gaze and stared at his hands gripped on the table in front of him. "She kept hoping I'd turn into a docile husband. Always patiently waiting for me to be different—to get the wanderlust out of my blood." He shook his graying head. "I am what I am! I can't stay in one place, in one house, tied down to a—"

Trish could have finished the sentence for him. Wife or daughter. It was the same difference. He didn't need or want either of them in his life.

"You're like your ma," he said quietly.

No, I'm not, Trish raged silently. She wasn't like her mother at all—she was like Ben! Since babyhood she had railed against restraints, protested loudly when forced to conform, and had stubbornly refused to be shaped into something she wasn't. It was the heredity that Ben Winters had given her that had patterned her behavior. Now he was ready to deny the same yearnings that he had passed on to her. She had to make him understand. Taking a deep breath, she said patiently, "Papa, have you ever run the Colorado from Bend River to the mouth of the Big Canyon?"

"No, tried a couple of times . . . but gave up. We were halfway through Cataract Canyon when Teddy was lost. After that, we came overland, along the Gila River to the gulf."

"I want to tell you about it. Please, Papa, listen . . . and try to understand what it was like for me." In animated verbal pictures she took him with her down narrow chutes, through cathedral caverns, riding foaming cataracts and battling driving rain and lashing waves. Trish tried not to hold back anything and as she talked she found herself living again the ordeal of daily survival. In remembrance, the hunger, the fright, and exhaustion were only heights in living and feeling. There was not one dram of regret, just boundless exhilaration.

"You see, Papa, I'm like you. Not Mama! Just because I'm a girl doesn't mean I can't feel the things you feel. You were dying stuck on that farm . . . that's what would happen to me if I were shut away some place by myself."

Ben had raised his head as she talked and was looking at his daughter as if he were seeing her for the first time.

Desperately, Trish kept talking. "Please, let me stay with you on the *Excursion*. I could work. I could . . . I could be a mud clerk. And I wouldn't be a bother to you. You can go on just—just like you do now." She caught her breath and held it, knowing that she might ruin everything if she didn't give him a chance to digest what she had been saying.

The smile he gave her was a mixture of pride and regret. "You do a man proud, Patricia Lynne. But you're not a boy. You're my daughter . . . and I have to do right by you. First we'll buy you a decent dress and then we'll find a nice respectable family like the Gunthars who'll take you under their roof."

Twenty-two

Ben was frantic to find a place for Trish before the *Excursion* was due to depart at five that afternoon. All day the riverboat kept filling up with soldiers who were assigned to various stops along the river. Ben left his first mate in charge and hurried Trish to a store called Higby's Emporium, which was a fancy name for a barnlike store that offered everything from axle grease to lady's sunbonnets. Mrs. Higby was a seamstress of sorts and managed to outfit Trish in a dull gray gingham dress she'd made for herself as a day dress that wouldn't show the dirt when she worked in the store. Trish much preferred her Indian tunic but her father was adamant about getting rid of her "savage clothes." He couldn't approach any family to take in his daughter dressed like a squaw. He insisted that she wear a new sunbonnet to cover that fiery hair of hers.

All fight had gone out of Trish when she realized that nothing she could do or say was going to change her father's mind. He absolutely refused to allow her to remain on the *Excursion*. With Morgan and Jens gone, she had no one to turn to for support. She was as trapped as she had been in Bend River.

"You stay here, Trish, at the store," her father ordered when Trish was properly clothed in the ugly dress and sunbonnet. "I'm going to talk to Hattie Harrigan. Her husband was just killed in an Indian raid. Maybe she'll take you in."

Trish had nothing left to say to him. She'd said everything she could think of to change his mind. He had been adamant. No daughter of his was going to be exposed to the kind of riffraff that traveled up and down the river. He'd be amiss as a parent if he didn't protect her from such unseemliness, he had told her. He couldn't get her off the boat fast enough.

"You wait here," he said again. "I won't be long. I'll talk to Hattie and then come back for you." Her father touched her arm. "It's for your own good, honey."

She nodded wearily. That's what he always said to justify keeping her out of his life."

His tone held the edge of a rebuke when

he said, "You should have stayed in Bend River. I never had a moment's worry about you. I knew the Gunthars would treat you like their own."

Trish bit her lip as she sat down in an old wooden chair placed near the entrance of the store. She couldn't tell her father the truth. Even if she defended her actions, he'd probably think that she was to blame for tempting a man of God. She realized now that he had never understood her, never would. Somehow she had to take care of herself—no matter where he dumped her.

He left her looking out a dirty window at the miserable town. Dust rose under the wheels of wagons going by and swarms of flies tormented the horses and mules. Soldiers were all over the place. Across the street uniformed men were going in and out of an ugly saloon identified as Brigg's Saloon. Some of the soldiers sauntered down the board sidewalks or came into the store, asking for tobacco.

As gawking soldiers passed her chair, they nudged each other but Trish refused to meet their eyes or respond to their friendly, "Good day." When a soldier stopped and stood in front of her so close she could hear his breathing, she

raised her eyes and gave him one of her
withering glares.

"Trish . . . Trish, is that you?"

The caustic remark died in her lips. The
old wooden floor under her feet seemed
to gave way like quicksand.

"It is, isn't it?" insisted the young cavalryman. "Trish Winters?"

No, it couldn't be. But it was.

She couldn't say anything.

"What a surprise!" Billy McIntyre, the
young soldier whom she'd met in Bend
River nearly a year ago, was smiling down
at her. The same strong-smelling grease he
had used to smooth down his hair wrinkled
her nose and was a poignant cue to the past.
His narrow, freckled face and gawking
stance had not changed since that day in
the parlor when he had clumsily kissed her.
How could he be here, in Colorado City,
looking at her as if it had only been yesterday that they'd walked hand in hand along
the river?

Billy peered under her sunbonnet as if
to reassure himself that this lovely creature was indeed the girl he'd flirted with
while on patrol out of Laramie. "I can't
believe it. You, here in Colorado City."
He sobered. "Everyone's been hunting for
you."

In her nightmares, she had lived this

moment. If he had swung a hanging noose in front of her ashen face, she would not have been surprised. The arm of a posse had stretched all the way to this hellhole to grab her. Her frantic flight down the river had been for naught. She had murdered a man of God . . . "the mills of the gods grind slowly—but exceedingly fine."

"What . . . are you doing here?" she asked with wooden lips.

"Stationed at Fort Yuma now. Just arrived . . . first day in town . . . and I find you."

"Yes," she said with bitter resignation.

"When they told me what had happened, I couldn't believe it, Trish."

There was something in his voice that gave her encouragement. Maybe she could handle this situation, after all. Her shock thinned and her agile mind began to work on a plan. She needed time! She had to try and manipulate his feelings—so he wouldn't turn her in to the authorities. "I'm glad we . . . we met like this," she lied, trying to force some softness into her stiff lips. "I've needed someone to talk with . . . explain what happened." She searched his face, hoping for some indication that he might be persuaded to accept a different story from the one he had heard in Bend River.

"I'd like to hear your side of things," he admitted.

"Let's take a walk—give us time to talk." Trish stood up and slipped her arm through his and gave Billy a strained laugh as she led him out of the store.

Other soldiers looked at him with envy as they walked down the sidewalk. They shook their heads. How had that sandy-haired corporal managed to tag a pretty filly like that?

Trish kept a smile pasted on her face. She asked Billy questions to keep him talking while some kind of strategy took shape in her frantic thoughts. One thing was vital. She had to keep Billy from turning her in. He was all army. How could she keep him from doing his duty? She desperately needed his help to keep out of the clutches of the law.

Trish's mind sifted and sorted at a frantic pace. How much of the truth would Billy believe . . . how could she twist everything to her advantage . . . would it do any good? These clamoring questions filled her head with a throbbing ache as they walked. He gave every indication that he would be stiff-necked enough to bring a criminal to justice—no matter what his personal feelings might be. He would probably interpret any advances as proof that she had worked on the parson and invited a seduction. She had to tread a fine line between persuasion and feminine appeal.

They walked a short distance downriver and then she sat down on a rock and patted a place beside her.

"Billy," she said softly. "I guess you think I was pretty forward . . . that day at the parsonage . . . when I let you kiss me. I was young and taken by your uniform. You understand, don't you? A handsome cavalryman . . . how could I resist?"

A pleased flush accented the freckles on his face. He put his arm clumsily around her shoulders. "More than once, Trish . . . I wish I'd told you how much I cared about you. Especially when I heard what had happened."

Encouraged, she managed to turn and whimper into his shoulder. "It was awful . . . just awful. I have nightmares about it. It all happened so fast. There was nothing I could do. You have to understand." She looked up at him beseechingly.

"I'll try," he said gruffly.

She was encouraged. She took a deep breath. How could she sway him to accept her side of the story? Her word against a man of God. She despaired that he would never put aside his duties as a U.S. cavalryman, but if she didn't try, he would surely turn her in. The memory of Gunthar spread-eagled out on the floor with a knife sticking in his guts made her weak.

"Tell me about it, Trish." Billy's arm tightened on her shoulder. His voice was quite gentle. "Tell me who the bastard was who took you away—and I'll hunt him down like the snake he is!"

Trish blinked. Her contrived whimpering stopped in her throat. What was Billy talking about? Hadn't they found the parson murdered in his own kitchen? Billy's words held no meaning. "What—?" she managed, raising her head and sniffing tearfully.

"Who was it? Who abducted you? Was it the same fellow who stabbed Parson Gunthar?"

"Abducted me . . . stabbed the parson?" she echoed.

"What really happened that night? There're a dozen stories going 'round."

She didn't dare speak. Hope suddenly dispelled the sense of doom that had settled on her. She had to find out his version of the killing. "I—I don't remember . . . very clearly," she stammered, stalling. "What are they saying?"

"It seems that woman, Winnie May, came to the parsonage for some reason . . .

and found the parson drowning in his own blood. She managed to get the bleeding stopped. Saved his life, she did." A chuckle coated Billy's words. "Kinda hard on the parson being grateful to the town whore for saving his life. They say he was so red-faced, he couldn't even stammer his thanks."

Trish had pulled away from Billy's arm and was sitting straight, staring at his face as if she needed to read his lips to verify what he was saying. "He didn't die?"

"Nope. Don't look so worried. The parson's fine."

"He's fine. He's not dead?"

"Nope. I told you that saloon gal saved his life."

"And he didn't say . . . who stabbed him?"

"You were there . . . taking a bath, weren't you?" asked Billy with a frown. "The way I understand it, this guy came to the parsonage and attacked you . . . just about the time the parson returned unexpectedly. He tried to rescue you—but the fellow caught him in the stomach with a bread knife. They found your shawl caught on some branches and decided the fellow must have carried you off on his horse. Who was it, Trish? Give

me a description and the army will find
him!"

Trish suddenly choked on hysterical relief. She covered her mouth with her hand
and tears of relief spilled into her eyes.
She wanted to laugh, cry, and shout all at
the same time. She wasn't a murderess!
They didn't know she had stabbed Parson
Gunthar and left him for dead. Rich
laughter bubbled up in her throat. She was
tempted to tell Billy the truth. Let everyone know that the parson had assaulted
her. Why should he get away with playing
the hero? Trying to save her, indeed! The
deed had been his evil doing and everyone
ought to know it. Then she thought about
Winnie. No, she couldn't upset any story
that her friend had put together. Besides,
the parson was sweating enough knowing
that Winnie May knew him for the rapist
he was.

Trish started laughing and crying at the
same time. What a picture! The parson
sweating and lying his head off! Trying to
make himself out a hero while the town's
prostitute stood by with her sides heaving.
If only she had been there to share in
Winnie's deep laughter. "Oh, Billy, you're
wonderful! Thank you so much."

"For what?" Billy stared at her as if she'd
lost her mind. "It's time you told your story,

Trish. Who abducted you? What happened? How did you get here?"

"Yes . . . yes . . . well, I didn't know the man." Trish was thinking rapidly as she wove a story to match the one Billy had just told her. "He must have been a trapper . . . yes, yes . . . that's what he was. Anyway I got away from him and . . . fled downstream till I came to a couple of boats. I climbed in one and hid until I was safely away from that horrible man." She laughed, delighted with how well the story held together. "Two river men brought me safely to my father—and here I am!" How simple it sounded in condensation.

"You came down the river . . . all the way from Bend River?" Billy's mouth had dropped open. "I didn't know that anyone had ever made it through the Big Canyon."

"Well, we did!" In her exuberance, she eagerly described the river's grandeur, treachery, and challenges. She was unaware of the dynamic energy that spilled out from her like the white foaming cataracts she was describing. As Billy watched her vivacious beauty, an expression of deep regret coated his homely features. Once this gorgeous creature had led him to believe she'd marry him if only he'd take her away from Bend River. He wondered what his chances would be if he offered a delayed proposal. Fort Yuma might not be so bad after all if he had Trish settled in some shady hacienda.

Twenty-three

At the same time Trish was walking down the street with Billy, Morgan was accompanying Major Hamilton on horseback to the mouth of the Colorado River where pieces of the government craft, *The Explorer,* had been unloaded from a schooner and were being reassembled on the muddy bank of the river.

He had promised the major to share all the knowledge he had gained firsthand about the Colorado River and the lands that bordered it. All data about the region was scarce and he felt it his patriotic duty to pass along any valuable information he possessed. Once that was done, he would return to Colorado City, tell Ben that he wanted to marry his daughter, and they would be on their way. A new idea had begun stirring and he could hardly wait to tell Trish about it. He hoped that she and her father would mend some fences now that they had a little time to spend together. Trish had certainly proved that she was made of the same strong fiber as her river-man father. Just thinking about her made him want to hurry up and do his duty and then rush back to her.

Morgan took one look at the government craft and struggled to control a belly laugh. The iron boat had been designed in Philadelphia and when the workmen tried to reassemble it, the craft threatened to break apart midship so they bolted a thick beam on the bottom.

"You need a light, agile craft," Morgan told the young commander, Lieutenant Ives. "The river is filled with sandbars that will hang you up with that much appendage stuck on the bottom."

Ives had been hoping to further his military career by this expedition and he didn't appreciate Morgan telling him that the enterprise was doomed to failure. Major Hamilton introduced Morgan to the party of eight men and immediately questions flew at him like a swarm of nettles. Any hope that Morgan had of returning quickly to Colorado City faded as the days passed.

There was so much they didn't know. He drew maps, shared his knowledge, and offered his advice. "You'd do better to plan an overland exploration of the area when you reach the Big Canyon. Forget about taking any boat farther than Callville."

Lieutenant Ives listened to Morgan's evaluation of the cantankerous river, thanked him for his interest in the project, and gave orders for the expedition to proceed as planned.

Morgan could tell from the young man's military manner that he wasn't going to take advice from anyone, especially someone who had no rank authority over him. Since Major Hamilton had no responsibility in the project, his opinion that they would do well to listen to Morgan fell on deaf ears.

Two weeks had passed when Morgan finally wished the members of the exploration well, took his leave, and returned to Colorado City with the major.

He told the officer that the government was wasting its money and he predicted disaster for the entire project. Major Hamilton was to remember Morgan's prediction when Lieutenant Ives's iron boat ran full speed into a hidden rock, sank, and threw the whole party overboard, ending the government's exploration of Big Mud.

Morgan and the major arrived back in Colorado City late in the evening. The *Excursion* was in dock after completing several runs up the river during the time that

Morgan had been away. Relieved that he
had done his duty, even though it had had
little impact on the government exploration, Morgan bade the officer goodbye.
"I'm anxious to get on with some personal
business so I'll be taking my leave."

"You're welcome to be my guest at the
fort for as long as you wish, Mr. Wallace.
I'm sure there are many ways a man of
your caliber could be of great value to our
country."

"Thank you, Major, but I have to make
some plans that involve a young lady. I
hadn't planned on being away this long."

The major smiled. "A beautiful, tawny-
skinned redhead?"

"The same."

The officer held out his hand. "Good
luck, then."

Morgan took a room at the Sagebrush
Hotel and Saloon, and took time to bathe,
shave, and change into some new clothes.
He rehearsed a speech that he hoped would
not raise Ben Winters's hackles when he expressed his feelings for his daughter. He
had the feeling that Ben suspected that everything had not been completely platonic
between him and Trish even though Morgan had tried not to show any familiarity

toward Trish the night he left with Major
Hamilton. He didn't want Trish's reunion
with her father spoiled. Ben might be ready
to avenge his daughter's honor before Morgan had a chance to express his feelings in
a calm, sincere manner. Maybe Trish had
already prepared her father.

Moonlight spilled over the barren land
and stars were reflected in the leisurely
flow of the river as Morgan hurried down-
hill to the wharf. The riverboat was dark
without any sign of crew or passengers on
any of the decks. Lantern light flowing out
of the boiler room led Morgan to its door.

"I'm looking for Trish Winters," Morgan
told the Scotsman as the little man swung
around.

Freckles stood out on Scotty McPherson's dirty face as he eyed Morgan without
speaking.

"Where is she?"

He gave Morgan a pugnacious frown.
"Well, now, that ain't for me to be saying."

Morgan's mouth hardened and his eyes
snapped. "Do I have to tear up this ship
board by board to find her?"

"Won't do you no good."

A cold chill went through Morgan. "Isn't
she here?"

Scotty shrugged.

"He sent her away, didn't he?" Morgan

swore, spun on his heels and bounded up the main ladder to the wheelhouse.

During the few days he'd been gone, he had visualized Trish plying the river with her father, delighting in the swish of the paddle wheel and the white wake trailing after the boat. They had so much to share and from what Trish had said, the two of them needed time to mend some past hurts and become reacquainted. He remembered the longing in Trish's voice as she talked about her father. The pride she showed when she claimed he knew the Colorado better than anyone. More than anything Trish needed to feel an acceptance from her father. If he's hurt her again—! Morgan swore as he reached the pilot's quarters. He pounded on the door and then flung it open. "Where's Trish?"

Ben was half dressed, sitting on the edge of his bed. At Morgan's explosive entrance, he grabbed an army revolver out from under his pillow. "Stay right there . . . or I'll blow your goddamn head off," warned Ben.

"If you think waving a gun in my face is going to keep me from finding out where she is, try me," Morgan said, standing over him. "Now where is she?"

Ben's black eyes narrowed as he kept the

gun pointed at Morgan's middle. "None of your damn business."

"I'm making it my business." All the smooth, polished speeches that Morgan had rehearsed left his mind like a flight of wild birds. His tone was as cold and sharp as pointed ice. "You turned your back on her again, didn't you? You selfish—!"

"I'm looking out for my girl the best way I know how," Ben countered.

"She went through hell trying to find you. And you didn't even let her stay with you a few days."

Ben lowered the gun. "I couldn't."

"You don't deserve a daughter like Trish."

Ben's shoulder's slumped. "You've seen the kind of drinking and whoring that goes on a boat like this. It's no life for a decent girl. She should have stayed in Bend River."

"And be raped by your holier-than-thou Parson Gunthar?"

"What—?" Ben's head jerked up and he looked as if Morgan had kicked him in the guts.

"You put your daughter in the hands of a lecherous son of a bitch. She told Jens the whole story and he decided I ought to know what happened so he told me while we were in the Indian camp."

"I don't believe that Parson Gunthar—"

"The bastard came home one night when she was bathing and attacked her. Trish defended herself by stabbing him and running for her life. That's when she climbed in one of my boats and we didn't discover our stowaway until we were miles downstream. She's the most courageous woman I've ever known. She kept Jens and me going when we would have given up."

Ben looked stunned. "Why . . . why didn't she say something?"

"She was probably afraid to tell you. Now, where is she?"

Ben hesitated and Morgan took a threatening step toward him. "We can do this the easy way . . . or the hard way."

At that moment, Morgan heard breathing behind him. He turned around and saw Scotty standing there with an iron pipe in his hand. "Reckon ye ain't goin' to find out nothin' lest the captain wants to tell ye."

If Ben had given the word, the randy Scotsman would have plowed into Morgan with both arms swinging. Even with the weapon in his hands, the little man was no match for Morgan's hard physique but his freckled face was scrunched up like a ferocious mutt and fire flashed in his eyes.

"Easy, Scotty," Ben cautioned, knowing

that Morgan would deflect the first blow and that would be the end of it. "Hold your temper."

"I can take him . . . I can take him," Scotty sputtered. "He ain't gonna cause trouble for our pretty lass. I'll protect her."

Apparently Trish had acquired a red-headed knight to do battle for her. "It's Ben who should be looking after her. She should be here on this boat with her father . . . and a good friend like yourself."

Morgan couldn't tell from the Scotsman's expression that he agreed with him.

Ben studied Morgan. "Trish was full of talk about you and that blasted river. Pleaded with me to let her stay on the *Excursion,* had some idiotic idea about being a mud clerk."

"Why don't you quit treating her like a simpering female that doesn't know her own mind? If she were a boy—"

"But she isn't. And I couldn't stand the way these no-good, swearing bastards were looking at her. I had to get her off the boat—"

"Where is she, Ben? I'll find her. You know that?"

"How do I know you're good for my girl?"

"I'll bring her back so you can ask her."

Ben thought a long moment, then nodded. "All right. Maybe we should get a few things straightened out." He told Morgan that he had arranged for her to live with a widow, Hattie Harrigan. "The older woman's between husbands now and was glad to have Trish. She has a small house in back of the livery stable."

Morgan didn't wait for any polite good-byes. He pushed past Scotty and hurried away from the riverboat, setting a fast pace down the shadowy Main Street. Crowded saloons were the only buildings with any light and the smell of liquor and unwashed humanity assaulted his nostrils as he strode along the muddy sidewalks.

Morgan had no trouble finding the tiny dwelling. The smell alone left an odorous trail to the livery stable. At the back of the lot, an adobe house stood on a barren plot of land adjoining a horse corral. The heat of day remained in the parched earth and a night breeze only stirred suffocating waves of air.

Trish would shrivel up and die in a place like this, thought Morgan. He cursed her father for not keeping her at his side. She must feel herself completely abandoned. No telling what she would do to escape from this miserable end-of-the-world. He wished he had stayed in Colorado City instead of going off with the major.

The house was dark and silent. A few mesquite bushes softened the crude exterior and he could see two narrow windows cut into the front. The door was weathered and sounded hollow under his knock.

"Trish . . . Trish," he called. "It's Morgan." He waited and then knocked again. A flicker of candlelight shown through one of the panes of glass and then he heard a woman's voice on the other side of the door. "What do you want?"

"I want to see Trish Winters. Open the door, Mrs. Harrigan. Her father told me she was here."

Morgan waited impatiently for the woman to open the door. The candle she held in her hand flickered over a weathered face and two long braids of graying hair falling down over an ample bosom. She was clutching a wrap shut with her other hand. She made no move to let Morgan inside.

"Will you tell Trish that I'm here to speak with her?" Morgan asked politely as if he were calling on a home where such manners were required. Then he said loudly, "I'm Morgan Wallace."

"No need to shout," the widow snapped in a belligerent tone. "She ain't here."

"But . . . but I thought Ben Winters put her in your care?"

"He did, but Ben ain't paying me enough to watch her every minute of the day and night. Besides, she's a sneaky one, she is. Every time I turn around she's slipped away. That gal ain't been much around . . . not since that young cavalryman came courting."

Morgan couldn't believe his ears. "What?"

"Yep. She's taken up with a soldier . . . got him heated up like a hot potato. He'll be putting his shoes under her bed—"

A peal of jealous thunder went off in his head. "Do you know where she is . . . tonight . . . this minute?"

"Of course, I do. There's some kind of goings-on at the fort tonight. She got all dolled up, hoity-toity like and went off with her soldier boy. Don't know when she'll be back. Sometimes those army parties go on all night."

"I see," Morgan said in a voice that was controlled anger. "Well, thank you very much, Mrs. Harrigan."

He strode away from the house toward the spot on the river where the ferryboat navigated back and forth between Colorado City and the government garrison on the other side. He was ready to shove his fist into somebody's face even if it meant taking on the whole U.S. Cavalry.

Twenty-four

Earlier in the evening Trish and Billy took the ferry across the river and walked up the hill to where the buildings of Fort Yuma were silhouetted against the night sky. A United States flag whipped hotly in the night breeze over ugly barracks that formed a square around a dusty parade ground. When they reached the long, low building that served as a social hall, a half-dozen musicians, mostly fiddlers, were sawing away at one end of a square, unadorned room that was already filling up with uniformed men and townspeople. Trish wore the green silk dress and more than one pair of eyes turned in her direction as she entered the hall.

Trish was reminded of her birthday party the night that the Suttons' house had vibrated with laughter and song. That night in Jacob's Ferry was the first time in her life she had ever really felt that she belonged to a family. The first time anyone had made a fuss over her. Given her presents. She envied Jens and Rebecca who had found each other and she wished she could be there to see their happiness.

Memories stabbed at her and she stiffened against a loneliness that was like a painful ache. There had been no word from Morgan. Not that she was surprised. She'd heard the excitement in his voice as he talked to Major Hamilton about the government exploration. There had been new life in his eyes when he left with the officer. She remembered how he had carefully recorded all kind of data those early days on the river before they reached Jacob's Ferry. All that had been left behind but she was certain a lot of valuable information remained in his head. He would be a valuable asset to any exploration party.

As the days passed, she accepted the painful reality of the night of passion they had shared in the Indian wickiup. It had been of the moment, readily put aside by Morgan when the world intruded upon them again.

Trish put a fixed smile on her lips as she walked beside Billy. She wouldn't think about Morgan now. The only thing that was important was making her escape from the miserable place her father had left her.

She'd die by inches if she had to live with a querulous old woman in this miserable outpost. Dependent upon her father and without resources, she had no choice. As a single woman she was denied any honorable means of supporting herself. The situation was intolerable. After sleepless nights of worry, she had decided upon the only escape open to her. As the wife of a cavalryman she could become a camp follower and go wherever Billy was sent. There were rumors that soon his patrol would be sent on to California. She didn't care where they went, just so she got away from this suffocating hellhole and the river that taunted her with memories.

"You look mighty pretty," said Billy, parading her proudly around the room. "There's the reverend." He nodded toward an army chaplain. The older man wore a clergyman's collar and gold cross dangling on his thick chest. He was standing near the refreshment table, obviously enjoying the array of food. "I told the reverend that we wanted to get hitched."

Trish moistened a dry lip and nodded.

"We don't have much time," Billy said. "I could be ordered out tomorrow or the next day."

Trish nodded again, some detached part

of her trying to break through the numbing shell that encased her.

"I talked to him," Billy continued. "He offered to perform the ceremony tonight in the chapel—if you're willing." Billy's eager eyes traveled over her.

"Tonight?" She went cold all over.

"Rumors are that we might be ordered out any minute. No telling how long I'd be gone . . . or if I'd even be back this way."

She could be stuck here for god-knows-how-long, she thought. That horrible, airless room could be her home for years. Her father would never relent and take her on the boat. He was perfectly happy with his life as it was. Morgan had been right. Benjamin Winters had no need of a daughter.

"Tonight would be fine," she said with dry lips.

"I bragged that you were the prettiest gal west of the Mississippi." Billy laughed. "And if he has two eyes in his head, he'll see I was telling the truth for sure." He gave a swipe at his oily slicked-down hair. "I can't believe all this is happening." He took her arm. "Come on, let's tell him."

They walked around the edge of the room, avoiding several squares of dancers stomping and twirling in the middle of the floor, and joined the chaplain at the refreshment table.

"This is Miss Winters," Billy said proudly. The round-faced army chaplain beamed at her. "So you're the lucky lady Corporal McIntyre has been telling me about."

Trish forced a smile to her tense lips and managed to make the right responses as Billy and the chaplain arranged for a quiet ceremony in the nearby chapel within the hour. Her gaze went to the heavily laden table and the array of tempting food spread out along its boards. A huge punch bowl was surrounded by trays and trays of thick sandwiches, sliced meats, fresh cakes and popovers, and a variety of cheeses. Food had always been a solace for Trish and as the men finalized arrangements, she accepted a glass of punch from a smiling young Mexican and began filling a plate with all the offerings. A full stomach would help her endure the ordeal that lay ahead, she told herself. She had taken a mouthful of food when she felt an undefinable quiver at the base of her neck. She swung around and her gaze met a pair of familiar, mocking, dark eyes.

"Good evening, Patricia Lynne Winters," Morgan said with a polite bow. A controlled anger flashed in his eyes as his gaze went from her to Billy McIntyre who moved possessively closer to her side.

The floor lurched under Trish. In that moment of paralyzing shock, only his name would come to her trembling lips. "Morgan."

His smile was sardonic. "I'm glad you remembered. I thought you might have forgotten me in the few days I've been away."

"Two weeks to be exact," she countered. Her breath was suddenly short as she looked up at him. His hair fell in smooth blue-black waves around the crisp planes of his face, now smoothly toned without gauntness or strain. His new clothes fitted his broad shoulders and the long, lithe body she knew so well. He could have reached out for her and she would have gone into his arms. Nothing else existed for her. They were alone in a crowded ballroom with people gawking, laughing, and talking. She must have been leaning toward him for suddenly Billy tightened his grip on her arm and pulled her back against his rigid side.

Morgan's dark eyebrows quivered. He would have grabbed the young soldier by his collar if the chaplain hadn't moved in a protective way. "I don't think we've met, Mr.—?" said the reverend.

With great effort, Morgan reined in his

emotions and managed a civil reply. "Morgan Wallace . . . a friend of Miss Winters."

"Nice to meet you, Mr. Wallace," said the chaplain smoothly. "Have you come to congratulate the happy couple? Perhaps you'd like to join the wedding party later, after the ceremony?"

"Ceremony?"

"Yes. I thought perhaps you knew. Corporal McIntyre and Miss Winters are getting married tonight . . . in the chapel. We were just agreeing on a few details."

Trish found her voice. "Billy is taking me away from this . . . place."

A slow smile curved Morgan's lips, his eyes lost their angry glint. He understood it all now. Another one of Trish's schemes to get what she wanted. Her father failed her and so did I, he thought with a pang of guilt. He should have declared himself before he went off to save the government exploration single-handed. She'd manipulated the poor boy into a proposal of marriage. "Well, now, this is a surprise. You see, I spoke to her father about my own intentions."

Trish blinked. "You what?"

"I've just come from the *Excursion*. He told me you were staying with Widow Harrigan until I returned."

"And what is your business in this area, Mr. Wallace," prodded the chaplain.

"I'm on my way to San Francisco. I understand that there is a need for a transportation company along the western coast up to Alaska. I plan to put several riverboats into operation as soon as possible. This is the opportunity I've been looking for." He smiled at Trish. "Do you think ocean travel might overshadow the joy of river running, Miss Winters?"

She tried to speak but her mouth wouldn't work. San Francisco? Alaska?

He grinned. "And what do you think about living on a riverboat named *The Stowaway*?"

He was going to take her with him. "I might be persuaded to give it a try," she conceded with her eyes glowing like rich emeralds.

. "But you've already decided to marry me," protested Billy.

The reverend cleared his throat. "Really, Miss Winters, you must make up your mind."

"I have," Trish said softly. Her eyes caressed Morgan's face and her mouth softened as she gazed up into his face as if it might disappear at any moment.

Morgan felt his chest tighten. She was captivating in the green silk but for an instant his eyes stripped away her finery and he saw her naked in his arms as he gently bathed the rancid brains and cornmeal from her body. The heat of desire sluiced hotly through his body.

Trish turned to Billy. "I'm sorry . . . I really am." She kissed his cheek and then turned away from his perplexed expression.

"May I have this dance, Miss Winters?" Morgan held out his arms and she glided into them as he led her out on the dance floor. He gazed upon the face that had never lost its power to haunt him. As his hand rested lightly on Trish's back, he could feel the rippling of her supple body moving in waltz time to the rhythm of his steps.

Tears brimmed on her long eyelashes. "I thought you'd forgotten me."

"I might say the same thing," he chided. "I go away for a few days and come back and find you about to marry some pimple-faced soldier."

She sobered. "I have something to tell you. Maybe you won't want to have anything to do with me when you know the truth."

"The truth? My, my, you have changed, my love. I've never known you to depend upon the truth for what you want."

"Don't tease me." Her lips quivered. "I

couldn't tell you before . . . because I thought I'd stabbed someone to death with a knife. He came after me . . . and I didn't know what else to do. Anyway, that's why I was running away . . . why I hid in your boat." Then her eyes brightened. "But the swine didn't die." Trish began to chuckle. "My friend Winnie May saved him and made up a story that he'd tried to save me from some drifter who had carried me off."

"Parson Gunther didn't die?" said Morgan surprised.

She missed a step. "How did you know his name?"

"Jens told me."

Her eyes widened in surprise. "You knew all along?"

"He told me on the hunt. Said that I ought to know about your past and his own."

"Did he tell you that he—?"

"Was on the run himself?" Morgan nodded and gave her a wry smile. "I was in the company of two outlaws and didn't even know it. Jens confessed about his own unfortunate past and worried that he wasn't good enough for Rebecca."

Trish tossed her head. "Jens is as good as they come. Rebecca's lucky to find someone like him. Despite everything that happened, he never got over her."

"It's hard when a woman gets under your skin," Morgan said with a knowing grin. "We can't talk here. Let's get some air."

Deftly he guided Trish out a narrow door at the end of the hall. They sped down some steps and across barren ground into a sheltering clump of Joshua trees at the back of the building. Somewhere in the tree branches a bird thrashed about as if the couple had no right to be there but a flaming comet could have descended upon them at that moment and Trish wouldn't have noticed.

Out of sight of glowing windows and open doors, Morgan swung her around. Then before she could answer, his lips captured her half-open mouth. Her arms came up around his neck and her lips clung to his as if trying to devour the warm, moist desire that ignited there and sped down into the limbs pressed against his. His powerful male energy invaded every pore of her flushed body. Remembered desire responded like a lighted flare, bursting and spilling in flaming bits. His caressing hands burned through the soft silken folds as his fingers traced the curves of her waist and thighs. His breathing thickened and her heart beat madly against her rib cage. The intensity of his kiss sent quivers of aroused desire into her limbs.

He tore his lips away from her mouth and pressed his face into her sweet, shiny hair. "My God, Trish, do you want me to ravish you right here in front of the United States Army?"

"Yes," she murmured in a passion-laden whisper.

"No. We're going to do this right. Patricia Lynne Winters, will you do me the honor of becoming my wife?"

A smile curved softly at the corners of her mouth. "I'll think about it."

He kissed her again, harshly, mocking her with the pliable softness that curved under his demands. He touched his tongue to her lips in a demanding quest, darting between her even teeth, sending spirals of sensation plunging through her. Then he lifted his head as her hands curved around the nape of his neck. The wonderful, virile length of his body pressed against her breasts and thighs.

He took the glow in her eyes for a definite "Yes."

WHAT'S LOVE GOT TO DO WITH IT?

Everything . . . Just ask Kathleen Drymon . . . and Zebra Boo

CASTAWAY ANGEL	(3569-1, $4.50/$5.
GENTLE SAVAGE	(3888-7, $4.50/$5.
MIDNIGHT BRIDE	(3265-X, $4.50/$5.
VELVET SAVAGE	(3886-0, $4.50/$5.
TEXAS BLOSSOM	(3887-9, $4.50/$5.
WARRIOR OF THE SUN	(3924-7, $4.99/$5.

Available wherever paperbacks are sold, or order direct from Publisher. Send cover price plus 50¢ per copy for mailing a handling to Penguin USA, P.O. Box 999, c/o Dept. 171 Bergenfield, NJ 07621. Residents of New York and Tennes must include sales tax. DO NOT SEND CASH.